Mrs. Bundle's Four Seasons, Vol. I:

The Secret at Mount Holly Mansion

ALLISON CESARIO PATON

Other books in the Mrs. Bundle Mystery Series:

Mrs. Bundle Takes a Hike:
The Case of the Singing Swans (#1)

Mrs. Bundle's Dog Days of Summer:
A Case of Artful Arson (#2)

Mrs. Bundle's Maine Vacation:
Subterfuge at the Seashore (#3)

Mrs. Bundle's Hair-Raising Adventures:
Peril on Skitchewaug Mountain
and other Tales of Mystery (#4)

Mrs. Bundle's Midnight Mystery:
The Case of the Springfield Shock Jock (#5)

Mrs. Bundle's Four Seasons, Vol. I:
The Secret at Mount Holly Mansion (#6)

Copyright © 2015 by Bundle Publishing. All rights reserved. This book or any portion thereof may not be reproduced or used in any manner whatsoever without the express written permission of the publisher except for the use of brief quotations in a book review.
ISBN 978-0-9790270-5-5

Design: Univoice History | www.univoicehistory.com
Cover illustration: Donna Stackhouse Illustration and Design

For more information about the Mrs. Bundle series, please contact bundlepublishing@yahoo.com

Bundle Marketplace: https://squareup.com/market/bundle-publishing
www.mrsbundle.com

Preface

This novel is an homage to the bygone era of the 1930s and 40s: where most events, actions, and possessions were not simple but simpler; where the written word really was written; where items were used, reused, and then repurposed with equal enjoyment; where games were hands-on and entirely tactile; where weather was predicted by the naked eye and depended upon to be changeable; where country beings were accustomed to travel on two or four legs; where foodstuff was real and cooked at home; where much conversation was left unsaid, to be later understood by nuanced conjecture or intellectual deduction; where stories were told and retold and meticulously handed down generation to generation; where information and gossip were passed along via the grapevine; and finally, where Family was Everything and one and all Stuck Together.

As always, many thanks to those who have gifted my books to others—my labors of love and imagination, meant for pure enjoyment for you, your friends and family, mystery lovers, animal lovers, Vermont lovers, and other kindred spirits. I thank you all for passing along the stories of Mrs. Bundle and her comrade, Cracker.

All characters and other entities in this novel are entirely fictitious, as are all current events within the story. Some locations and local landmarks are real and are used solely as an authentic framework for the author's intention of telling this fictional tale. Although the historical events described within are based in fact, this is in no way a historical work and the author has no intention of portraying it as such.

Dedication

*To
Anthony John Carlucci,
our Uncle Tut-Tut:
Unique and
special Uncle,
excellent Camp
Projects Manager,
Gentle Soul,
Decorated
World War II
Serviceman.*
1924–1981

PART ONE
The Calm Before…

Prologue
January, 1940

For days the air had been thick and cold, viscous and unmoving, a stalemate of heaviness dying for the release of precipitation from the skies. In its infancy, the ogre had first reared its head thousands of miles from a bucolic New England scene. Vowing to continue to strengthen and conquer everything in its path, the white behemoth's belly was a growling, churning cold mess. Forming cell by cell with deadly assurance it was capable of much more, each squalling mass was wildly joined by another, and another, compelling the fickle beast to grow, to be feared, to surpass the usual.

Far away from this madness, an ardent couple greedily stole their kisses, one holding the other desperately whilst crushing cold stabs of wind snuck through the knot holes and rough wall crevices and like mischievous spirits sought to derail them. The hazy glow of the rising Vermont moon backlit their rustic surroundings. Surrounded by secrecy on all sides, the allure of the night liaison beckoned to them and could not be denied.

To her, it was nothing short of incredibly romantic; she felt unbelievably warm and safe, completely compliant—truly, this was their time. To him: the challenges that stood in his way would not deter him. He was sure he would conquer them all.

Chapter 1
A New Year In An Old Place

For those who live in the modern-day williwags of Vermont, "getting away" is a charming concept and habitually little else; rarely accomplished, even more the case in wintertime than the other gentler three seasons. In the land of the cold, the trendy concept about taking one's pasty, sun-deprived body far away to bask on a balmy Caribbean beach is in deep and mortal battle with the basic concept of survival of the fittest.

Entertain first this pleasant vision: Vermont's peak summer months in which no one has the slightest desire to exit the Green Mountain state's lushly vermillion landscape—awash with sunshine, framed with masses of bursting perennials—all whilst the cleanest air passes through every being's nostrils. During those stellar months of warm weather, Vermonters can enjoy and watch their budding vegetable gardens grow with great pride, beaming with optimism for abundant resolution.

Now feature on the other work-worn hand, winter's offering: an entirely different animal, one that presents for even the hardiest of the hardy a challenging dilemma. Should one stay and cozy up with Jack Frost, or throw in the trowel, drain the pipes, and go?

Firstly, most stick-in-the-mud Northerners will acknowledge that getting away in winter suggests the departing party actually has a hankering to leave. Truth be told, most Vermonters will, until the end of time, find a myriad of compelling excuses to stay put and put up the good fight against the primary nemesis: *The Weather*— defined as freezing, unrelenting winter gloom and doom interspersed with milliseconds of sunshine (believed to be a diabolical deception intended to confuse and convince the resilient masses that warmer weather is just around the hopeful corner) with the goal, in a nutshell, to survive without going stir crazy—leading to the subsequent deadly opponent: *Winter Things To Do List*, which is as long and work-intensive as an ironman triathlon.

Herewith, kind reader, find the items on the *Winter Things to Do List*:

1. Keep the home fires stoked and (at all costs) the oil tank full (a sore subject but much-discussed)
2. Finish up canning the summer bounty and fill the pantry, organize the edible gourds, legumes, and root vegetables in cold storage and stock the refrigerator and cellar freezer to the brimful "just in case"
3. Knit, sew, darn, or patch all available winter survival apparel
4. Complete all the inside painting and repair that no one wanted to tackle during the summer respite and systematize a comprehensive spring plan of action for anticipated outside jobs caused by winter's wreaking havoc
5. Plan, re-plan, revise, and obsess over the upcoming spring planting (vegetable garden and annuals)
6. Make sure the furry friends are happy and fed (both domesticated and farm variety) all whilst keeping at bay the miniature rural vermin scrambling for coziness inside
7. Ready and maintain all vehicles, both pleasure and work (snow tires, antifreeze, emergency kit, snowblower parts, plows, and the like) with a leaning toward snow machines, which light up the night's back mountain roads like juggling votives
8. Cope with all the above fluff while attempting to find creative ways to move limbs—i.e., discovering the latest exercise craze, which, combined with the final arch enemy— *Resistance to Leave the Comfort of One's Cozy Home*—is truly problematic; a challenging brainteaser, and if not accomplished, will result in exhaustion, loss of motivation to go anywhere, and that age-old spiraling-downward malady called Stinkin' Thinkin'.

❄ 7 ❄

These dreaded winter challenges are offset against the humanely inherent search for the elusive sun. Coupled with a desire to create fun-filled activities to stave off the throes of winter glumness, the search climaxes in the discovery of new and different things to do—or even better, a yet undiscovered place *to go*. Hence—*The Getaway, But Not Too Far Away* will magically materialize to break up the winter monotony like the joy and ecstasy of bowling a perfect strike… focus, line it up, step purposefully, and let it go—fist pump!—you've found gold in them thar hills!

Mrs. Bundle had (notwithstanding, in an odd way) come upon such a *Getaway But Not Too Far Away* and was (albeit, less than joyfully) getting away—with everyone's wholehearted encouragement and good wishes. In point of fact, it was *how* Mrs. Bundle had been made privy to the delightful getaway locale that made it even more unusual and noteworthy. In Vermont, discreet word of mouth and provincial subterfuge are the best way to find out-of-the-ordinary nuggets. The common rule of thumb in the boondocks: put your need out there, ask around, and eventually the "just what the doctor ordered" solution appears. Even more opportune was to be given a treasure destination without even having to ask, one readily shared between old friends, seasoned locals, or, in Mrs. Bundle's case, a grateful return favor.

The particular recommendation had come from a past client: Mrs. Millicent Pettyfer, better known to locals and her rural neighbors as Granny Milly. Well into her nineties, she had been previously well-known as the proprietor of the Honey-Do Motel And Campground (now defunct) located on Grasshopper Lane in the backcountry of North Pillson Corners. Back along two summers past, Mrs. Bundle had helped protect Granny Milly in a touchy situation involving grand theft and elderly exploitation. Their friendship had grown. Mrs. Bundle enjoyed the eccentric woman's company and insight (not to mention, Granny's homemade medicinal brew), and generally liked to keep an eye on her. Her biggest challenge was monitoring what Granny liked to do best: give away to anyone with a smile, and some who merely asked, her most cherished possessions. So, Mrs. Bundle had been compelled to find creative ways, without offending her, to make sure possessions stayed in Granny's keeping. She often enlisted her friend Sheriff Will O'Malley in the hunt down of pricey articles that might have been advantageously accepted by the dubious receiver—i.e., vintage motorcycles, jewelry, and collectibles. As her unofficial protector, she herself was not exempt from Granny's benevolent giveaway sprees, so she would surreptitiously return and reload Granny's gift arsenal—ranging, in the last year, from a Ronco salad spinner to a Spanish lace mantilla, a wiffle ball and bat, a weed wacker, and most recently, a wax-sealed fruit cake in a tin dated 1954.

Over time, serious one-upsmanship had developed as each tried to out-do the other with kindnesses. No amount of mollification could deter Granny, but Mrs. Bundle knew one surefire way to make her happy: the amusing woman loved to dine out. Mrs. Bundle was happy to accommodate this guilty pleasure with a weekly jaunt to their favorite local eateries. During one such visit to Hartland Four Corners and the newly-refurbished Tuddy's Diner, Granny (between bites of her favorite sandwich—a BLTCE: bacon, lettuce, and tomato triple-decker club topped with cheddar cheese and a fried egg) had subtly slipped something to her under the table. Mouth full, she mumbled, "For you, dearie. But mind you keep it under your hat."

Amidst the diner hustle and bustle, Mrs. Bundle tried to inconspicuously view what had been passed. Under the shadow of the shiny new countertop, she made out what appeared to be an old landscape postcard. The scenery, reminiscent of an idyllic Currier and Ives winter scene from yesteryear, was that of a perfect Victorian mansion set on a perfect woodland knoll with a perfect pond below. In the lower right hand corner, antique Engravers font captioned **THE MOUNT HOLLY MANSION INN.** She couldn't place it immediately as a local landmark. Upon further scrutiny, she took in the details: a full moon's light cast a gleam on the mansard-roofed, Gingerbread-style, turreted dwelling with wraparound veranda, all set on a wintry knoll with an iced-over pond. A bonfire glowed against the shimmery light as a lone, silhouetted skater (gloved hands clasped behind his back, muffler flying in the wind) executed a figure eight on the frozen pond. The old *Photochrome* colored scene, so pristine and trouble-free, couldn't exist in today's modern world, she concluded.

"What an exquisite photo. Very vintage. Thank you, Milly," she said, assuming it was another gift, but not yet understanding why. However, she was sure there would be a spirited if not convoluted explanation. What she did know was that Mount Holly, a quaint and beautiful village, was more remote than even her neck of the woods. Located not too far away one county over—Rutland County—Mount Holly included the hamlets of Belmont, Healdville, Hortonville, and Tarbellville, a total area of 25 sparsely populated square miles. If there were 1400 total residents they were lucky. Back roads and mountainous nooks and crannies ran rampant throughout the remoteness. Even a lifelong Vermont hiker such as herself was challenged by and would never master that rough country; one could get turned around and lost very easily on the plethora of old tote roads and trails.

Granny swallowed and licked a bit of errant mayonnaise from her peach-fuzzed upper lip. "Now, listen, girlie." She lowered her voice, tapping the table lightly. "The way you're goin' with all you got on your plate, you're goin' to need this here spot someday soon. You're dang lucky you ain't kilt by now. I been tellin' you to slow down with all that detectin', but you don't wanna listen." She licked a drop of egg yolk and continued. "Okay, okay, some people just got to have their adventure. I did in my day, don't ya know. But it can catch up, let me tell you. So! If'n it's ever quietude you're lookin' for, that's—" (she tapped) "the—" (another tap) "*ticket!*" Rough knuckles rapped the table a final time in emphasis. "You just write to them." She displayed a toothless grin. "I'm a-tellin' you. It's one special place. Y'see," she puffed up proud as a hen laying a gilded orb, "they's cousins to my Homer. That's how *I* know 'bout it to tell you. Otherwise," she winked, "it's a secret."

Homer would be Milly's husband (who Mrs. Bundle knew was long gone even though Milly sometimes forgot), a most likeable fellow who'd always been at the ready to lend a hand in the community. Sadly, one such obliging good turn had been his demise. During the 1956 July 4th parade whilst hauling the Super Heroes float, his farm tractor had jackknifed, killing him instantly, poor soul. She said, "So—cousins to Homer were they, now?"

"A-yup. But growing up they was just young'uns compared to him. Let's see now, there's Aurelia…a dite flimsy, but prettier 'n dew on a primrose…then Olivia—all business, direct and proper-like. Then there's that darlin' Woodsum, such a gentle, kind soul. Gee, willikers! What a handsome young devil he was—well, after he grew into them big ears. And cooler 'n a polar bear's toenails—'specially in a pickle." She took another bite, mostly bacon, and gummed away. "*Mmmm—hmmm!*" Once able, she continued, "See, they's just the three of 'em together. Born on the same day. That's what makes 'em The Pettyfer Triplets. They run the Mount Holly Inn here just like their folks did afore 'em. Have most all their lives. Born there; more'n likely they'll all die there." She raised her glass of milk, toasted the ambiance of Tuddy's, drank with a long slurp, and ended with a resounding lip-smacking. "Uh-huh. Quite a place in its day. Homer and me stayed there on our honeymoon—1934, it was. And special? You betcha—right elegant! Mind you, them three triplets was jest teenagers at the time but worked like the dickens. And now, after all these years? They's still there. Never left; probably never will." She lowered her voice a tad, "'Course, that kerfuffle back when was just a bunch of—" she dry-spit in the most unladylike of ways. "manure! Homer never held store with any of it."

"Kerfuffle?" Mrs. Bundle's ears picked up; she hadn't the foggiest what Milly might be referring to. She raised an eyebrow. "What kerfuffle?"

Granny Milly gulped at her slip-up. "Oops. Can't be sayin'." This holding back was indeed unusual, as Granny Miller was known for not having a filter—fact was, she was forthcoming on most any subject. But now, with restraint, she abruptly put on a classic Yankee-poker-face, gestured the universal locking-of-pursed-lips sign, and threw away the invisible key.

Even though Mrs. Bundle would have loved to broach the subject further, she didn't; she knew better. To try to pry information out of a Yankee was a futile endeavor. Sometimes it was just best to move on.

Meanwhile, Granny had retrieved the last BLTCE crumb from her sandwich plate with an expertly-placed thumbprint; it caught neatly thereon—a delectable final prize. She stuck out her tongue and licked it clean off. "Gaw, that Ger Tudhope! Don't he make a good sammitch?" Wholly satiated, she stabbed a bony finger at the post card. "Y'know, anyone and his brother can't help but love that spot. In its heyday, paying folk come from all corners of the earth for such a fancy-schmancy place." She cackled, "Tee, hee, hee! Retreat is what they called it back then—all peaceful and soothin'. Imagine that. And the food," Granny's gums smacked appreciatively, "like you read about! A body'd think she up and died and gone straight to the Promised Land. We took some of their pointers back to the Honey-do." She paused, exhaling, "Yuh, yuh. Them Pettyfer Triplets are gettin' along in their years. They just pick and choose who comes. That's how they do it."

"I see." Mrs. Bundle had followed Granny Milly's winded accounting as best she could and she had to admit it had piqued her interest. There was a curious phenomenon in Vermont: many estates Milly termed "fancy-schmancy" could remain anonymous, tucked at the top of remote peaks or down in the isolated hollows and valleys, verdant deep pockets of forest found by few, many unreachable during the winter months. Come to think of it, many years ago she vaguely recalled hearing about a remote mysterious inn with an incredible reputation for fine dining, located somewhere near Plymouth, which was a stone's throw from Mount Holly. Could this be one and the same?

"Where exactly is it?" she asked.

Milly described the countrified version of how to get to Mount Holly Mansion Inn. Turned out, it was one of those places "you can't get there from here," unless you knew the rolling back roads and steep shortcuts. It was a destination only the hardiest of visitors could expect to find. Once nearby, she promised, one came to a plateau with magnificent views of the surrounding mountain ranges and the only building, a large, well-kept barn. Parking their vehicle of transport, one would then hike (or snowshoe in wintertime) up another long, steep trail. Everyone was kindly asked to leave every semblance of modernity behind—with zero tolerance otherwise—so visitors could experience the simplicity nature offered without modern impediments. It was definitely remote—as Milly put it, "in the sticks with none of them new-fangled cell phone towers spoilin' the air"—a hidden jewel. Nowadays, it sounded like it was the kind of place only a handful would appreciate for its simplicity and remote environment. Milly concluded, "Yup. It's way up on top of Saltash Ridge. See here, girl! I wrote their address on the back for you. You make sure, now."

Mrs. Bundle read *Mount Holly Mansion Inn c/o The Pettyfers, P.O. Box 3, Mount Holly, Vt. 05758.* Noncommittally, she hedged, "Okay. You never know…"

"I'm tellin' you straight." Granny Milly directed a stern gaze at her friend. "You go on up to the Saltash when you need it. It'll do you a world of good. Them, too." She burped loudly. "Ahhh. 'Nuf said."

Lunch plates were removed by the snappy and skillful table girl, Bonita; like magic, two smaller dessert dishes replaced them.

"Now," Granny peered critically at her portion, "let's see what we got here." She brought it closer, inspecting the confection from one end to the other. A satisfied grin emerged as she blinked twice, highlighting the mass of tiny crinkle lines at the corners of her eyes. Her fork dove like a seagull into the pile and resurfaced with a big bite of her favorite lemon meringue pie and straightaway filled her mouth. Mumbling blissfully, "Oh…my…word! Lordy, lordy!" her lips smacked together. "Jest like weensy fluffs of heaven goin' down. I got to bring some back t'home." She winked, "My Homer'll kiss me for it and then some!"

Chapter II

Winter Malaise Takes a Stranglehold

After an unexpected business trip to North Carolina's Inner Banks in October that quickly turned quite harrowing, Mrs. Bundle had found it difficult to get back into ordinary life. Three years earlier, she and Cracker had begun B & C Detectives, a fanciful concept hatched from Mrs. Bundle's desire for more allure in her life. Whimsical imagination had quickly turned to imminent danger as they became embroiled in a mystery involving international deception—a first case, beyond doubt, of "fantastical" proportions. Since solving that first mystery, she had never looked back, basking in each mystery, challenging her mind and spirit—even through dodging near-mortal wounds, murderous villains, and a number of extremely hazardous conundrums.

Truth was, this latest mystery had nearly done her in—firstly, physically (including but not limited to nasty cuts and bites, bruises, and a pesky infection, all acquired whilst slogging through, of all places, a remote, muggy swamp), leaving those around her asking whether this quest for more intrigue could be considered a healthy vocation. And, she was done in mentally, too. Sharp noises caused her to jump; her usual calm had been compromised; she found her heart beating wildly if things didn't go just so. She looked to others in her life for support, but had found, in addition to their help, varying opinions offered free of charge, which uncharacteristically left her even more unsettled.

Her loyal Cracker seemed to be perfectly content with things status quo; he was always there with plenty of responsive purrs, companionable nudges, and comforting ankle rubbing—more likely because, as her sleuthing comrade in those dangerous situations, he knew the score.

On the other hand, there were others to consider. As Karen (Mrs. Bundle's one and only daughter who happily resided in Alaska) had put it, "Geez, Mom, women of a mature age like you just don't go off gallivanting at the drop of a hat—and they certainly don't *voluntarily* put themselves in the middle of unfeasible life-threatening situations. God knows you always encouraged Les and me to follow *our* dreams, and far be it from me to ever tell you what to do, but…holy cow! Couldn't you find something less stressful to do? Love you muchly, Mom, but I wouldn't be truthful if I didn't let you know I'm concerned, very concerned! And what do you think *Dad* would think? Really, Mom. How would you feel about relocating to a colder climate?"

And then there was Les, her equally happy son, who checked in regularly with a typically innocuous perspective. Not only a devoted family man, he was as busy as a political beaver in Washington, DC, which kept him sufficiently occupied, after returning from a five-year stint of diplomatic service in Japan. He had enough on his plate; however, she couldn't help but hear the concern in his voice when she had shared a few of her last episode's less-dicey details. He had approached The Subject (quite tactfully) during the holidays. "You'll be joining us later in the year for a visit. Do you think it might be time to, em, consider selling the old farmstead and moving here permanently to be closer to us? We've got plenty of room," (their stately mansion in upscale MacLean, Virginia, home to many diplomats and high-ranking officials due to its close proximity to Washington and the Central Intelligence Agency, was five times the size of her little farm on the knoll) "and I know, I know," he'd chuckled with just the right dose of diplomacy, "you and Cracker like being constantly on the go. You'd both fit in like two peas in a pod with our busy lifestyle," then deftly added the final zinger, "You know Junior would be *over the moon* to have his Gram here!"

She craftily, in rebuttal, did a reasonable amount of hemming and hawing interspersed with questions about her only grandchild Les, Jr. (who she adored) and his more recent adventures on the baseball field, thereby adroitly sidestepping the potential change in lifestyle from frugal fun in the williwags to shoulder-rubbing with high-end mall shoppers.

She was so proud of Karen and Leslie. It was true: she and Arthur had engendered a sense of confidence and independence in both their children—and the end result was that both had traveled very far away from North Pillson Corners to follow their dreams, rarely to return for a visit. Although a close-knit family in spirit, Arthur's death had given pause to Mrs. Bundle's perspective on life and, more importantly, what to do with it after finding herself alone as a woman of a mature age. What ultimately had shaped her conclusion was that she knew she would require more allure to keep her happy. Creating *B & C Detectives* had certainly fit the bill—big-time. As her nearest neighbor, Walter Andersen had lectured one day (using his poignantly comical Walterisms with his bulbous head wobbling in bafflement), "Gawd, Lettie, I jest don't get it. You're busy as a dang bull's butt in fly season. Allure, you say? You got that allure thing up your detectin' *ying-yang* like you read about! Don't know why you ain't happy just hangin' around Pillson drinkin' coffee and gettin' the latest gossip like the rest of us yokels."

Mrs. Bundle was inclined to underplay the gory details of her cases, preferring to focus on the successful end result which, she had to acknowledge, was extremely satisfying and, from her perspective, worth every black and blue, headache, and sore muscle. Her impetuosity could lead her into danger—there was no doubt about it—and she chose to embrace rather than suffocate that quality. Still, she couldn't ignore those closest to her and their admonitions; if nothing else, it had given her pause.

16

While recovering in November, two simple, quickly-solved cases had come her way—neither bringing her much excitement (although she never trivialized any problem-solving opportunity). The first involved the disappearance of little Sissy Sprenkle's rabbit Mrs. Picklepopper (discovered quite cozily ensconced inside Sissy's mother's prized mouton stole). The second case, another of a growing list of woeful instances of delinquent Howard Snargle's light fingers finding their way into unsuitable places—this time, the Garden Club's money box (which had been entrusted to his mother, who also happened to be the club's treasurer). Howard's subsequent woeful confession came with an overly sincere promise to Mrs. Bundle that he would "turn his life around" if she would only give him one last chance. Dubious but determined, she had agreed. Her conditions had been firm—a commitment from him that he report at the first sign of spring thaw to the Andersen men for maple sugaring season for a more honest approach to money-making.

During this time of quasi-inactivity, a lingering malaise set off by the October events in North Carolina seemed to initiate a deeper, prickly dissatisfaction within her with…what? It wasn't so much the residual effects from the injuries she'd suffered while imprisoned in that treacherous place; moreover, the challenge was a certain restlessness that had set in, a feeling she couldn't seem to shake. Her "little world" of North Pillson Corners seemed to be closing in too tightly around her. Those closest and most dear to her had noticed her demeanor was different; they resolved with each other privately that it all would pass in good time. However, as the holiday season came on in full swing, her preoccupation was still evident; thinly-guised sunny disposition masked wary fretfulness.

"I'm just saying, everyone needs to back off," Althea Swain Kelley (her best friend, "Allie," who knew her inside and out) recommended to those near and dear. "Good grief! Let things sugar off on their own. And no questions!"

Christmas came with little change to her down-in-the-dumps attitude, as much as she tried to hide it. Ultimately, feisty little Erin Corrigan, the young Irish dynamo next door, brought the getaway idea to the forefront. In point of fact, Walter's granddaughter, Angie Andersen, and his favorite young spy Erin (both of whom had a united, unselfish interest in seeing that their dearest friend, neighbor, and mentor was happy) put their heads together. What they had come up with was a loosely improvised plan to spirit Mrs. Bundle away for some R&R. However, for the plan to succeed, both knew it had to be handled very delicately.

Three blustery days after Christmas during afternoon tea at the Bundle farm, the drama played out, with Angie first asking innocently, "Mrs. B, did I tell you Natalie Hufferman just got back from a remote mountain cabin in Idaho? A bunch of them did a winter backpacking journey. She's quite the traveler—she's been all over since high school. She said this was the best trip she ever took. Very peaceful. There's lots of quiet in the mountains of Idaho." She sighed longingly. Having had an especially grueling semester at Bowdoin, she herself was exhausted. "Oh, wouldn't it be just *so* lovely to get away? It's so nice to go somewhere peaceful and quiet, isn't it?" She slid a glance sideways. "No phone, no textbooks to read, no problems to solve? You know, no stress. You'd enjoy that, I'll betcha."

Mrs. Bundle, wary of more advice, gave a dubious look. "Me? Get away?"

Erin eagerly chimed in, "Aye, Angie! Sure and away, we all need a wee break, don't we? Ach, life's just so…crazy! Some alone time does the body wonders, doesn't it now? That is, for us *all*, mum. You, Angie, with all your school work done—you're totally knackered, right?"

Angie nodded too enthusiastically. "Yes! Totally." She leaned backward into the deep cushion, sighing. "Boy, could *I* use a nice quiet break before I go back to school. Gaw—New Year's Eve! Right around the corner. I can't believe it. After that, more challenges… and *stress.*" Again, the key word.

"Aye, a new year. And me with me own stress—ach!" Erin tapped her forehead with deep weariness, in full actress mode. "Ah, mum!" She squeezed her lids shut. "Don't ya know, as I sit here and put my thinking cap on…I'm getting an idea….it's brilliant!" She brightened, ready to spring the newly-hatched thought. "What we need is an escape…aye, a getaway for just the *older* lasses!" Having become increasingly touchy about including younger sister Aineen (only four), she gave a huff of tolerance. In her eleven-year-old mind, there was a huge chasm between their ages—and life experiences to date. *She*, on the one hand, was in the category of *older lass*; Aineen, regrettably, was still just a babe. However mature Erin wished she was, she still, on more occasions than not (to the perturbation of her elders), suffered from Foot in Mouth disease.

"She's a work in progress," Mrs. Bundle continued to remind everyone.

Erin had a keen, bright mind; that said, her unchecked outbursts of excruciating frankness often led her into trouble. All those who loved her were committed to gently but decisively muffling her whenever she chewed, sputtered, spattered, or spit out those unsuitable thoughts before thoroughly thinking them through. To a person, all closest to her were of the same mind: the malady would resolve itself in time and with maturity. Meanwhile, they were perpetually on guard.

"You know who I mean," Erin went on with emphasis, "you, Angie, and *Me*." She squared her newly-acquired butterfly glasses back on center. She was still getting used to them; her increasing near-sightedness had necessitated this new look. At first, she had balked at the idea that she really needed to wear glasses fulltime, but in true Erin fashion, she had ultimately embraced the idea after picking out the most distinctive style of frame in the lot—and made it even more unique with her choice of the modish emerald green hues. "And our precious C-Cat agrees, don't you now?"

Cracker, lying lazily close at hand, blinked his shrewd topaz eyes dispassionately as Erin reached down and stroked him in the special spot between his ebony ears. He flipped his tail in silent acquiescence to the cue. If Mrs. Bundle took the R & R bait, Erin and Cracker had a solid agreement in place. A resounding yawn issued forth from deep within his portly body, after which he wriggled his whiskers to and fro.

Yes, yes, I know the drill, he cat-thought, having been recruited by Erin to be Aineen's designated best buddy and stay home to keep her company whilst they whisked Mrs. Bundle away. Despite the cat's persnickety nature and sometimes snobbish behavior, everyone knew he was exceedingly fond of Erin's diminutive little sister. It would be a pleasure to keep her busy. And, it didn't hurt that she gave him extra Liver Lover cookies from the fridge when no one was looking. He ambled over to his mistress and rubbed his noble head against her ankle in encouragement. *Meeeoooowwww! Go ahead; live a little!*

"And Gumpy," (the girls' nickname for Walter Andersen) "said he would...well, I mean now, I *imagine* he would take care of Frolicky." The Percheron draft farm mare, now-retired but used to hard work, occasionally still dipped her hoof in for some heavy labor with Erin at the reins.

"Hmmm." Mrs. Bundle caught the slip and cocked her head pensively. "Well, I must admit in theory it sounds like a lovely idea... just to get away from all that's so *predictable*. With no complications or strings attached." She adjusted the pearl necklace round her slender neck, rolling the smooth balls resting at the soft depression in her throat. She smiled wistfully, thinking. *Yes. To get herself out of her own head and into another world—but not too far away, mind you.* "It *would* be nice for us girls to get away for a couple days. Somewhere simple," she nodded, warming up to their idea. "but remote."

"Exactly! That's settled then!" Angie thumped the arm of her chair and asked eagerly, "Where would *you* like to go? I'm sure you have a special place in mind... maybe somewhere you and Mr. B went back along. Any ideas?"

"Well, I'm not sure. It seems so long ago since any kind of a getaway." A look of surprise came into her eyes. "I'm drawing a complete blank. Isn't that always the way it is? Whenever you're put on the spot to think of something special, all the beautiful ideas suddenly fly right out the window." She sighed and sipped her tea. *Where indeed? Remote and simple? With no worries? Was there really such a place?* She clucked her tongue absentmindedly, "Oh, I don't know. I used to know where to go to get away from it all…but those places are probably long gone. Today, it's all hustle, bustle, and big business."

Looks of uncertainty passed between the two girls; getting their mentor to *agree* to go had been way too simple. Expecting to be met with solid objections, they hadn't gotten as far in their plan as to have an actual destination.

Angie offered, "Well now! Let's put our minds to the task. We'll come up with something. Right, Erin?"

Erin's tea spoon clinked as frantically as a school house bell against the side of her china cup. "Aye, that we will! Em….let's see. Em…" Suddenly she lit up, her back a lightening rod, causing a chain reaction of the dark curls on her head to bounce. "Say, I've an idea! Blimey! How about us going up to Canada like Uncle Carl when he travels to his music festivals? Only, we could go to Saskatchewan!" She nodded knowingly. "Aye! Saskatchewan—it's soooo romantic-sounding—and very remote! How do I know, you might ask? Well, now, I've just read a book about this fine lass—an immigrant—who journeys across Canada on a train all by her lonesome to live with her strange—but so funny—uncle in a sod home in Saskatchewan. It surely was the remotest of places—in the book, mind you. And in the 1880s—imagine that!" There was no doubt Erin, an avid reader—and talker—was in love with words: from the sounds, to the way they formed a story and opened up a totally new world—as a result of which, she had naturally become an even more passionate speller. Hence, she took full advantage of any opportunity to demonstrate her aptitude to spell an exciting new word, and now recited carefully: "S-A-S-K-A-T-C-H-E-W-A-N. Ah now, such a lovely spot it was, filled with plenty of quiet."

"Uh-huh, okay." Angie smiled encouragingly. "But Saskatchewan might be a bit too far for us to go—unless we flew there. Um—" she caught herself, sensing that subject might have inadvertently hit a nerve, "I mean, not that there's anything wrong with flying—" she moved on quickly, "Y'know, Mrs. B—I have to be back for practice by the 11th, so our window of opportunity for a getaway is limited.

I'm thinking we need someplace local, y'know, but still remote." True enough, she was on semester break from a very busy sophomore year at Bowdoin College where she excelled academically and also played for the women's lacrosse team. Add into the mix her special man, Jack Corrigan. Even their dueling school schedules—hers in Maine, his at Norwich in Vermont—didn't deter them from remaining close, albeit often by phone and certainly in spirit. Not that they didn't have their struggles (as Mrs. Bundle had been made privy to during her last chat with Jack). She was in hopes they would be able to work everything out over time.

Angie bit into her shortbread cookie, chewing appreciatively. "Mmmm! These are *so* good! We have to make sure wherever we go there'll be lots of desserts and pots and pots of tea...while we're there just *pondering*." She lingered on the word as though it was just beyond her reach. "You know, life and things."

"Desserts!" Erin's tongue darted, deftly licking some residual shortbread sugar from her lips. Her eyes glistened. "Aye, someplace with lots of *sinful* treats!" Sobering to this lofty task they'd been given, she nodded heartily, adding, "And a bit of ponderin' sure sounds good to me, don't ya know."

"I do so like ponderin'." Mrs. Bundle's mouth corners turned slightly upward. "I'm sure we could arrange our away time to correspond as an early birthday gift for you, Angie luv, too." She reached out and gave her shoulder an affectionate tap. "My dear, twenty years old—can you believe it? No longer a teenager...my word! And to think I knew you when you were just a babe in your father's arms. Good god, time flies!"

"Gaw! I'm getting ancient!" Angie grinned, a young woman quite happy with all that she was and had become, a natural beauty with classic features combining her Italian, Scandinavian, and Anglo-Saxon heritage. Large brown eyes held green-yellow flecks like a dewy fawn's within a lustrous olive complexion that shone with young vibrancy. Her hair was a rich chestnut brown streaked with natural blonde enhanced by the hours she spent playing her favorite outdoor sport. "I can't imagine what Jack has planned. He's going to come home special. He's being very mysterious." She poked Erin. "Do you know what your brother's up to?"

"Blimey! D'ya think me *bráthair* and me give two figs about that day?" Her eyebrows rose innocently. "Ha! You'll get naught out of me!" Unable to contain her enthusiasm, she jumped to her feet. "So, me darlin' Mrs. B..." she gave a broad wink over her head at Angie, "what about our getaway? We still haven't decided where we're going?"

"Oh! Now wait just a minute." Mrs. Bundle paused in thought. "Hmm. You know, I happen to have...something...somewhere, where did I put that?" She placed her cup in its saucer, rose from her chair and went into the hallway. Rifling through the telephone desk top drawer, she muttered, "Somewhere here...ah!" She'd found what she was looking for under the address book—it was the picture postcard given to her by Granny Milly. Yes, it certainly was lovely, its scene tranquil, the location remote, away from everyday worries. Granny's smacking lips entered her mind's eye, along with her words: *And the food—like you read about!* She nodded. "Yes. This could be just the ticket." While the girls bantered in the next room, she studied the postcard. How perfect it all appeared; a retreat in the mountain woods...there wasn't a phone number on the card, only the address Milly had written in longhand. She consulted the small calendar from Wheeler's Drug Store on the desk. A tinge of anticipation seeped into her pool of melancholy. If they were to have a proper getaway vacation before Angie left, she would have to get a note off right away!

"Say, Mrs. B! Did you find what you were you looking for?" Angie called from the den.

She placed the postcard in her pocket and returned to the girls.

Her eyes had taken on a sparkle of anticipation. "My dears, I think I may have just the place to begin the New Year with some old-fashioned flair. I'm going to see if I can make arrangements for us to stay at this very special inn recommended to me back along. I know the area, about a half hour drive from here—over the old Tyson Road, past Echo Lake through Plymouth, and then straight up 103—not too far away, mind you, but remote, to be sure. I think it might fit the bill perfectly. Keep your fingers crossed, luvs, and leave it to me." She raised hers in the air; with a burst of promise, she cried out, "Here's to a fun escape—one to remember!"

Spontaneously, Angie and Erin raised crossed fingers, too.

Angie rooted, "Woo-hoo! Here's to fun!"

"And here's to lots and lots of treats! Cheers!" Erin offered with gusto.

Chapter III

Things Are Looking Up

Just days later, Mrs. Bundle received an answer to her note of inquiry to the Pettyfers. Their return correspondence was written on one sheet of lilac-colored stationery, the script in perfectly formed cursive:

> Dear Mrs. Bundle, We've been waiting to hear from you. Of course we have rooms here at the inn for you and your two young protégées. It is a most opportune time for you to visit; the pond and the woods are especially lovely at this time of year—a momentous long weekend, to be sure! We've included a map on the back. When you reach the bottom turnaround, the barn door will be open; leave your car inside. You'll then snowshoe in from the lower path; it's about a fifteen minute hike. Follow the blue painted arrows on the tree trunks—up, up, up. We trust you will find it an invigorating jaunt, and yes, rest assured we will have most hearty beverages and flavorsome delicacies upon your arrival. Dress warmly and bring only the most essential items for your visit. If you haven't already guessed, we can't abide anything newfangled or modern. Please leave it all behind in your world. We are confident you will find everything you need for your stay right here in our humble establishment. We shall expect you on Friday the 6th for high tea.   Cordially all yours, The Pettyfers.

"Oh, heavens!" She merrily clasped her hands together. "It sounds...utterly perfect! But..." she reread the last sentence. "Oh—wait! January 6th—my goodness, that's tomorrow!"

Cracker (who was known for thoroughly enjoying every modern convenience put before him), swished his tail and cat-thought, *Capital plan—mind, for you. Methinks I'll greatly enjoy holding down the fort in our little modern world—with all its creature comforts, thank you very much.*

Mrs. Bundle reviewed the map on the back of the correspondence—it was very detailed, smaller than she could comfortably see, so she scanned it on her printer, enlarged it to 8"x10" size, and printed it off. "There!"

Immediately after, she put in a call to the Andersen farm. Angie was on the kitchen wall phone, with Erin listening on the upstairs extension. She filled them in, finishing with, "It's all arranged. But we've got to go tomorrow!" There was a flurry of excited exchange, and she continued, "Yes! That's right, tomorrow! Now, the innkeepers are very strict about one thing. We must make sure we leave *everything* modern behind—cell phones, CD players—everything electric."

"My hair dryer?" Angie asked; Erin echoed, "Really, mum? Everything?"

"Yes. Everything, girls! We'll have no use for items like that."

Angie, unconvinced, asked, "Why?"

"It appears there are no conveniences where we're going, that is, nothing from the present day way of life—as they say, 'anything newfangled or modern.' We have to respect their wishes. Embrace them, in fact."

"Surely you don't mean," Erin squealed with delight, "we're going back in time?"

"Yes, in a sense, we are."

"Oh, won't that be grand!"

"We'll be home Monday. So," Mrs. Bundle asked, "are we all in or are we all out?"

"In! Definitely in!" Their voices collided, "Yes, yes! Aye!"

"Well, then. Pack your backpacks for a long weekend of fun. And bring snowshoes; we'll be hiking in the last leg to the inn."

She answered their questions as best she could—given that it was mostly blind faith and adventure that had offered up the green light to travel into the deep williwags of Vermont. Bordering remote Coolidge State Forest, the Saltash Mountain area was noted for precipitous terrain, huge forests and connected wetlands. With a peak of 3000 feet, it was the area's highest mountain, so she knew it would be a challenge. "Oh, it's definitely remote," she assured them with rising excitement. "But not a fair distance away—just up the road a piece through Plymouth, the foothills, then Mount Holly and up the mountain near the tippy-top. Yes, indeed—an adventure! Saltash Mountain here we come!"

Chapter IV

Something In the Air

That evening as they cheerfully prepared for their trip another event of as yet unknown proportions appeared to be in the making. A fickle winter Midwestern storm was unexpectedly wreaking havoc on the heart of the nation, a storm bearing down, gaining unforeseen intensity, bent on stirring the pot. Freezing rain and sleet were already bombarding several states from Texas through Ohio. Southwest Missouri had six inches of snow and more was coming. Over 20,000 homes were without power from Iowa to Oklahoma. Snow shovels, backup generators and ice-melting salt were selling out fast in all the hardware stores. Shelves in grocery stores were emptying of staples. Ice-covered roads were virtually impassable in a number of states. Forecasts predicted more than two feet of snow in some places, up to an inch of ice plus snow in others. Making matters worse was the expectation of brutal cold and winds gusting to near 60 mph. At the same time, two hundred miles off the coast of Florida, a Nor'easter meant to acquiescently head out to sea was apparently changing its mind. Collectively, when and if all the conditions came together, the two storms' mutually menacing purpose would be attained, thus creating a monumentally brutal wintry collision. If that happened—and the jury was still out on this one—it could indeed be the monster storm of the season and even, possibly, unparalleled for many decades past and to come—perhaps, what they would label, "The Storm of the Century"—even as the

New Year of 2006 had barely rung its bell. The worst case scenario? The blizzard from the west: dropping potentially huge proportions of snow and ice, falling all the way from Colorado to Maine by the weekend; the tempest from the south: disrupting millions, a logy behemoth that could promise a deadly wake of destruction as it charged into New England and further north to Canada without mercy or discrimination. Roll the dice and pray, Martha.

To tough New Englanders like Mrs. Bundle, the threat of snow was just another day in frozen Margaritaville. In fact, it was a stone-cold reality, a given in the wintry little world of North Pillson Corners, that being just over the crucial elevation line where altitude and latitude defined a perfect snow opportunity resulted in a dusting of snow almost every winter day.

Before they left, the last conversation she had with Walter Andersen had not been out of the ordinary in the care she took to make sure everything and everyone was covered in the event of inclement weather. "Are you sure you don't mind keeping an eye on things while we're gone over the long weekend? And Cracker, too? It's just for a few days, but there's the threat of snow—"

"Oh, pshaw—snow, schmow! We haven't had a real whiteout for decades! Between Royal Hudson,"—Pillson's all-around mechanic and emergency vehicle guru, do-gooder and most eligible bachelor—"and me and the boys, we can take care of things here— don't you worry one *ioter!*" Walter Andersen assured Mrs. Bundle as they'd departed North Pillson Corners, "You'll be gone up Saltash way to some *board and breakfast*, you say? Nope! Don't tell me no more—you're supposed to be *dislocated* for a few days and so it shall be. Y'know, I did meet a gal from over that way—oh, t'was eons and eons ago! Ice cream social or some such thing. Back then that was what we did for fun." He guffawed, "Didn't I love them *mara-squino* cherries!"

She could just see his wistful smile through the phone. Walter's middle name could have been Digress, known as he was to go off on tangents until and unless someone reeled him in and got him back on track, which she cleverly did now.

"Walter? They're saying the weather could be dicey."

"Right-o. Them so-called weathermen and their weather reports are a pain in the keester! We're talkin' Nor'easter? *Phhhttt!* You watch, it'll just *skun on out* to sea. Pesky little storm coming in from out west? We'll just see what that brings. Ha, ha! Never you mind. You'll feel *all brandy new* after this retreat. Have a good one!"

An old Yankee like Walter knew Nor'easters that came up the Atlantic Seaboard were old hat—sometimes in a fury, but very often, even with all the newfangled weather radar and expert forecasters after lots of hoopla from the weather stations, fizzling out to nothing. Storms came and went like crazy clockwork in Vermont.

She settled back into packing mode, assured things would be just fine. Junebug, her dependable, emerald green VW bug, was used to all manner of Vermont weather and road conditions. Once at the Mount Holly Mansion Inn on Saltash Mountain, high drifts or no power would hardly be an issue; according to Milly Pettyfer, the innkeepers not only embraced but celebrated this hardy life with no modern conveniences. At the Mount Holly Mansion Inn, she envisioned, life would be sublime in its simplicity.

Chapter V

The Arrival

Aurelia, Olivia, and Woodsum Pettyfer, known as The Pettyfer Triplets, came from good hardy New England stock. They were the descendants of the original Pettyfer clan of Worcestershire and Plymouth—Plymouth, England, that is—and then later, those first who came to Plymouth, Massachusetts and afterward settled in Plymouth, Vermont in 1797. The later generation migrated slightly westward to nearby Mount Holly, a picture of rural simplicity and natural beauty featuring Star Lake and Lake Ninevah, where the Mount Holly Mansion Inn was eventually built.

"We saw a red fox on the way up!" Erin exclaimed immediately to her greeters.

Upon their worn-out guests' jumbled arrival—dropping snowshoes, boots, hats, gloves, in the vestibule and knapsacks near the mirrored, carved hall stand and breakfront at the front door—the innkeeper trio had lined up in the inn's grand front foyer to formally greet and introduce themselves. Like Matryoska stacking wooden dolls made to nest inside each other, they were oddly similar except each sibling's height increased, beginning with petite Aurelia Pettyfer, then slightly taller Olivia Pettyfer, and then the human version of a stringbean, Woodsum Pettyfer.

"Welcome to our home!" They warbled in unison, like three

veteran macaws on a short branch.

The shortest and most prim stepped out first and offered her soft handshake to each of them individually. Formal and petite with wispy white locks shaped round fragile, sweet features, she was dressed in a mid-calf black skirt and matching lightweight kid leather boots with two tiny side buttons, and a crisply starched, long-sleeved, buttoned-to-the-neck, white blouse with delicate lacy collar. Round her slight shoulders was draped a vintage knit shawl matching the color of her strikingly deep blue eyes, fastened at the exact height of her third blouse button with a hexagon-shaped amethyst antique brooch. Her cheeks were a healthy pink, smooth as a polished apple against translucently alabaster skin. "Welcome, dear hearts!" she trilled brightly, "I'm Aurelia. We hope you have brought good appetites with you."

"Starvin'!" Erin blurted out, her voice echoing in the cavernous space. "Aye!" Her eyes were wide with expectation; her face was sweaty from the afternoon's exertion; curly locks stuck to her forehead like sap to pine bark, giving her the look of a ravaged raccoon—which, on first impression, didn't appear to intimidate the Pettyfers at all.

"Very good! We especially like starving guests. Can't abide lollygaggers at the table." She returned to her spot. "Sister dear?"

Olivia Pettyfer stepped forward, her features less attractive, her expression deadpan. She too had deep blue eyes; hers, though, passed through them like a piercing laser. A roughly-sharpened pencil was stuck behind her ear. More noteworthy was the rustic wooden mallet—primitive, distressed, and of the kitchen variety—that she held in her sturdy hand.

"*Welcome!*" Her bark was penetrating. "I'm Olivia Pettyfer." Although there was a smile on her face, her voice, flatter than Aurelia's, was in direct contrast to her face, pinched and sharp, and her manner, decidedly more businesslike, more edgy. White finger-waves, fashioned and cropped just so below her ears in a classic 1930s hairstyle, highlighted her no-nonsense approach. She wore a loose-fitting, tweedy cardigan with deep lumpy pockets filled with who-knew-what, casual trousers, a brown turtleneck and sturdy brown oxfords, all designed for less restriction, made to wear well with few frills—in essence, a quintessential old-time spinster look. Attached to the sweater front was an enamel ribbon watch pin, to which she gave a quick eye. Her chin jutted out and she viewed them with cynicism. "Well! You're right on time." She lightly tapped the mallet in the palm of her hand as she inspected them from head to toe. Under close scrutiny and not knowing what (if anything) they should do, they stood quite still and collectively held their breath.

At long last, Olivia gave a firm nod and stuffed the mallet into the deep cardigan pocket. She pronounced, "Cousin Milly was right. You'll pass muster and then some." She performed the same ritual handshake, going down the line one at a time just as Aurelia had; hers, though, was stronger, her squeeze a bit more wince-evoking. Her chin settled back into her neck and she said solemnly. "We like you." She stepped back in place. "Brother?"

The gentlemanly octogenarian spritely stepped forward; it was his turn to be on stage. In a rare moment that those loved ones at home would be proud of, Erin held herself in check. *Sure and he looks like Abraham Lincoln*, she opined inwardly—tall and skinny as a beat-up broomstick with a big shock of white hair—*but, aye, much more of a looker!* He had been blessed with the same midnight blue eyes; his, though, twinkled with rakish fun behind round, wire-rimmed spectacles.

He saluted smartly. "Woodsum Pettyfer at your service. Welcome, welcome ladies!" He took Mrs. Bundle's proffered hand and pumped it enthusiastically. "Boy, oh boy! What a thrill! We've heard lots and lots about *you*, ma'am. Cousin Milly tells us all about your harrowin' exploits! Regular Tuppence Beresford and Emily Pollifax all rolled into one! Quite the gumshoe, ain't y'now? I'm a lover of Sam Spade myself. And how! Used to go down to the Nelson's Hardware on Friday nights and listen to him and Nick Carter and," he modulated his voice downward in perfect radio announcer emulation, "'*Master Detective!*' Yup, on their radiogram! Everybody knows they was the best of the best. Yes sir—they was the cat's pajamas!"

Erin covered her mouth and repressed a snark with great difficulty. "Cat's *pajamas*?"

"You never heard of that? It's quite the goin' saying—real hotsy-totsy! I ain't no wet blanket, that's for sure." His vocabulary, peppered with slang from a long bygone era, was both confusing and endearing. He focused his specs and smiled at Angie, "My, my! Here we are. Yuh, yuh—oh, we know all about you—you're a celebrity! Angie Andersen. Just like the pictures in the newspaper! In big print—big, *big*!—as one of them stars up on the big screen—love readin' about you in the *State Standard* and all! What a girl, *what a girl*! MVP—first at Woodstock Union, and now Bowdoin All-Region! Ain't you somethin'! Y'know, we played lacrosse, too—in our younger days, didn't we, sisters?" He made a nifty lacrosse swing and his arm swiped a nearby candle stand. Both he and the stand almost tumbled over. He recovered just as Angie grabbed to steady him. He guffawed, "Whoopeee! Ha, ha! I still got it!"

Olivia interjected, "Oh, I never!" She rolled her eyes. "Word of caution. Woodsum tends to go on and on." She clucked like a hen about to lay a whopper and shook her head disapprovingly. "Just give him the old elbow anytime. You have our permission to let him know when he's being a bothersome ol' nincompoop."

"Hardy har har! Horsefeathers and humbug to you, dear sister!" Woodsum interrupted, grinning and unscathed. "It's my job to provide the entertainment here. Mind you, we do like to have a bit of fun," he raised a hand, covering his mouth in a jesting manner, "especially with our *feisty* guests." He paused, glowering at Erin (a look inconsistent with the twinkle in his eye), "Jeepers creepers! What's your story, mornin' glory? Are you here to cause *trouble*? You're not a *flapper*, are ya?" He squinted over his specs in a vain attempt of intimidation.

"A *flapper*? Haw!" Erin burst out, giggling, unfamiliar with the nametag but figuring it might not be particularly flattering. "Sure, and I'm just a wee angel! Can't you tell?" She'd expeditiously crossed her fingers behind her back.

"An angel you say? Says you! Well, now, if that's the case, you come to the right place. This here's been called heaven on earth by those in the know. But just in case you're not one," he waggled his finger at her, "we'll all keep our eyes on you."

"Aye, Mister Woodsum! That's a good idea, I'll wager I'd do the same!"

He winked; she winked back. With that, a solid friendship was formed.

"Well, then, I'll bring your backpacks upstairs to your rooms while all you ladies go in to tea."

Suddenly, from somewhere in the further sector of the big mansion, mournful sounds burst forth. There was a frantic succession of dull scratchings and loud, crotchety whines, followed by a plaintive baying like a sick baboon. "*Aurrrrrooooo! Aurrrrrooooo!*"

"Blimey! What *the divil* is that?" Erin asked, nonplussed.

Woodsum, cool as a country cuke, paused and tapped his nose. "Well, now. And so you might wonder. Should we bring out the little man? Sisters, what d'ya think?" he asked expectantly.

Olivia let out a sigh, "Yes, yes…let the little monster loose for a bit. But," her voice became stern, "back in jail he goes if he's naughty."

Woodsum moved to a door at the farthest end of the house and opened it just a hair. It opened a tiny bit more and a petite indescribable creature stepped through. A *click, click, click* on the hardwood floor grew louder as "it" came closer. Stumbling down the long hallway, the Pettyfers' "little man"—a ball of fur, mostly mange—arrived to investigate the new arrivals.

Olivia's tone and face seemed to transform magically at the sight of a scruffy animal. "Yes, yes, yes," she cooed. "You are a tiresome little devil, aren't you?" She sat down in a nearby thickly upholstered wing chair and held out her arms.

The scrunchy black animal consisting of long body, short legs, and distinctive topknot on his head, found his way to her and snuffled in at her ankles, making a variety of funny, gruff noises. He had about the ugliest dog's mug they had ever seen—certainly not the most loveable.

The guests watched skeptically as Olivia lavished pats of affection on the snarling little grump. "Oh pipe down!" Over her shoulder, she said, "He won't nip at you 'cuz you're ladies. He likes ladies."

Aurelia further assured them. "But if you were man or mouse… you best watch out!"

Olivia added, "We don't abide cats here at the inn. Absolutely abhor them, in fact! So Possy fits the bill to a T. Goes right after little critters! And men. We don't abide men with hats, and neither does Sir Possy. Excluding dear brother, that is. Isn't that right, *sweet* little dear Possy?"

Woodsum gathered up the potbellied domestic animal and placed him gently in Olivia's lap; in a huge display of affection, she soundly kissed his topknot and hugged him to her. "Grrrrr!" she said with affection.

Equally demonstrative, Aurelia genuflected, cooing and tribbling with obvious warmth. "Oh, Possy, Possy, *Possy!*" His response was a growl worthy of a skid row bum. Olivia hugged him even tighter, fussing and clucking.

The casual observer could conclude that, contrary to their initial protestations about the consequences of bad behavior for Little Man, the Pettyfers seemed to cave like medieval serfs under his beguiling personality.

Erin shook her dark curls and exclaimed, "*Pussy?* Why Pussy?" She raised a cynical brow at the shabby creature whose protruding teeth gnashed like a crazed warthog. "Mum…he *is* a dog…I reckon?"

Gathering much-mustered patience, Olivia answered, "Yes, dear heart. He is a dog—a very rare dog, indeed." She grabbed his paw, forcing him to wave it in greeting. "Meet our little man, Sir Postlewaite! It's *Possy* for short, though. We can't abide long names."

"Sir *Postlewaite?* Aye, I know that's Scottish, isn't it now? And you say he's somethin' special?"

"I should say. That's a *proper* Scottish name for proper gentry," Olivia sniffed, "to be sure."

"And next to me own dear homeland of Ireland!" Erin reached

out to shake the paw, warming slightly to the dog. "Hmmm. Possy." She tried it again. "Possy! Rhymes with *bossy*." He groused grudgingly and his belly growled. She went fearlessly eye-to-eye with the old codger. "*Hmmmph!* I'll just bet and then some, aren't y'now? Em, aye, that you are a rare one, too."

She looked up at Miss Aurelia, who offered, "Well, yes, can't you see oodles of nobility in those expressions?"

"Aye, I'm tryin', mum. Such a *nice* Sir Possy," Erin's voice lilted upward, "aren't you now?"

Aurelia said fondly, "Yes, yes! We have loved them all, each and every one."

Their puzzled stares reminded her that they were unaware of the afore-mentioned fine lineage. "Beginning with the *original* Postlewaite. Possy the First." Aurelia reached into her pocket and the dog quickly gobbled whatever was in her hand. "Our *breathing* Postlewaite here is the great-great-great-great-great—"

"—and so on!" Olivia waved, impatiently motioning her to move on.

Aurelia said, "He is the *eighth* generation—and very sadly the last, we fear—of a very long dynasty of Dandie Dinmont Terriers." She bowed her head toward the pile of mange in tribute, "The Omnipotent Sir Postlewaite the Eighth and Great! All hail!"

Erin and Angie bowed their heads reverently—*when in Rome*, Mrs. Bundle thought.

"Also known as Cranky Franky on a good day." Woodsum added, eyes crinkling. "Look here." He produced a yellowed folder from behind the front desk and proceeded to give them a lengthy history page by page of their dogs' lineage.

By all appearances, they catered with great love to their cantankerous purebred very likely in the last stage of his dog years. According to the Pettyfers' official certificates, even Cracker the King of Snobbery might have been overcome with the dog's impressive lineage (even though, frankly, Sir Possy's dog-thoughts weren't quite fit for churchgoers' ears and are thusly unprintable).

They explained that nowadays the old dog spent his days in one of four places: sunning himself in the solarium, the innkeepers' quarters in the back of the house, the warm kitchen, or on a plush round bed on the other side of the front desk underneath the prominent "*No pets allowed*" sign.

Little Man Sir Postlewaite the Eighth had it made in the shade. In point of fact, it was apparent the grubby bugger ruled this kingdom.

"Are y'sayin' now, he's like that king? Em, like Henry the VIII, right?" Erin queried. "We studied him. Aye, that bloke had a passel of wives!"

"Well, yes, you might say rather like that. *Our* Fostlewaite is the final lone descendant in a long line. Two of his ancestors met with early demises—Possy the 4th and Possy the 7th. We won't offend you with the details. Sadly, they'll be no more Postlewaites here at the inn."

"Why not?" Erin asked naively.

Aurelia sniffed as she treaded on sensitive territory. "Our little Possy here couldn't…sire an offspring, at the time."

"And now, 'course, he's past his prime." Woodsum added tactfully.

"Aye. He's bloody old, isn't he?" Erin added, "Em, so he's too old now for—?"

"Ahem." Mrs. Bundle coughed.

"Right, Mrs. B! So," she scrunched her nose, "shouldn't we call out 'Possy, Possy, Possy'—y'know—like eight times for this one that's left? C'mere," She demonstrated loudly, "*Here Pos-bos-possy, Possy, Possy—*"

"No need, dear heart." Olivia's arched eyebrows and tight clenched fists belied her patient tone. "One Possy is quite sufficient."

"Eight Postlewaites. Imagine." Angie marveled. "When did you get the first Possy?"

"Before the war." Aurelia said, blushing. "World War II, that is."

"The Big One." Woodsum said solemnly.

"Wowser." Angie gingerly patted the bundle of grunge. "I see why you're so attached. You've been through so many. Possies, that is."

Olivia smiled lovingly at their pride and joy. "You can't help but love his funny face, can you? Like all the ones before, he's really *quite* special, don't ya know."

"And sweet as sugar!" Aurelia added.

Erin said doubtfully, "If you say so, aye."

"Well, you know what they say...'It's hard to convince a hungry person.' Tea, everyone?" Olivia asked, back to business.

Chapter VI
Tea and a Top-Notch Tour

Afternoon high tea, usually served in the dining room, had been set out in the solarium today to take full advantage of the last vestiges of the winter afternoon sun. Better described as a conservatory with full greenhouse benefits, the sclarium, located just off the informal parlor, was steaming with humidity—a verdant jungle! Grand exotic plants and lush shrubs were closely housed within southerly exposed windows.

Miss Olivia seemed to be the plant expert. She gave them a quick tour. "We have a veritable who's who of exotic plants, shrubs, and small trees, most from southern climates like Latin America and South America. We have even cultivated many varieties, like these short sunset and banana palms—lovely, aren't they? And this is a tropical hibiscus. Here, our aloe varieties—so many good uses. This is prickly pear cactus indigenous to the Galapagos. Ah, sister!" she acknowledged Aurelia, who had joined them quite unobtrusively, "Are we ready?" Following her lead, they left the steamy area and moved toward the windows.

"My word! What a view!" Mrs. Bundle exclaimed.

From the unobstructed solarium windows, the sweeping panorama of the sloping hill down to the pond was spectacular. From this vantage point, one could also take in the windmill generator located at the top of the hill, which caught the maximum wind currents and provided power for the most essential things, including the few light bulbs scattered throughout the large house, which emanated a rosy hue during nighttime. Indoor plumbing and hot water were an absolute luxury at Mount Holly Mansion Inn, installed in Victorian form and then revised in the 1930s to accommodate the growing number of posh clientele.

Inside the conservatory, two trays had been set on side-by-side spider gate-leg tables opened fully to accommodate high tea; both were surrounded by comfy cushioned rattan chairs. Knitted cozies covered two pots of steaming hot Earl Grey—amazing what a bit of deeply scented leaves steeped in boiling water, a tad of honey, and a smidgeon of cream could do for the souls of the three weary travelers. Fresh cinnamon bread was sliced and spread thickly with cream butter. Also offered were savory cheese and herb scones, broken apart in heavenly crumbles as the hungry trio slathered homemade marmalade. Stilton cheese was served on the side. It was just enough to satiate their grumbling tummies without spoiling their appetites for dinner. While they sipped and supped, a spontaneous but spirited game of Parcheesi ensued—set up on the nearby game table—between Erin, Angie, and Mister Woodsum, who had also happened along *most* conveniently.

Woodsum chuckled. "We pride ourselves here by sayin' if you're wantin' to come lay your head and rest your body for a few days, we're the bee's knees! We got about as much adventure as an old stick, but there's always somethin' fun to keep you busy." He was a Parcheesi whiz, at the same time providing a running banter about the inn in its heyday and the everyday duties involved in running such a place. He was most entertaining, and the girls were captivated by his charming ways. The way he described it, Woodsum ambled about, up, down, and around making sure all was running smoothly; he did heavy lifting, maintenance, and outside chores. As he put it, he was always "fiddling with something": there were well, septic, and heating systems to watch out for; pumps to tinker with; wood to cut, split, and stack; and chores galore. The women of the house took care of the daily operation and bookkeeping, meal preparation, and a welcoming environment (which seemed to have dwindled significantly since the "good ol' inn heydays" that Woodsum referred to). As a rule, both women prepared all the meals and, judging by their first high tea, Mrs. Bundle had no doubt of Granny Miller's promise that the food would be fantastic.

Mrs. Bundle watched, enjoying both the enthusiastic repartee and competitive gamesmanship exhibited by all. Surprisingly, it was Erin who handily beat the pants off her opponents in the final round, with a solemn promise to "Mister Woodsum" for a rematch.

"Well I know when I'm beat!" he said good-naturedly. Excusing himself to "take care of my outdoor duties," he left them.

Moments later, as if on cue, Aurelia entered the room with anticipation. "Are you all ready?"

They looked expectantly and she motioned for them to rise and follow her. Thus began the The Official Grand Tour, coined by Aurelia and juxtaposed with a rich historical account. "Mother and Father believed, as did all those between the Victorian and Edwardian era—that's when this house was built, ladies—that the outdoor living space was very healthy—and bringing the outside in was even better! That's why you see the huge outside porches with lots of wicker in nice weather, and always lots of houseplants everywhere. We love green and leaves, lots of leaves! In the warm weather, many a time we'd all sit outside in the evening counting shooting stars and sharing stories and gossip. Gossip in those days was just a way of communication. And, of course," she looked round the space with affection, "our lovely solarium brings the summer inside during the cold winter months. We love all the flowers and exotic plants collected over the years. Father built the solarium especially to capture every bit of winter sun he could; he got rather melancholy if he didn't have the sun."

Angie sighed. "I like it. It's...peaceful here."

Mrs. Bundle knew the stress the dear girl had been under in the last year. Angie was very dear to her, and their last heart-to-heart conversation had been deep and somewhat worrisome. Between school, the long distance relationship with Jack, and decisions looming in the near future, the girl needed this retreat as much as she did.

"Yes. Again, that was always the way, here at the inn." Aurelia went on, "Well, most of the time, anyway. Come this way." As dusk turned to early darkness, they left the softly lit solarium through the informal parlor, and she pointed out, "As you can tell by the well-worn carpet, this room was used quite a lot, being that it's between the front foyer and the solarium. Yes," she said wistfully, "a great deal of traffic over the years. There was a time when we had…fun!" Her eyes moved, flitting round the room as though watching imaginary guests, "Please make yourself comfortable in this area anytime. You see, that's been the goal of the inn since my parents built it. They always wanted it to be a place of welcome, a place for memories to be created, to embrace good times." She led them back into the huge front foyer and opened her arms. "All the rooms on the first floor have 11-foot ceilings; the rooms upstairs are 10-foot."

"It's like being in a museum!" Erin exclaimed. "In a good way."

Aurelia smiled, "If you want progress, Mount Holly Mansion's definitely not the place. I daresay them types'll be much better off at that motel with all the bells and whistles up the road a piece in Killington. This of course, is where we meet and greet our guests."

They stood in the huge open foyer's great space where they had first been welcomed. There were so many doors, leading to other rooms, auxiliary closets, or storage rooms. They had an opportunity now to appreciate the grandeur of the foyer's features: darkly stained woodwork, impressive black and white diamond inlaid floor, the relic of a massive front desk amidst a high tin ceiling. "To welcome everyone individually and to keep it simple. Informal, and home-like. This is where they could drop their boots, hang their hats and scarves. 'Course, seeing as we don't abide change, every bit of the inn is just like it always was. That umbrella stand and coat wardrobe there, the front desk—why, Father ordered the pine all the way from North Carolina! And the dinner gong," she pointed to the large Victorian gong atop a four-foot-high cabinet—"you will become accustomed to hearing that whenever meals are ready. Olivia usually wields the striker. She's got those big hands." Behind the Jacobean style gong hung the striker mallet. "*Every* stick of furniture and the furnishings here have their own very old story." Her mouth twitched, "Excepting if some of the pieces are gone because they became so overused and broke, or just disintegrated with time."

"Y'mean," Erin asked, looking around, "every chair and table in the place…every single piece has a story?"

She nodded. "Yes! Pretty much. We even have some pieces from the Arts and Crafts period—very progressive, wouldn't you say? All ten guest bedrooms were outfitted with lovely items to make the guests feel at home. *Every* piece was lovingly handpicked by dear Mother and placed with care in its appointed spot. Same with the other rooms: parlors, dining room, den. As a rule, we've kept things exactly the same—"

"Right, now! Just as," Erin interrupted excitedly, "if we all closed our eyes, we could imagine we were back in the olden times, right? Sure, and I'd love to travel through time, to go backwards and live like…like, when *you* were a wee young lass."

"Exactly, dear heart." Olivia had arrived as though on cue; an overly long and very thick screw driver was tucked casually under her armpit—apparently, she always came prepared for any given emergency.

Aurelia said, "Sister will show you the rest of our tour while I go check on how things are faring in the kitchen."

"So! Let's begin with what everyone calls 'the pride of all Victorian homes.'" Olivia opened French doors to reveal the other matching front parlor, albeit much more formal with lots of grand antiques. A plush-covered round table graced the center of the room. Numerous Queen Anne richly silk chairs, two matching Sheraton couches and loveseats, tea tables and glassed wall cabinets, all filled the room amidst its nooks and crannies. Heavy red velvet drapes with swag and jabot overlay hung on the windows, pulled tightly closed to counter the north wind drafts. The fireplace mantle was draped in the same swagged velvet; logs had been neatly laid in the grate, ready to be lit. All was impeccably clean, giving it a somewhat staged appearance. A fancy organ with lots of tabs and pedals was just one of the many showpieces in the room busy with silk throws, tchotchkes, and doodads. "Back in the day, this room was used for all special occasions, not to be confused with the family parlor which we just came from. We saved this room for holidays, wedding receptions for those who married while at the inn, and formal family events like celebrating birthdays and funerals. This is where they would be laid out." She pointed to the center of the room and raised a finger in anticipation, "Yes, Erin, to answer your question. Dead people. The organ was used. I happen to know almost every dirge, spiritual hymn and sacred song. And," a hint of a smile appeared, "I have a few pop tunes in my repertoire, too." She moved on quickly, "The formal parlor has the walk-through window," she pointed, "to the eastern porch and veranda. And this is our portrait area." In one corner an area had been set up as though staged in a typical Victorian vignette: formal deep burgundy velvet loveseat, a marble-topped fancy table, twin high-backed upholstered chairs. Directly in front, a tripod had been set up with an old wooden boxed camera, complete with bellows, long lens, and sliding plate; the beautiful wood patina on the box gave them the impression it was lovingly shined regularly.

They walked round the staged scene, the girls especially fascinated with the antique camera. Underneath the front lens was an oversized brass plate that read: *Cheer up. Things might be worse.*

Angie gave a giggle, "Imagine the folks that stood there and read that before they had their picture taken."

Olivia continued, "That's what they call a studio camera—top notch for its time, so they said, used in the most *progressive* photo shops. Brother is very proud of it. Back in the day, tourists would go to a particular vacation destination—for example, Niagara Falls—and then have their photograph taken in the poshest of circumstance. So, Woodsum begged and begged for it, saying he could do the same. He'd caught the photo bug when he was going for his Eagle Scout badge, used a little Buster Brown box camera to start with—cost two dollars. But he desired something bigger and better. When he saw that modern camera in the Montgomery Ward Catalog, there was no question that he had to have it. Finest cherry with an adaptor for all that newfangled Polaroid film—quite the thing! Father finally gave in, with Woodsum's promise that he'd photograph any guest who desired a souvenir of their stay. Over time, he became quite good at it—we always like to call him a *very serious* amateur. He even did a *Photochrome* postcard back in the day!" She shook her head, "Not for advertising, mind you! No, no. People just loved takin' a few home with them as a memento of their good time spent here."

"Oh, yes! I have one, in fact. Granny Milly gave it to me." Mrs. Bundle said. "It's just lovely!"

"Yup. Brother fancied himself quite the shutterbug—dreamed about getting his photos in *National Geographic*. Nevertheless, he was just the resident shooter for the inn." Olivia shrugged good-naturedly. "Lots of families—hundreds undoubtedly—have sat in those chairs and had their photographs taken for posterity. Of course, nowadays it gets little use."

"Hundreds, you say?" Erin cocked an eyebrow. "Blimey! That would be a lot of photographs Mister Woodsum has taken, hasn't he!" Primping like a glamour queen, she sat on the ornate couch and struck a dramatic pose. "Aye, like this? Surely, I'd just *die* to have me photograph taken in this grand setting!"

Angie stepped up and looked through the lens. "I can see what a drama queen you are from here!"

Erin's eyes keenly surveyed the room; portraits of flowers and nature scenes were all that adorned the room. "But where are his photos? Did he give 'em all away?"

"Not at all. Brother always saves everything." She paused as though considering some pros and cons. A strangely youthful look transformed her countenance. It was devious and full of fun, belying the stern outer nature that had likely developed with old age. She whispered conspiratorially, a sneaky smile on her face. "Would you like to see his bits and pieces?" At their nods, she closed the parlor door and turned, her sharp features more relaxed. Cocking an eyebrow at them which emphasized the significance of this stretching-of-the-rules, she moved quickly across the room toward a set of grandly ornate panels. Decorated with a handsome raised-copper verdigris relief design, the three-section piece was a fine example of Victorian metalwork. The varying hues of raised trellis design were masterfully executed, artfully disguising the entrance — to a private area!

She reached up to the top right cornice, sliding a delicately curled metal bolt to the left. Suddenly, the accordion-like panels folded effortlessly to reveal an anteroom, darkened and without the benefit of outside natural light. "Welcome to Woodsum's private lair. As I was saying, brother was quite the serious amateur. He needed his own space. So, he and Father created this darkroom right here in the parlor closet. Kept it cozy." She stepped aside so they could see. "He's shy about it, is all. Keeps it all, as they say, close to the vest. But I don't think he'd mind if you took a peek inside — just so long as you don't touch anything on his developing table. He's darn particular like that." She lit the kerosene lantern on the side table and handed it to Angie. "Here you go."

"I took a photography class freshman year at Bowdoin." Angie said, peering into the space, Erin at her heels. "Besides digital work, we learned how to develop our own stuff. I loved it."

"Me, too!" Erin added, having never developed anything but willing to try at the drop of a hat, and they entered the modest space. "Whoa, this is *so bad!*"

"Bad?" Olivia questioned with a start.

"Not to worry," she said with the assurance of a tweenie trying out some slang, "Nowadays, when kids say bad, they mean it's good, really good."

Besides the long wooden work table flush against the wall that dominated the room, shiny pans and china trays and an aged egg timer were first obvious; wooden boxes of various sizes held photographic measuring cylinders, chemicals and stirring rods, and other tools and gadgets to make a positive image from a negative. A device that Olivia called a photographic enlarger sat nearby. Everything was as neat and orderly as a scientist's lab. Below the table were slots holding paper in a range of sizes; above, old clips on a line ran the length of the room, presumably to hang prints but now empty of any photography. Built-in shelves lined the far wall, filled with many generic cardboard memory boxes, a white front label documenting the month and the year. Angie held the lantern high, revealing that the top shelf boxes held the earliest photos dating back to 1935, proceeding chronologically shelf by shelf. On the floor sat an ancient wooden crate, perfectly intact: *Kodak 9A Century Camera* was embossed on the outside and stamped with the *Montgomery Ward* logo.

The girls chattered back and forth busily; Olivia sighed and, leaning in, spoke softly in Mrs. Bundle's ear. "Brother went great guns with the picture-taking for a time. After that, things just rather petered out. I daresay he hasn't got the shutterbug fire in him anymore. The years they go by, bit by bit." She clucked with regret. "As they say…'Wishing isn't doing.' And here we are now. Nonetheless," she brightened, "he just might be convinced to take *your* photos before you leave us. The young ones might like that." Suddenly, she smiled—finally, a genuine one.

Mrs. Bundle smiled back, replying, "Yes, I know they'd love that. That's very kind, Olivia."

Suddenly Erin shrieked. "Is *that* Mister Woodsum? Ho-ly cow! Look at his hair!" she exclaimed, pointing at the lone framed photograph in the room, positioned distinctly in the center of the work table. It was a 5"x7" black and white close-up of two young men laughing, heads together, one arm slung casually round the other. It was another time, a genuine slice of jolly repartee: both without a care in the world, buddies hamming it up for the camera. The fellow on the left was a striking blond chap in his own right: hair cropped closely and very neat, sporting round rimless spectacles giving him a studious look; wearing a white open collar shirt, he seemed the more reserved and mature of the two. With his tall stature, he had a commanding air about him; he would be the one most in charge. But it was the second young man who had caught Erin's attention: spectacle-less with a copious head of black hair dominated by a shock cascading recklessly over his forehead, he possessed a playful grin and vibrant blue eyes that sparkled with fun, indicating only trouble was afoot when anyone entered his world. The features were distinctive; it could only be Woodsum Pettyfer—in his much younger years.

"Oh, yes, that's him." Olivia chuckled, "He was a handful of fun back then, brother was."

"He's a piece of work! Aye, and it sure looks like a long, long time ago." Erin said. "Oh! It says '*Happy Times*' on the back."

"Oh, yes, it was. August, 1939." She smiled wistfully and her eyelashes flittered; a memory had again softened her stern exterior. "It was such a fun time…for us all. Ahh, summer…free and easy."

"Sure, and Mister Woodsum looks like he's got a wee bit of the divil in him!" Erin peered closer, "I'll bet back then he and this older chum here gave the lasses a run for their money, didn't they now?"

Angie added, "Definitely. They're both gorgeous!"

"Who's the young man with him?" Mrs. Bundle asked harmlessly.

As though the shutter slapped shut, Olivia's face and demeanor changed and the pinched look returned. She clutched the screwdriver to her bosom, hiding how stricken she *really* was. She griped, "Oh, him. Just another sorry mate." Her affectionate air and ease seemed to have transformed to…was it bad temper, Mrs. Bundle wondered, or just plain melancholy? She thought, *her happy, carefree memories have turned to…pain…or hurt feelings. She wasn't about to talk about that man — no two ways about it. Poor Olivia.*

Suddenly the floor throbbed beneath them, issuing forth a solid thrum strong enough to cause their feet to buzz. Rhythmic *thump-a thumpa* sounds, like the bass in a marching band, played out in full reverberation below. Erin reached for the nearby chair, unsteady.

Without explanation and ever-efficient, Olivia crooked her neck and glanced down at the enamel ribbon watch pin on her breast. "My, my! Isn't it getting on now! All this dilly-dallying won't do. We still have much, much more to see. Shall we?"

The girls nodded good-humoredly. Mrs. Bundle was not so easily sidetracked. *There's a story here, to be sure…but probably not one to be heard today.*

Locking the panel behind her, Olivia, yet again the trained tour guide, led them back into the foyer's great space and they proceeded further down the hall and through a grand door. "This is the formal dining room. It's a large yet intimate space. In its heyday, we provided seating for fifty guests."

"Wow." With care, Erin ran her fingers along the huge, sensual Aubusson tapestry hanging on the complete section of wall, which helped provide soundproofing for the grand space.

Olivia pointed out the swinging door, "That leads to the kitchen and our innkeepers' suite of rooms out back." She grabbed the large screwdriver from under her arm and gently waved it in figure eights, placing stress on her words with quiet singsong emphasis, "*Off limits*...to guests for now, *except* in emergencies." Without giving them a chance to respond, she suddenly turned on her heel and ordered, "This way, ladies!"

They followed her obediently back to the main foyer.

"Now!" she said pointing the big screwdriver instructively, "There's one more area we have yet to visit after the den. Come along." She moved quickly as they crossed the large foyer into an informal sitting room. "This is the guests' den—you know, a place to congregate, a hangout of sorts." The vintage wallpaper was of multihued birds in flight; pleasantly-shabby easy chairs—with comfortable cushions in a variety of barkcloth floral prints—dotted the room like colorful shrubs; twig-inspired tables and lots of hanging plants gave the room a relaxing "nest" impression. "Come join me over here," she lowered her voice expectantly, "to the quietest but most distinctive room at Mount Holly Mansion." She had reached the far side of the room and they were right behind her. She turned the brass knob of an imposing mahogany door. "This was Father's pride and joy. Behold, The Grand Library!"

The juxtaposition between where they were coming from—the small, unimposing den—to this new space was striking. It was a colossal room and it took their breath away. They stepped into an academic world of wonder filled with large, impressive ten-foot-high bookshelves interspersed with deep hardwood-paneled walls and doors. The walls housed a treasure trove (catalogued and organized) of every grouping of text, prose, and varied content in a variety of languages. There were leather bound editions of reference books in history and philosophy; large tomes of geography and maps; books of fiction, novels, and mythical classics of literature—hundreds (notwithstanding, pages in the thousands) of literary gold pieces.

"Even as little-traveled as we were up here on the mountain—mind you, it was only once a year we journeyed to the big city during the holidays—regardless, Father, at all times, wanted us to be," she held up her fingers in quotes, "'*well-read*, well-spoken, and worldly.'" It was as though she was reciting a script, one she had repeated many times, "Oh, yes. Especially about history and key world events over the centuries. We learned to speak and write French, and German, and the rudiments of Latin, of course. Father was a bit of an enigma, plainspoken but very passionate about his own beliefs and politics, a true isolationist who loved sharing the knowledge within the walls of the library with all of like mind who came to visit. He was a man with principles who created his own utopia up here on the Saltash. He passed on those views and perspectives to us." Olivia bowed her head humbly, "He quite liked it when our guests—from all over world and quite learned, mind you—were taken aback by the scope and breadth of his collection. You can believe this library has seen a lot of action over time," her breath caught. She blushed, "reading activity, that is."

"Holy moly!" Erin shrieked with glee, "Is that a library ladder, Miss Olivia? I've always wanted to go on a library ladder! Oy! I'll be gobsmacked!" She ran her hand along the ten-foot tall ladder's sturdy rungs. "Look, Angie! It glides, see now?" She gently pushed the wheeled ladder; it slid effortlessly sideways along the wall-long track. Olivia watched patiently, evidently used to the reaction to this novelty.

"Well, will you look at that." Angie said. "Love it!"

Erin moved it slowly down the long wall. "See? It travels all the way, even around that corner!" She faced her host. "Miss Olivia, can I climb it?"

Olivia nodded slowly. "Yes-s-s, my dear. But only if you're very careful."

"Oh, no doubt!" Erin was off—with caution, as promised.

Olivia nodded toward the nearest corner where an ornate Chippendale chair was paired with a massive desk which housed a tremendous amount of cubbies and small drawers like little apartment doors in a dollhouse; a supersized hutch above held old ledgers. "Mrs. Bundle, this is where Mother sat and conducted all her correspondence, kept the inn records. And where Aurelia still does exactly the same."

In a far corner, an imposingly large lantern hung over darkly plush leather armchairs. Kerosene lamps on tables dotted the literary landscape throughout the room; the dangling crystal pendants did double duty, beautiful to look at but functional to intensify and reflect light. In the middle of one of the tables an elaborate, leather bound bible, elevated on a table stand, displayed its calligraphy-inscribed pages left open with an embroidered marker. Olivia pointed with pride. "That's the Pettyfer family bible. Father was always very proud of our unblemished roots, dating back to the Norman Conquest in England of 1066. Mother's lineal descent was from an American Revolution patriot named Potter—even though she never cared much about all that DAR hot air. All the family history has been meticulously entered on the flyleaves." The wall above was graced with a large ornate carving in fantastic gold squiggles amidst a crimson background—in the forefront, the large carved head of a dark knight, very impressive. "That, for what it's worth," she pointed with the screwdriver, "is the Pettyfer coat of arms." Her voice held a tinge of weariness at re-telling the Pettyfer family history.

Delicately tracing her fingers over the thin yellowed page, Angie gulped, "Wow! This is so cool."

"Now, you all go ahead." Olivia urged, "Help yourself to any of the books while you're here. They're all on permanent loan." She casually added to Mrs. Bundle, "If you're interested, we have quite an extensive mystery and children's book sections, too. The library is set up on the Dewey Decimal Classification just like a real library—ten classes, each divided into ten divisions, each having ten sections."

They were off like a shot to explore, and a good amount of time passed. Olivia unobtrusively left them alone, allowing them to explore the neatly-catalogued shelves at their leisure. They gleefully chose books to read, lingering on one, and then another, and another. Two heavy oak tables in each corner afforded areas for privacy, spreading out oversized books and maps, and contented study. Even as their searches brought out the occasional exclamation of delight, they kept to their own discovery while sounds throughout the rest of the inn were muffled and faraway. Angie became engrossed in a Montgomery Ward Catalog that was dated 1922. Erin squealed with joy before disappearing deep within the pages of an original 1939 first edition of one Nancy Drew novel she had not yet read: *The Clue of the Tapping Heels*. She added this to her collection of five other vintage mystery series heroines, including Trixie Belden, Beverly Gray, and Judy Bolton.

A classic mystery aficionado, Mrs. Bundle was enthralled with the vast collection, many of which were long out of print. She thoroughly enjoyed flipping through coveted 1941 monthly editions of *Ellery Queen's Mystery Magazine*, setting aside a half dozen for good measure.

As she randomly perused the lower shelves of vintage children's books, a book caught her eye, almost jumping out at her. She paused, then gasped. "No! Oh, my!" Her hand shook slightly as she chose the thin but larger than normal children's book. "I can't believe it!"

Here in this library, was a copy of a book she had searched for, given to her by her Aunt Nancy, one she had read and shared with Karen and Les. They had read theirs so often together it had fallen apart over the years. Both children had put their own scribbling touches in the book. Years later when she went looking for it, it was no longer in the old toy chest or on their bookshelves. Since then, she searched every yard, library, and jumble sale, but had never been able to replace it. Recently, it had come into her memory again and when she searched online, she discovered as she suspected, it was no longer in print. Rare copies were pricey and very dear to those lucky enough to own one.

But now, here was that exact book, appearing as if by magic! She held the like-new copy, carefully caressing it in her hands. This, she marveled, was truly a treat and a half! Her fingers traced the title: ***Deegie And The Fairy Princess*** by Ruth W. Rempel ~ Illustrated by Dietrich G. Rempel and James A. Wiley, 1949.

With an overload of anticipation, she opened the cover. Ah, she remembered these pages! The illustrations were lit up with still-vibrant color, enough to charm any five-year-old. The story, both mesmerizing and troubling, was about a little boy named Deegie living in a castle with a plethora of barnyard pals: Perky the Pup, Cuddly the Cat, Yippy the Chick, Squawky the Duck, Hoppy the Rabbit, Chubby the Pig, Fleecy the Lamb, Milky the Cow, Frisky the Horse, and Balky the Mule. Deegie leads a happy life with the animals as his only friends and family until one day, a mean North Wind comes along, and blows all the animals away.

She skimmed the pages; at the mid-point, she sighed with delight. "Ahh, yes!"

It felt wonderful. Like any good book, the anticipation was in the turning of every page, the smell of the paper, the denouement of the story and the familiarity in its retelling over and over. There was nothing like a good solid book in one's hands! Favorite stories that you could pass around, and pass down to loved ones! She set the precious book in her lap, savoring the thought that she would spend the next few days with this special best friend nearby. She couldn't wait...but, in true reader passion, she would!

Mrs. Bundle relaxed, reflecting in the quietness of the library with Angie and Erin nearby. It was as if there was no time here. There was no ticking away of clocks, no clicking or buzzing of phones, no whirring or beating of appliances, and—God forbid!—no clamoring TVs or brightly lit computer screens; nothing to cause distractions or invade one's senses.

"Oh, no," Aurelia had offered earlier in her dainty voice, "Father and Mother didn't believe in all of that nonsense. And we seem to have taken that belief to heart, too." Everything important was planned around meal and tea times, and the rising and setting of the sun (a most delightful concept, Mrs. Bundle decided, one that should be employed more often). Indisputably, Mount Holly Mansion Inn wasn't like stepping back in time; it was truly a living, breathing, working relic that embraced early 20th century practices and ways, shunning all qualities of modernity. It was both charming but work intensive; enlightening in its minimalism but quite complicated; peaceful and simply remarkable where time had stood still in such a delightful manner. The house was run on pure early-1900s ingenuity in which all three Pettyfers had their roles to play.

Mrs. Bundle couldn't help but note that the Official Grand Tour had been perfectly led by each of the three like a professional tag team and was flawless in its intent to make them feel welcome but ever-so-gently pushed where they were allowed within the confines of the inn's vast space.

"There's a lot to see here." Woodsum had said during teatime, "It takes a while to get acclimated."

After a pleasant hour, they heard a distinct step and merry whistling and the lone man of the house joined them again. He pointed out even more treasures within the library, for later perusal during their stay. "But that there," he pointed with disdain at an unusual door with dappled leaden glass, "is the gun cabinet. Off limits if you can't tell by that big padlock. We keep it locked up tighter 'n Fort Knox. Father was quite the collector, which *some* people seem to appreciate." He smiled at Erin's crinkled nose.

"Guns—ugh!" she said.

"I'm with you, missy. I can't abide guns either."

Erin swept her arms like a windmill. "Sure and me head's spinning. There's doors everywhere here! How do you keep track of it all?"

"Oh, don't you worry," he tapped his nose; there was a bit of mischief in his voice, "we know where everything and *everybody* is. We know where to go and when to go, and who goes where and why. But I ain't no stool pigeon. I keep it under my hat till I need to spill the beans. Say, speaking of just that! I bet you'd like to see good ol' grandfather. Mind you, he's something of a hermit." Woodsum's eyes shone with glee. He moved across the large room, then stopped at one of the many doors. "We got him right over here…he likes to nap in this here closet."

"You keep your grandfather…in a closet." Erin pronounced with one eyebrow quirked comically.

Angie added doubtfully, "Uh-huh. Right. Um…he sleeps here?"

He slapped his thigh. "Ha! Right-o! C'mon, now, don't be afraid. He won't bite ya." He turned the knob slowly while they stood well behind him, peering into the shadows. His tone was furtive, "We used to hide in here when we were kids."

"Goodness gracious!" Mrs. Bundle exclaimed.

Looming at over seven feet in height, a large, happy moon face gazed back at them.

"Okay…it's a grandfather clock." Angie confirmed. "Funny, Mr. Woodsum. Very funny."

"Oh, Grandfather!" Erin giggled with relief.

Certainly, it wasn't just another odd occurrence here at the inn that the handsome, massive clock was not only hidden from view, but located far away from all the hustle and bustle of the inn, and Mrs. Bundle had to add, "We haven't heard a thing from Ol' Grandfather since we arrived."

Erin's observation was more blunt, "C'mere now, that's odd. How come he's not tickin' and tockin' out in plain view?"

"Well, because we don't like to wind him up for no reason. Noisy fellow! He's an old relic and we like to give him a break. Let's give it a whirl just so you can see." He deftly pulled the chains and tinkered with the innards. Suddenly, it came to life. Its quarterly chime had a faraway sound, a tinny and sweetly muted version of Westminster Cathedral chime. Woodsum reached in and removed an old wooly blanket, then stepped back from the open face door. Ol' Grandfather really let loose. The sound roll inside, similar to a music box, was connected to 12 chime rods cut at various lengths intended to produce different tones. It was loud as all get-out and they winced at the earsplitting harmony. He winked and yelled above the din, "Y'see what I mean? We can't abide loud noises here—especially from Ol' Grandfather!" Quickly, he shoved the old wooly blanket back inside and placed it strategically; immediately the sounds were diminished as the hammers struck the chime rods. He readjusted his spectacles and nodded. "There. Much better."

The three guests' keen observation was that the Pettyfers' list of what they couldn't or wouldn't abide had grown fairly long in just this short time since their arrival. This most recent non-abidment wasn't lost on them, causing them to ponder what else the Pettyfers couldn't tolerate.

Woodsum gave Erin and Angie a tutorial on the history of "windin' up Ol' Grandfather."

As she watched, Mrs. Bundle noted that peace and silence had been brought to the highest level at the inn, and the silence was considerably more golden than one could ever imagine. That said, there truly are some things that never change from one generation to the next. The old bones of the inn, the stately walls, the high ceilings, the ornate furnishings from a bygone era: history was here, right here...so much had occurred in these rooms, *here*.

A gut feeling niggled at her brain. For certain, the inn had its own story to tell; the fact of the matter was, the inn had a personality of its own! Eyes shut, she imagined what it must have been like sixty years before. She took a deep breath and cleared her mind. Even as there was an innate sensation of comfort—a sunny sense of hospitality, further layered by the charming furnishings and amplified by the invigorating power of mixed aromas throughout (scented natural pine, lemon oil polish, the comforting smells of home-cooking from scratch—all tantalizing to noses begging for more)—she perceived an underlying feeling of...*yes*...it was a feeling of *conflict*. No doubt about it.

The room became larger in her mind, not threatening, but certainly imposing. *Yes*, she thought, her sixth sense kicking in, joining the gut feeling, there's some unrest here—or, something unfinished...and *even*, Mrs. Bundle couldn't help but acknowledge and embrace that familiar intuitive twitch, an aura of apprehension. Someone was...or had been...very *fearful*. It was elusive to Mrs. Bundle's thoughts, but possibly...she shivered as a breath of cold air passed through her like a knife, something quite *dark*. This house was an enigma—warm and loving yet cold and...yes, secretive! She tried to open her mind further but was abruptly interrupted by a familiar deep, very sane voice, loud and clear, resonating like an alarm and overcoming her thoughts—*Dearest Letitia, you know full well once you cross that unsettling threshold, there is no turning back....take care, dear....take care!*

It was like a cross between words of warning and advice; she knew she should pay attention to both. *For goodness sake! Shame on you,* she told herself, *you're here to enjoy a few days off with the girls and take a nice rest—certainly not to go snooping into others' private past.* The off-putting thoughts dissipated quickly as she brought herself back to the present conversation and the distant tolling of the gong.

"There's the warning! Here at the inn we can't abide stragglers, especially when it comes to eating. Are you dames ready for dinner?" Woodsum was asking.

"Really?" Mrs. Bundle asked, "Dinner already? My word. I can't believe I'm hungry!"

The hours had flown by; they were so busy learning about all that the inn had to offer, and exploring the library, that they still had yet to get to their rooms.

"Now that you mention it," Angie touched her growling tummy, "I'm ravenous!"

"Time to eat again?" Erin pondered the quandary, and then said amiably, "Aye, that's a good problem, right!" Placing her hand through Woodsum's proffered arm, she exclaimed, "Aye, *this* dame is ready!"

Chapter VII
Settling In

Ah, the food! Like magic, superior cuisine appeared, as though created by a food genie with Olympian culinary ability. In point of fact, everything about the Mount Holly Mansion Inn was beyond this world, as though a magic wand had been waved and they were in a winter fantasyland of fun.

The delicious supper was served promptly at eight o'clock, and consisted of fried smelts (Woodsum's wholesome reward from a recent ice-fishing expedition to nearby Echo Lake), creamed scalloped potatoes, and warm yeasty brown bread. Simply put, it all felt like being at home and they dug in. With no holding back, dinnertime passed pleasantly as they all ate together family-style. Lively warm conversation melded amidst deep hums of complete gastronomic pleasure. The main course was followed by a lovely light dessert of lemon curd topped with raspberry conserve. By the time the stream of food came to an end and the last bites were taken, the guests felt completely at ease in the company of the innkeepers.

The Pettyfers were thoroughly delightful human beings somewhere around their mid-80s—if Mrs. Bundle's quick calculations were correct based on the trio's stories and recollections. Figuratively and literally, the Pettyfer line ended with them, as there were no more Pettyfers to carry the torch or the Pettyfer name. Their health seemed incredible, almost Herculean, if one took into consideration the heartiness of their spirit and physicality of the jobs they were required to perform at the inn. Depending on which sibling they were addressing, they simply called each other brother or sister. Everyone else, it seemed, was referred to as Dear Heart, Young Gal, Girlie, or Missy. The most odd phenomenon Mrs. Bundle noticed immediately was that the Pettyfers spoke in the collective We, a pronoun transformed and reissued in a curious way, expressing the singular tight-knit entity they personified as The Pettyfer Triplets. All three seemed ageless: their hearing seemed acute; their eyesight no worse than others half their age; jointly, they had plenty of pluckiness. Mrs. Bundle was left to wonder: how on earth did they do it?

Sharp as tacks, they could remember details of the inn dating back many decades. Mrs. Bundle wondered if they took some kind of magical memory pill, their recall was so remarkable; they shared delightful trivia about their antecedents in nearby Plymouth Notch, and its famous history.

"Oh yes, we met President Coolidge when we were very young. He was born in Plymouth Notch in 1892 by the same midwife as Father." Aurelia blushed. "Father fished with Calvin, Sr. when he came to visit the family homestead periodically. Grace, his wife, was talkative, and lots of fun! Mother said she was quick-witted and quite amusing, nothing like Silent Cal. 'Course no one ever talked politics, being on opposite sides. As just a boy in knickers, brother went to the Grange with Father for the Masons once and Mister Coolidge was there. John and Calvin, his sons, were much older than us." She used her silver fork like a teacher's pointer. "Oh, Father always said they were both fine young men. Mister Coolidge was in Vermont when he got word by messenger that Harding had died. Shortly after that Calvin, Jr. got a blister playing tennis and got the sepsis and died. He's buried right down in Notch Cemetery."

"Sepsis?" Erin, unaware of the ailment, asked.

"Infection of the blood. Tragic." Olivia pronounced flatly. She went on, "Uh-huh. President Coolidge was just a country lawyer who worked his way up the political ladder. Popular because he believed in small government. Didn't waste his words. I like that. Father said he was good to fish with because he didn't talk much. This was only in the summer, mind you, when he came to visit. Certainly, not one for smelting. Too cold for him. Father always said there was nothing to show a man's true colors than jigging for smelt in a cozy shanty in the dead of a frosty winter day."

"We all love smelts." Woodsum declared. "There's a secret to the batter. That's the key."

Mrs. Bundle's taste buds told her there might be beer, crushed saltines, and cornmeal in the mixture. "Whatever the secret is, they were delightful."

"That was just about the best smelt I ever tasted!" Angie exclaimed and sat back, glad she had worn her loose jeans today. "Well, that is, besides Gumpy's—but he might like to know your recipe."

"We'd be happy to share it." Aurelia offered, then paused. "That is, um, sister?"

"I'm sure we can share it." Olivia confirmed.

"Uncle Carl and me go smeltin' all winter, aye. We get a big pailful! At Knapp Pond we get rainbow and brook trout in the summer. Sometimes, the Clancy twins tag along." Erin sighed resignedly, "Sure and I can't get rid of the lads, much as I try! Ach! Mister Woodsum, you would *not* want to meet them dodgy Clancy twins. Talk about trouble! Forget about fishin' quiet when they're around. Me brother Jack says he'd like to knock their blocks clean off sometimes with all their foosterin' and fightin'. They are truly annoying beasts." Erin patted her full tummy and slouched back in her chair. "Whew!" She gave a sly grin. "I just can't *abide* them Clancy twins. Not one bit." She huffed in disgust, causing a chain reaction that made her dark curls quiver; her quick look monitored the impact of her use of *their* special word, "I absolutely *loathe* them!"

"They sound like trouble—capital T." Woodsum nodded sympathetically, drawing a slow toke on his pipe. "Ayuh. Being as you ain't no pushover though, you probably keep 'em in line. I'd wager a good sum on that. Had a similar situation in my younger days. Here's what you do." He waved a thumb over his shoulder, and yelled, "*Scram!* And don't let the back door hit you on the way out!"

There was a healthy guffaw of camaraderie between Erin and Woodsum, a bond firmly cemented by their mutual non-abidement of annoyances that fell into the Clancy twins category.

"My, my. An incredible meal." Mrs. Bundle murmured, covering an escaping yawn. What more was there to say? Everything at this minute was…perfection.

Aurelia picked up the leaded glass decanter filled with cherry cordial from the sideboard, motioning toward Mrs. Bundle's empty glass. Two magenta spots (courtesy of her third glass of same) dotted her cheeks, giving her a youthful glow. "Another, dear heart?"

"Oh, no, no! I couldn't put away 'another' anything." She stifled a yawn. "Oh, dear! I'm so sorry. Between the hike up, the Official Grand Tour, and this splendid dinner, I'm thoroughly tuckered out."

"Happens every time." Olivia sipped her cordial delicately.

Aurelia added with a smile, "We aim to please."

"Erin." Angie nudged her sister gently. "You're not falling asleep at the table, are you?"

"Ach, I've got sleepy sand in me eyes!" Erin removed her eyeglasses, carefully placing them on her cloth napkin; her eyes were glazed. "It's so grand here, sure and away I feel like…I'm dreamin'! Am I dreamin'?" She sat up straight in her chair, struggling against nature to stay awake, afraid she might miss something even more wonderful.

"Well, then," Woodsum declared, rising. "As ol' Benjamin used to say, 'Early to bed, early to rise…'" he paused as a mischievous grin played across his face, "'*work like heck, and advertise*'"

"That's not what Benjamin Franklin said!" Erin chided, alert again. "He said, 'Early to bed, early to rise, makes a man healthy, wealthy, and wise.' You're pulling me leg, aren't y' now, Mister Woodsum?"

He hooted. "Gotcha! Ha! Girlie, that was Benjamin *Champagne* who came up with that one. An old school pally—lived up to his name and then some—spifflicated most of the time in his younger days—" At Erin's confused look he clarified, "too much of the giggle water. Then he became a big cheese—made all his money selling tractor tires in the 40s." Erin was following his every word. "Why, he could sell paint off your barn door! Fact is, you remind me a bit of him—and how!"

"Y'know, Mister Woodsum, people say I'm a hard lass to understand, what with me Irish accent and all," Erin scratched her head, "but I think you surely got your own way of talkin'—what language is it, em, exactly?"

"Ha! You slay me, kiddo!" he slapped his knee. He mimicked her light lilt, "'*What language is it?*' Hardy har! That's a swell one!"

"What that is, is enough tomfoolery for one night, brother. You know what they say…'Talk less and say more'." Olivia scolded, with a hint of a smile behind her eyes. "You go on. The bottles are already filled. Then you can take the ladies up to their rooms."

"We'd love to help…" Mrs. Bundle rose.

The two women protested loudly. "Oh, no! You couldn't. We don't abide helping!" Olivia picked up the hefty tray with apparent ease—even after a long day of work. They watched them gather everything up; Aurelia added, "This is *your* time to rest. It all gets taken care of; don't you fret."

As if on cue, Woodsum returned from the kitchen, hands full. He handed each guest their own towel-wrapped round package, out of which peeked out a solid black plug. "Here you go!"

"What's this?" Erin asked, taking hers. "Oooh! It's so nice and warm!"

"It's called a hot water bottle—excuse me for saying—the old-fashioned copper kind. Thank-you!" Mrs. Bundle said gratefully, stifling another yawn. "Good Lord, I'm bushed! Not to mention very sore from head to toe from that hike." She flexed her foot, which felt tender—one of her recent injuries rearing its ugly head.

"Yessir. Your own personal bed warmer. It'll keep you toasty." Woodsum said, "C'mon, follow me."

"Erin, don't forget your glasses." Mrs. Bundle reminded the girl, who reinstated the specs into their proper pretty groove above her nose.

Woodsum led them up the formal front hallway staircase, the first time they had traveled upstairs; Erin clung to the elaborate twisting balustrade. Their respective rooms had been readied in anticipation of an early night. The lighting was very hazy, lit only by one muted electric wall fixture, making the trip somewhat spooky.

At the top of the wide grand stairway was a landing opening to an exceptionally large common area, a great room comprised of a number of comfortable armchairs with ottomans, side tables, another area presumably for all guests to share. Two large wings, West and East, came off this area, running perpendicular. Five solid wooden doors lined each respective side—there were ten bedrooms.

Toward the rear of the common area where the wide hallway converged, Woodsum pointed out two full baths. "Here are the johns. During peak season, this one's for Gents; this one's for Ladies. But you all go ahead and feel free to use both." He pushed opened the Ladies door. "See? Water closet, all marble sinks with brass fittings—and you got your clawfoot bathtub—all original. Best to wait until morning unless you got an, um, emergency. It's kinda dark with the low lighting at night." He motioned to another nearby door, "That over there leads to the *Swiss Family Robinson Suite*. That was what we used for the big families—its got its own living room, bath, and two bedrooms. 'Course, we keep it all closed up now—being wintertime, y'know."

"Someone must have enjoyed that book." Mrs. Bundle said. "To name it that."

"Yup. That would be Father—Mother, too." They followed him. "They were partial to European fiction—father was savvy enough to read the native German edition by Johann Wyss. He fancied that other German author who wrote stories set in the Wild West, too."

"Carl May?" Angie asked. "We studied him."

"Yes, that's it. Man, he could write a good western better 'n anyone." He was now at the end of the corridor. "That, my friends, is the old dumbwaiter. Got its use over the years." He paused at the large door, "I'm showing you now so you'll steer clear of it. Basically, it's a movable frame inside a shaft; the cart gets dropped by rope on a pulley that's guided up and down by rails." He spoke directly to Erin. "Not for passenger use, mind you. We used it just for heavy items — holds up to 500 pounds. It's controlled manually — slick. What's that notice say, Erin?"

Erin read the sign on the shaft's door, "Oh, dang! 'Out of order'?"

"Yup. That first step's a big one! Ha! As a rule, we don't use it. No shock absorbers so it's *noisy* as all get-out! 'Specially when it strikes the top of the shaft. Squeals and squeaks like a banshee on a rocket!" He stopped. "Okay, now. See, this is the back stairway. Going down takes us the back way to the kitchen — and to our living quarters. Now, watch out you don't get lost in the dark, miss the bathroom, and trip."

"Warning taken. We'll make sure we're careful. Right, girls?" Mrs. Bundle said, thankful to have been given the danger tour — and the caution to stay put unless it was necessary.

"Where does that go?" Miss Nosey Posey turned the knob on the door beside the back stair vestibule. "Hey! It's locked."

"Erin…" Angie warned, "Jeesum!"

"No, no, that's okay." Woodsum chuckled. "That door goes up to the attic where all you'll find is just a bunch of useless junk."

"Gaw! This inn is absolutely massive." Angie looked round her. "I'm overwhelmed."

"Yup! But you'll get used to it." Woodsum turned back to the task at hand. "This way, ladies. Over thataway is the men's wing — all vacant. This wing here is the more *feminine* side of the house. Your rooms are down the hall. Sisters wanted you to each have your own."

Their attention was focused as they followed him, clutching their water bottles.

"Look, Mrs. B!" Erin pointed as they passed the second door. "Oy! Our rooms have names. See? That one would be *Gibson Girl*. Who's a Gibson Girl?"

Angie said, "They were the magazine cover girls of the early twentieth century — it was always a feminine image of the beauty in that day. Much different from today's modern woman."

"Bingo!" Woodsum marveled. "Cousin Milly said you were a clever bunch, and she was right." At the third door, he paused and drew out the ring of old-fashioned skeleton keys. As if letting them in on a special secret, he winked, unlocked the door, and then bowed slightly. "Here we are. Angie. Sisters chose this one especially for you. See?" He motioned toward the door marked *Lady in Waiting* and stepped aside, "After you, Milady."

Three gasps of delight escaped as they stepped inside the lavender scented room in soft whites and welcoming pastels. The lemon yellow wallpaper featuring dainty 18th Century toile vignettes was totally enchanting. A toasty glow emanated from the fireplace.

"This one's just for me?" Angie asked, thrilled. "It's beautiful! And huge!"

"Yes, young gal." Woodsum's eyes sparkled at her excitement. "Pretty nifty, huh? Mother always had a way with decorating and Aurelia has followed in her footsteps keeping things real nice. She put all the personal touches in each room—flowers, soaps, and such. Makes 'em right special, doesn't she? So you just go ahead and enjoy it. Ready missy?"

By now, Erin was chomping at the bit. "Aye!"

Woodsum led her next door to the fourth room. "Go 'head, Erin. *It's the berries!* Enjoy!"

"Oh, my word!" Oozing anticipation, she burst through the door labeled *Little Lass*, and wasn't disappointed. The charming suite of bedroom and sitting area abounded with bright plaids, chintzes, and grosgrain bows; beside a massive built-in armoire were floor-to-ceiling shelves housing a collection of antique dolls, building blocks, old tin trucks and cars, wind-up toys, and other toys of a bygone era. A nearby vanity table with petite bench and oversized mirror held a collection of perfume bottles. She ran to it and sat down. "Oh, Lordy, I *am* dreamin'! Look, Angie!" It was a young girl's fantasy room, the kind of space even "adult" children would be thrilled to explore. There was an adorably chunky black stove set into the fireplace beside which sat a coal hod full of dark shiny coal and a small shovel.

"See that? It'll keep you warm 'n toasty 'til morning." Woodsum said. "You don't need to fiddle with it—okay?"

She nodded, taking in the room with complete pleasure. "Aye, sure and I won't fiddle with it."

"And there's your own lantern right beside the bed. In case you get spoo—"

Woodsum was cut off as Erin said, "Oh, I never get scared, Mr. Woodsum. You'll not need to worry 'bout me."

Mrs. Bundle was next. The final room was situated over the front hallway. "And you, Madam! We thought this one was best for you. It looks out down onto the pond and down to the valley." Eyes twinkling and smiling to beat the band, Woodsum stepped aside at the door labeled *Queen's Suite*. "After you…"

It was an oversized, grandly ornate, elegant bedroom with an equally ample dressing room. The furniture was exquisite in silk fabrics and tones of rich royal red. The room paint, chair rail, and wall accents were in pink hues. Beautiful vintage wallpaper—collages of lush roses—circled the room like natural rose vines upon trellises, traveling up the lower half wall from baseboard to chair rail. A posh candle chandelier, fully lit, hung above the vanity, casting streams of soft highlights, and creating a rosy blush, all reflected in the vanity's mirror—even the most plain visage could only be transformed into beauty within that mirror. The ceiling was a mural masterpiece of hand-painted cherubs, wood nymphs, and fairies.

"It's….fantastical!" Mrs. Bundle took it all in as the girls oohed and aahed. "Per-fect!"

"Well, being as you're the queen bee here this weekend, we figured it would suit you just fine." Woodsum's head waggled and nodded at her delight.

With their backpacks delivered to their respective rooms, all was ready: pillows were plumped high against carved headboards; warm satin comforters floated like fluffy clouds over each massive mahogany bed; soft hand towels and face cloths lay ready by each washbasin and pitcher; plush oriental rugs with nature themes provided a buffer between the cold hardwood floors and bare feet;

original bell pulls hung ready to yank beside each bed, which Erin couldn't help but execute.

"Missy, those don't work anymore, so pull away. And make yourself to home. Well! G'night, ladies," Woodsum saluted and turned smartly. "Don't take any wooden nickels!" His chuckling echoed behind him as he headed all the way down the long corridor, past the bathrooms and down the back stairs to his own quarters.

"Gaw—what a day. I'm so tired I think I could sleep forever." Angie embraced Mrs. Bundle. "I'm so glad we came!" She turned and put her arm around Erin. "Little sister, you're sure to be all right in that big, big bedroom all by your lonesome? You won't have Aineen in the bed beside you like at home."

"Of course! Surely, and I can't wait!" Fearlessly, she hugged her water bottle tightly to her. "D'ya think there might be ghosts here? Y'know, maybe a special ghost?" Her eyes, accentuated with purple tired rings and the emerald green rims, glistened in the soft light. "Ach! Murdered, star-crossed lovers. Could it be possible?" She tapped her bright red cheeks in anticipation. "No, wait! A wicked curse, surely there could be a wicked curse on the house!" Erin, with Celtic heritage alive and well, loved all things melancholic—the more macabre the better—and could never miss an opportunity to marry romance with ghoulish imaginings, thereby spooking herself to distraction.

"Oh, gaw! Go to bed! You'll give yourself conniptions if you don't watch out." Angie pushed her hair off her forehead, exhausted. "Okay, you guys. I'm out of gas. See you in the morning." She gave a worn-out wave, smiled, and disappeared down the hall and into her room.

"G'night, sister. *Oíche mhaith*, Mrs. B—a pleasant sleep to you." Erin edged past Mrs. Bundle with bravado toward the shadowed room.

Mrs. Bundle gave her a reassuring hug. "And to you too, my dear." She lowered her voice. "You know I'm right next door if you need me. Just give me the signal—right?"

Erin bunched up her hand and gently tapped three times on the wall. During overnighters at Mrs. B's, the distinctive triple tap, passed down from Angie, had become their special way of signaling distress—for emergencies of any kind. "For kindred spirits," Mrs. Bundle always assured, "always for those who need not be alone." They gave each other a conspiratorial wink and Mrs. Bundle nudged her. "Off you go, now, my luv. Have a pleasant sleep."

Erin's lopsided grin morphed even wider as she succumbed to a big yawn. As she closed the door behind her, her dimples sprung to life and she said out of the blue, "Aye, that Mister Woodsum, he's the funniest bloke. Wouldn't you agree? Sure, and we're bound to have ourselves an adventure here. G'night, mum!"

No more had Erin's door closed than there was a quiet knock at the door. Angie stuck her head in and said, "Do you have just a minute, Mrs. B?"

"For you, anything, my dear." She waited; Angie scooted in and settled on the bed.

Mrs. Bundle knew from their last alone time together that she had been weighing a most important decision. "Em...I just wanted you to know. You know, regarding that thing that's been bothering me?"

"Yes. Have you had a chance to talk with Jack?"

"I did but...he didn't agree at all. I thought you might help me talk to him when we get back. Y'see, I..." she paused. "I keep thinking 'what is my true purpose?'" Her voice was husky and very tired, "I love him. I want to make it work, but...I'm just not sure how." She paused, a tight little smile playing on her lips, "I think he's giving me a ring...for my birthday." She watched Mrs. Bundle's face to see if there was anything there to contradict or support that statement. A combination of fear and a frown played havoc with her features.

"Well, why so grim, my girl? That's what I'd call a good problem."

Here it came, all in a rush as she covered her eyes; her voice was emotional. "But before he begins his Professional Officer Course next year, it will mean field encampment the whole summer, and an intense orientation on an active Air Force base. Then, it's another *two years* of concentrated officer leadership training—that final year is extremely challenging, Mrs B. Oh, I've no doubt he can do it, but he's working so hard already! I just wonder if it's too much stress for him to worry about me being at school. He's a worrier—you know that, Mrs. B. I just don't want to...get in the way. It's his *dream* to be a pilot."

"It's his dream to be with you, too. All things considered, luv, he seems to be handling it all quite well—from what I observed over the holidays, he's happy. Yes, his schedule is maxed out. He's in and out of the house like a cat in the night. Has he given you any other reason to be so...conflicted?" She asked soothingly. "What bothers you so?" Mrs. Bundle loved them both and wanted them to be happy—and preferably together, if it was in the cards. They seemed to complement each other in so many ways.

"No, he hasn't given me any specific reason, or not so you could put a finger on it. But what I've been really struggling about is how *exactly* do we make it work? The long distance is so hard already. And the pressure between my studies, and lacrosse—traveling to games, getting good grades—gaw!" Her eyes drooped with total exhaustion. "It's just *really hard* to let go. And trust him."

Yes, there it was, the fear that still lingered, still held deep within after having weathered some rough times the summer before college during a Maine vacation. Would it ever leave her be so she could be totally without anxiety? "My dear, you are overtired to the nth degree. This evening is not the time to make any decisions or try to fix or figure out anything. I suggest you take the next few days, eat well, and get lots of rest. Just let this worry go for a little bit. You know," she comforted, pulling an old chestnut out of her hat, "I've always found there's nothing so important that a good night's sleep doesn't remedy."

"You're always *so* right, Mrs. B." She seemed relieved already, and rose promptly, "So I'll take your advice. Good night—" she laughed and they both finished another old but funnier saying in sync, "and don't let the bedbugs bite!"

Later, as the moon rose fully, very slight creaking sounds like little underwater baby belches betrayed a peculiar movement in the house. A series of elongated, softly scraping movements could be heard if one was acutely listening, steps plodding with difficulty from the upstairs common great room into the hallway toward the ladies' wing. Limping along with an irregular gait, progress was made.

Tentatively, the first bedroom door in the long hallway creaked open barely enough to show the slight silhouette of a woman who whispered furtively, "Come….come along. Just a bit further. You're late. I was wondering whether you'd come." She gave a low, encouraging chuckle. "Come in, you old thing, you."

"Old thing" peered suspiciously past her into the dimly lit room. Was everything ready? His heavily-lidded eyes searched, then ogled what was just beyond: yes, the glow of the fireplace, the ambient warmth…just perfect.

With new motivation, he chugged purposefully in that direction, craving the heat inside. *Ahhh, my dear, perfect, as usual! Never a complaint do I have—what patience, what caring as you attend to me—even after all these years! When it should be I that takes care of you. We'll always depend on each other, will we not…in one way or another…to pull us through all our challenges. Many a good time— we remember them, not the bad. We should never dwell on those.*

He raised his head very high and took in the image before him: the woman almost as aged as he, clad perfectly in a long-sleeved, chaste nightie, the dainty ballet slippers peeking out at the bottom hem, a shawl draped round her shoulders. *My, my,* he chided as he had many times before, *aren't we just the cat's meow? Now then, let's settle in by that very welcome fire and we can begin our reminiscing.*

She watched him with loving eyes, waiting patiently as, in bits and starts, he shuffled along. Dragging one aged appendage, then another, he grunted with relief. *Ha! There now, I've made it another time. I promise I won't stray far, my dear.*

The parched hinges squeaked as she closed the door slowly behind him. She pulled on the bolt, locking their shared memories within the room so aptly named *Golden Desire*...at least, for the while, all would be as it was.

The rest slept without knowing the more intense happenings occurring in the Midwest—a real thundersnow in Illinois with crashing lightning and all had wreaked havoc throughout the area. Chicago was already recording the blizzard as its second worse since record-keeping began—a huge twenty-three inches of snow. In Indiana, a freak tornado had touched down, with forecasters' earlier snow predictions blown out of the park with double the accumulation—two inches per hour. With the snow finally ending in the Midwest, bitter cold now set in with temperatures below zero by way of gusting winds as its whipping tail end waggled its way out of the region, leaving behind chaos and confusion not to be sorted out for days. Thousands of linemen came from as far away as Michigan. Strong winds and ice had knocked out power in large areas of Missouri, Illinois, Indiana, and Ohio. Eastward, chilling blizzard warnings in much of Pennsylvania meant a foot of snow or more. The storm expected to sweep solidly through the Northeast throughout the next day or two and had been upgraded from a winter storm warning to the real deal for all the large Northern cities, including New York City and Boston, with a mixture of snow, sleet and ice predicted. As the storm reached its northern track, visibility changed from clear to virtually zero. Travel across the United States had become a big wet mess and all were warned to just stay home.

Meanwhile, that little fickle potential Nor'easter that had been hanging about in the Atlantic Ocean was swirling round and round. Impulsively basing its mind solely on nature's whim, it veered drowsily to the west and then, with increasing speed, moved eastward with purpose, greedily eyeballing the coast. The center of the storm had taken on a circular shape more typical of a hurricane with a very small eye as its left-forward quadrant rotated onto land. Thus began a wider intense wake with its course straight up the Eastern Seaboard where it could eventually spar with its Midwest counterpart—timing was everything in this case. It moved with a fast clip as the winds blew their fair warning…we're coming for you, New England!

Chapter VIII
The New Day Awaits

They awoke early the following morning to the aroma of sweet, warmed maple syrup and buckwheat pancakes. Outside, a light snow dusted the property, forming soft white lambswool humps and deep folds amidst the frosted pines.

Like trained monkeys, the girls scurried downstairs at the sound of the gong, wearing the lovely quilted bathrobes laid out for them the night before. Mrs. Bundle followed behind, noticing her feet weren't moving as quickly as usual. In particular, the big toe on her left foot was especially sore and swollen; she chocked it up to the long snowshoe hike up the mountain the day before. *No big deal*, she challenged, pushing through the pain as she gingerly made her way downstairs.

Salivating with the intensity of food addicts, all three joined the Pettyfers in the dining room, where they were not disappointed. Platters laden with a real farmer's breakfast, replete with homemade sausage, roasted potatoes, and the afore-mentioned buckwheat pancakes awaited them on the gargantuan Chippendale-inspired sideboard. In between bites, when asked how she slept, Angie pronounced, "Like a log!"

Erin kept up a steady stream of chatter while they all ate together. "Aye, I love me room *so* much! And didn't I sleep just like a *babai!*" She chewed cheerfully. "Oh! I read all the doors! Aye, with all the names of all the rooms—I did it first thing when I woke up. Both sides—Ladies and the Gentlemen, too!" She recited them on each finger. "Besides our own three lovely rooms on the ladies side, there's the one called *Gibson Girl* and then the other before that—the first one—is called *Golden Desire*. Aye, I just love that," she sighed. "*Golden Desire*. So romantic. That would make the five total for the ladies. On the men's side, there's the big one opposite Mrs. B's—only instead of *Queen's Suite*, it's called *King's Suite*. Then let's see," she ticked off her fingers, "there's *Little Lad* and *Knight's Lair* opposite our rooms, Angie, didja know? And beside that is *Doughboy*. Ha! That's a good one, isn't it now? Would they be meanin' the Pillsbury Doughboy?"

"Well missy, doughboy is what they called the soldiers from World War I." Woodsum offered. "Another cup of joe, Mrs. Bundle?" She declined—her stomach was a bit queasy.

"You don't say!" Erin said, "And then…" she paused, "there's the last room—or the first room, whichever way you look at it." Her eyes shone, fully engaged. "Let me think…" She placed her index finger to her temple. "It began with an 'M', not a word I've seen before…"

Aurelia murmured softly. "*Michel…Michel's Choice*."

"Aye! Is that how you say it, Miss Aurelia? Mee-*khahl*? I love that! Mee-khahl." Erin's tongue rolled over the name deliciously. "*Mee-khahl's Choice*—it's exactly right across the way from my *other* favorite—*Golden Desire*. Like twins facing each other! C'mere, but here's an odd thing—*both* doors were locked! I couldn't get in to see either room like I did the others." At Olivia's arched eyebrow, she caught herself and covered her mouth. "Oopsy! Sorry, Miss Olivia. Of course, I took me a wee peek in all the other rooms. Well, I just had to, to see if they were as lovely as ours, didn't I now? Actually," she clarified, "I was looking for the darlin' kitty I heard in the wee morning hours. That's what got me up so early!" Her eyes gleamed with excitement as they returned skeptical looks.

"Kitty?" Olivia snarled, arching that eyebrow even higher in disdain.

"Aye, that's right! I heard a cat keening—ach, the poor dearie! For the life of me, I couldn't find it."

"*Kitty?*" Woodsum repeated and shook his head so profusely his ears waggled. "Oh, no, no, no! No kitties here."

"I—" Erin began, but was cut off.

"You're mistaken, child." Lips pursed, Olivia's acerbic side came forth once more as she said dryly, "There are *no* cats here at Mount Holly Mansion Inn. As we said yesterday, we don't abide cats in our establishment. Much, much too pushy and superior—the way they like to lord it over? No room here for that. Hmmpph! Our Possy just wouldn't stand for it!"

Sharing his disapproval from beneath the table, Sir Possy growled cantankerously, then licked his chops and issued a juicy burp, having enjoyed his own generous share of buckwheat pancakes. Snuffling like the quintessential old geyser that he was, he begrudgingly rekindled his interest in the already abused and mangled milk bone nearby. His old teeth chomped and gnawed, worrying it away one flake at a time.

Mrs. Bundle remained politely silent on Olivia's disparaging cat comments. She surmised the real reason they didn't like cats was because they didn't want to offend dearest Possy. Much as the Pettyfers were entitled to their opinion, she was *so* thankful Cracker had stayed home—likely as it was he would have been turned away—and wasn't there to hear his species maligned so unjustly.

Speaking of hearing things, she remained mute on a silly question she was going to ask about last night. Her overactive mind might have been playing tricks on her, but she could have sworn she'd heard other strange noises—definitely not kitty sounds—just as she fell off to sleep...as if something quite cumbersome was being dragged across the hallway floor.

Why, she had wondered half asleep, would they be moving furniture so late? So very tired from the day's activities and inside a bed so comfortable and warm, she hadn't had the oomph to get up and investigate. However, her psyche paid later as, during the night, she had dreamed of a very dead body being lugged up and down, up and down, the corridor—until she had finally rolled over and fallen into a deep sleep.

"Well, then! How 'bout let's get this all cleaned up. Sisters?" Woodsum stood up. "I'm sure our guests would like to head back upstairs."

Aurelia and Olivia rose as hastily as women in their eighties could muster.

"But there *was* a kitty around early, early this morning," Erin insisted, not used to not being believed. "I'm daft but not that daft. Not at all like your ol' Possy's wheezin', was it now?"

Olivia moved toward the kitchen door. "Dear heart, let me assure you, there are *no* cats within miles. And mind you, those doors upstairs are locked for a reason." Her lips thinned with the hint of a grimace, "We have no plans to open those rooms again...until late spring."

"Yes, sister is right." Woodsum added, clearing his throat. He blushed uncomfortably, "We like to conserve—heat costs, wear and tear, and such, don't y'know." He exited the room like a scared rabbit.

His manner had smacked of prevarication, or as Mrs. Bundle's Aunt Nancy always called it, "fudging."

"Of course." Mrs. Bundle nodded. "I do the same at my house. Always keep the doors closed in the upstairs rooms I don't use."

"But not locked," Erin said artlessly. "You don't lock the doors. If you did, a body would be sure to want to get in and see why."

Aurelia, quiet during this exchange, was shifting on her feet, fidgeting with her napkin. "Oh dear, dear." She looked at Erin, her eyes filled with upset, "I wish we—you're—of course, dear heart, you're right, it should be—"

Olivia broke in sharply, "Sister—?" She drew in a breath, and lowered her voice, placing a gentle hand on Aurelia's shoulder. "Would you like to go lie down for a bit?"

"But, ma'am, it's mornin' already—?" Erin countered, not holding back even at Olivia's sour look. She looked to Mrs. Bundle for support and said *sotte voce*, "I heard it, mum."

"Erin...ahem." Mrs. Bundle clucked a bit, conflicted that a nerve had unintentionally been hit. She said softly, "Remember what we talked about yesterday, luv. This isn't exactly like home. You can't go roaming around willy-nilly."

"It sure feels like home." Erin offered innocently. "Sure and away, Miss Olivia, that attic of yours looks mighty interesting! Can we take a gander at that, or is that off limits, too?"

"Erin! Jeesum crowbars." Angie blushed, and whispered. "Remember? Overstepping bounds?"

At Mrs. Bundle's cautioning and Angie's reprimand, the offender's hand went over her mouth again. "Oh! Right-o," she squeaked, crestfallen that she had let them down. "I've overstepped me bounds again."

"Erin dear, could you run upstairs and get my, em, reading glasses?" Mrs. Bundle asked. "I left them on the dresser."

"Sure, mum," she jumped up at the ready, "I'll be back in a flash!"

As she left the dining room, Mrs. Bundle turned to the Pettyfers. "I hope you're not offended by Erin's inquisitive nature. She can sometimes be a bit...impetuous." She chuckled, "I had the same characteristic when I was her age. Even now, I sometimes find it can be a bit of a...," she struggled for the appropriate words, "a challenge, you know, sometimes overcoming what might be a more sensible choice. Erin particularly enjoys daydreaming—losing herself in her fantasies. We try not to hold her back too much unless she crosses over too far."

Angie said apologetically, "Basically, she can't help herself. She's got a very fertile imagination."

'Please try not to hold it against her." Mrs. Bundle added, smiling contritely.

Aurelia issued a weary sigh. "Oh, yes." She gave a wan smile, "I had the same attribute—yes, I do believe it's an *attribute*—when I was a young girl. Daydreaming, imagining romantic things. Many's the time Mother would be compelled to rein me in and redirect me to more useful tasks." She giggled and her dimples showed, "Otherwise, I could sit under the biggest old oak tree and read about other fantasy lands and imagine myself a princess in a gilded carriage with many suitors, or go on long walks with pretend friends, my mind faraway. I always loved past civilizations, fancying myself a fearless ruler. Mother would bring me back to reality. And Father?

Oh my! He and I never did see eye-to-eye on the way we viewed the world. He was a very strong man, a realist. Couldn't find the joy in much of anything. Pragmatism was *his* middle name; common sense and order consumed him. Despite his control, I loved to be inquisitive, to wonder at the world and dream of all it had to offer. But that was considered too freethinking and frivolous for the time. I didn't care! I had my own vision. Quite off-putting to others, I knew, and very taxing for a young country girl. But I was willful and in my late teens finally—oh my word! Didn't I have such a time—sister and brother said it would lead to ruin. Ruin—can you imagine?" She gave her sister a rebellious glance, as though telling tales out of school.

"Shush now, sister." Olivia's voice held its sharpness, almost a warning.

A quick notion pursued Mrs. Bundle's overactive thought process: *Everyone has something to keep private, and often, to hide....*Were the Pettyfers hiding something?

Despite the charming veneer, there seemed to be a sad reserve surrounding Aurelia like an impenetrable bubble. Olivia, on the other hand, seemed to possess a surface of aloofness. And Woodsum seemed exceedingly happy stuck in an adolescent 1940-era time warp of fun. Was this a façade, a stiff way of buffering? *I wonder,* she thought, trying to winnow it down...*was it a protective mechanism for underlying hurt, a painful wariness?* What, she wondered, was *festering* under Aurelia's sweetness, Olivia's tough exterior, and Woodsum's humor?

Aurelia continued, "Oh, the fun we all had, didn't we, Olivia? Remember the skating parties, and the science classes, and all those wonderful ideas—"

"Sister has wonderful recollections!" Olivia interrupted, the corners of her mouth twitching. She abruptly changed the subject, "Mrs. Bundle, dear heart! I happened to notice. You were limping a trifle on your way down this morning...am I right?"

"Oh! I'm fine. Just a bit of soreness. It's my big toe, actually," she chuckled, lifting the offending appendage. "That was quite a hike in yesterday—on top of the hiking Cracker and I do every day. I may have overdone it just a bit." She stood gingerly in an attempt to play down the pain in her now-throbbing toe, but sat back down abruptly, squelching a small whimper. "Uh-oh! Oh, boy....that smarts!"

"*Hmmppph!*" Olivia moved quickly, sliding a nearby footstool toward her chair, and commanded, "Take off that slipper and put your foot up here." She knelt down. "*Hooo!* Look-it that! You got a blister on top of another the size of Siam—burst open from the looks of it. Swollen and red as all get out! What the *devil* have you been up to? Certainly not simply snowshoeing up here has got it this bad."

Mrs. Bundle looked sheepish. "Well, it's a long story. The short version is that I contracted a minor foot infection weeks ago from slogging around in a mucky swamp down south. Not my favorite trek, I guarantee. No big thing, but it's been the devil to get rid of. Antibiotics, soaking, etcetera…" she played it down, aggravated to have to explain something she'd prefer to keep hidden, to handle herself.

Angie peered over Olivia's shoulder, alarmed at the angry wound. "We've been trying to get Mrs. B to take better care of herself. It's more inattentiveness than neglect. She's had a rough couple months."

"It's all right." Mrs. Bundle reassured them. "The first blister came back just days ago after I resumed my daily hike. I should have attended to it better, but, as you've so rightly noted, Angie, I've been a bit inattentive lately." She strained to see. "Does it really look that bad?"

"Yes, ma'am, it most certainly does." Olivia made *tsk-tsk*-ing noises, nodding brusquely. "Angry red and *festering* as all get out."

Mrs. Bundle's antennae went up…there came that terrible word—*fester*—now spoken aloud. Her head began to spin and she sat back, fatigued.

Olivia went on. "Shame, shame on you for suffering in silence!" She looked up the woman and her demeanor softened immediately. "Ah, well. A good hot soak and Mother's poultice is what you need. Immediately."

Aurelia piped up from behind, "Don't worry. Olivia has Mother's gift for herbal remedies. You'll see."

"We'll just take care of that lickety split." Surprise—Woodsum was back, determined to help.

"A poultice?" Mrs. Bundle asked confused, then remembered where she was: this was Mount Holly Mansion where there were likely no antibiotics—only old-fashioned remedies. Poultices, in another time, took care of ailments ranging from joint pain and inflammation, abscesses, boils, bruises, and the ever-dreaded carbuncle. She was open to anything at this point; the pain was piercing.

"Yep! Got to draw out that angry infection you've got brewing there. Now, never you mind," Olivia said. "Let's see..." she muttered to herself, ticking off items on her fingers, "witch hazel, calendula, yes...comfrey, lavender, cherimoya, uh-huh. I've got just the poultice that will take care of that mess, and speed up the healing, too. Don't worry." She patted her good foot. "We'll take care of you."

Nearing footsteps reminded them Erin was returning.

Olivia said in an undertone, "And no matter about Erin and her...inquisitiveness. We don't hold anything against the girl, even though she is a nosebag."

Erin jogged back into the dining room, breathless and genial as ever. "Right where you said! Here you are, Mrs. B. Holy moly, that's some stairway you got there! Twenty-two steps! And that slippery banister? Surely, even as tempting as it is, I says to meself, 'I will *not* try sliding down!' Aye, I swear I kept clear away from it!" She paused at the scene of everyone surrounding Mrs. Bundle. "Em... what's the matter, mum?" She took in the footstool, Mrs. Bundle's wan expression, and the attention her bared foot was getting. "Gaw! What's wrong?" She elbowed her way in closer, "Em.....blimey! That's some ugly!"

"Oh, it's nothing." Mrs. Bundle did her own prevaricating, "Just a blister that's a bit 'techy,' as Gumpy would say."

"Infected is the real diagnosis. Lucky there's no poisoning." Olivia couldn't help but mutter under her breath.

Erin's face was stricken. "Infected? Just like Calvin, Jr.? Blimey! Will you be gettin' the sepsis and die, mum?"

"Oh, no, no, dear! No need to worry. Miss Olivia," she gave her nurse the eye, "has kindly offered to fix me up good and proper."

"Be right back." Olivia said, and the three Pettyfers left the room in a hustle-bustle mode, focused on their respective life-saving tasks.

Mrs. Bundle reached out and captured Erin firmly, who gazed at her with sweet concern; Angie boxed her in tightly on the other side.

"My dear girl," Mrs. Bundle said gently, "We need to talk."

The youngster with the long curly locks and bright eyes gazed at them. "Aye?"

"I appreciate your inquisitiveness. However, while we're here, you must try to use more restraint. You are in someone else's house. Agreed?"

"Aye, mum, but...d'ya mean even if it's an inn like this, with all this intrigue and history?"

Mrs. Bundle gave a nod.

Erin's voice was hesitant, "Including the old attic with who-knows-what in it?" She waved her arms, "And *everything* else?" Her brow, furrowed in concentration, forced her glasses to perch precariously mid-nose.

"Yes." Mrs. Bundle whispered softly, "And I'll tell you why. Remember what we discussed on the way here, and a couple other times, too?" She tapped her temple as a subtle prompt.

"Em, you probably mean that stuff about thinkin' things through first." She squinted. "Aye, now that you put it in front of me just so, I do remember. And the other, em...items on The List."

"Yes. Good. Consider this, my luv. It's the one *sure* way you get invited *back*."

"Oh, right, mum!" Her curls jiggled with gusto as she morosely shook her head. "Ach, I'll be *forgettin'* that thinkin'-things-through piece forever! But I definitely like getting invited back. Well now, don't you worry, I've got that list in me head right now." She thumped herself on the forehead. "Just have to pull it from the back of me brain to the front." She motioned and repeated, "Cuz, surely and I *do* want to get invited back."

"Mrs. B's trying to tell you in a nice way to just stop being so dang nosy." Angie spoke with sisterly frankness. "And you really should apologize to the Pettyfers. I would if I were in your shoes."

As if on cue, all three came through the kitchen doorway laden with items: Olivia, with a bucket marked *Remedies* chock full of tiny bottles of herbs, salves, and such; Aurelia, arms burdened with a large roll of cotton batting, hand towels, and an empty enamel foot basin; Woodsum, hands clenched round a large hot teakettle, his glasses steaming.

"Don't worry, Mrs. Bundle. We'll get you fixed up." he said, "You're the big cheese for the day. Our special patient."

"Oh my, I feel very special with all this attention." She exchanged a glance with Erin. "Let's wait... just a sec. Erin has something to say to you."

"Em...first things first." Erin stood at attention before them, checked her thoughts, eyes inquisitive but mouth firmly sealed with renewed eagerness to make things right. Fumbling with her robe in a supreme effort of gracefulness, she curtsied deeply. "Sorry, Miss Olivia. Truly!" Olivia quirked that eyebrow in surprise. She curtsied again, this time in Aurelia's direction. "Sorry, Miss Aurelia! And Mr. Woodsum, too! Surely, and I'm really, truly, *honestly* sorry for bein' such a terrible nosebag. Please don't be takin' too much offense — I'm working on doing better. Ach! It's a terrible cross I bear."

The triplets' assurances came in a flood, "Oh, of course, of course,", "No offense taken,"; "Nobody's perfect, mornin' glory!"

"Thank you." She edged back, close to Angie, cocked a quizzical brow, and whispered. "How's that — okay?" Angie sighed and nudged her with approval. Erin turned back toward the threesome. "But, em, I'm wonderin' one wee thing."

The trio froze and Woodsum squeaked, "How's that?"

"Well, I never heard that word before. ...*Meee — khahl.*" She let it roll off her tongue. "I'll wager it's foreign, right? Could you tell me, what exactly does *Michel's Choice* mean? Is it a book I have yet to read?"

Olivia fussed with her herbs, focused completely on measuring. Aurelia, who had been fidgeting with her load, dropped it all on the floor, at which point the cotton batting and towels went flying and the basin spiraled round like a top midst the silence.

Woodsum set the kettle atop the trivet on the table. "Hey now, whippersnapper! How 'bout you gather the pan and things for sister? Let's treat you and your wound in the parlor, Mrs. Bundle, where you'll be more comfortable. Would you like some help getting there? Maybe Angie could hold your arm."

Angie sprung into action, helping Mrs. Bundle to her feet.

"Thank you, dear." She winced, "Oh, that is quite tender. I know enough to stay off it today. Some quiet time in the library will do me good this morning, Would you mind, girls?"

"Of course not." Angie said, "Erin and I can find lots to do. We'll go outside and explore, get some exercise. We just want you to get better."

As they followed carefully behind the hobbling detective, Olivia asked, "What *about* the young ladies, Woodsum?"

He piped up promptly. "Say! How 'bout goin' for a hike with me? I got lots of keen places to show you. There's some nice new snow out there making things real pretty."

"Sure!" Angie and Erin agreed enthusiastically, and Olivia added, "Perfect."

Later, while the girls got ready and she soaked in silence, Mrs. Bundle's mind wandered. Once again, things had seemed a bit too orchestrated, as though they were all being gently led. It wasn't enough to be annoying, but...food for thought. As kind and attentive as the Pettyfers were, there was an eerie prevailing tension that permeated the inn like a chloroform cloak. It was cordiality bordering on control. The three were like mind readers in their uncanny ability to know what their guests needed or desired—often, even before they did! Yes, this *was* definitely a developing pattern. Could it just be the way they did things here at Mount Holly Mansion Inn? That, she supposed, would be the simplest explanation. Her gut, however, told her things were off kilter here. Mrs. Bundle's inquisitive mind couldn't help but wonder (and then conclude with reluctance) that all was not perfect—*they're hiding something, and whatever that something is, it was* big.

Chapter IX

A Tour of the Grounds and Beyond

Satiated aplenty and in need of a tough workout, the girls had welcomed the offer to explore every inch of out-of-the-way Mount Holly Mansion Inn's property consisting of fifty forested acres just shy of the Saltash Mountain's pinnacle. With Woodsum as their guide and accompanying sandwiches in their rucksack, Angie and Erin set out on their outside tour of the property. The view from the front porch was spectacular, looking south westward toward a small pond glazed with an ice-blue sheen. A light snow was peppering the peaked sky; there was little hint of wind. The air was crisp but not freezing, comfortable for a brisk hike.

During summertime the inn was surrounded by cobblestone walkways leading to gardens. "That'd be the butterfly garden over there. And down thataway near the summer kitchen, that's the herb garden." He pointed a gloved finger, "We always plant real pretty annuals over there near the solarium." Now, pods of perennials lay like dormant jewels underneath the massive white landscape. For the first leg of their tour, Woodsum wended his way through the garden paths down to the icehouse near the pond, where abundant supplies of ice blocks were stored in anticipation of the inevitable warmer seasons to come. Around the perimeter of the pond, cat-o-nine tails stuck out of the shoreline snow like wayward swords. A section of the pond had been cleared of snow "if you've a mind to go skating while you're here," Woodsum offered.

They reconnoitered up the south hill to the rear of the inn where the back ell came off the main structure. Woodsum extended his gloved hand, "During the summer, we got an outside cistern up on the back hill that stores rain water. It's brought down on a gravity fed line to the outlying gardens, sheds, and the main house summer kitchen. Works pretty slick if I do say so."

The girls provided suitable approval sounds and he continued. "Look right here, little ladies. I'm 'specially proud of this." They looked around; the only thing visible was a very healthy grassed area the size of a king-sized bed, surrounded by the whitened, frozen ground.

"You mean this here?" Erin pointed. "Say now, it's just grass, right? But, in the winter—very odd."

He chortled, "Just grass? Hee-hee! That's right! Don't let anyone ever say us Pettyfers are 100% in the dark ages! Only 95%—because, this here, girlies, is our *piece de résistance*! This—is our newfangled septic tank! Baffle system and all! It's the bee's knees!" In detail, Woodsum delightedly described all the ins and outs of his new 1000 gallon concrete tank septic system, the crisscrossing, hand-dug lines running underground, and its quality operation. "Yep. Back five years gone, we made an executive decision. This here's the only thing we've caved in on modernizin'—and it's a honey of a system!" He pointed. "Ain't it nifty?" Without doubt, this one feature and benefit the Pettyfers had been willing to deviate from was appreciated by those loving a properly functioning loo.

After suitable admiration, the three moved toward an old barn-boarded shed, its door adorned with a large vintage metal sign whose subject was a male skater in black silhouette, the distinctive Olympic rings below. As they got closer, they could see the lettering: *III Olympic Winter Games, Lake Placid, USA February 4-13, 1932.*

"Wow!" Erin breathed frosty air, "That sign's old!"

"Pretty keen, huh? Father brought me to the Olympics that year. I was just a youngster of twelve but I remember it well! What a time we had. It was the aces!"

"What about Miss Olivia and Miss Aurelia? Didn't they go?"

"Oh, no. They weren't allowed back then." He saw their looks of disbelief. "Yuh, times sure have changed." He shook his wool-capped head, then went on. "I especially loved ice hockey back then. Don't ya know, most all of the U.S. team was from New England. The U.S. took home the silver, Germany the bronze. 'Course, you can't fault the Canadians for taking the gold; they got hockey in their blood. Well, Father knew somebody who knew somebody and don't you know, I got to meet some of the players at a private luncheon! Yuh, that was quite a time." He pulled on the jagged door. "C'mon in and take your pick."

He entered first, then stepped aside. Ice skates dangled from the exposed rough wood beams. Leaning against the four walls were a dozen or so pairs of downhill and cross-country skis—different lengths and sizes, the old-fashioned maple hardwood kind made for touring, with leather bindings fitting one's boot size—antiques in perfect condition. "We used to run a rope ski tow for the guests—started it in the 30s. Called it quits in '79—no snow did everybody in. Nowadays, we just cross country when we feel the urge."

"Sweet!" Angie searched the larger ones while Erin picked through the smaller sizes.

"C'mon, you tomatoes," he motioned energetically, "let's get a wiggle on. Times a'wastin'!"

Matches were found; skis were waxed and slipped on; and they were off!

Following a well-worn ski trail, they shooshed quietly along into the backwoods of the Pettyfer property, deeper and deeper into the forest. New snow fell quicker with denser, thicker white flakes. Amidst the swish, swish movement of her poles and skis, Erin caught snowflakes on her tongue, giggling; Angie couldn't help joining in as they slogged.

"Are there any moose out here?" Erin asked. "Aye, we see them all the time down where we live. A mother and her baby. Two meese together."

"With all due respect, missy, they don't ever call 'em meese. Or mooses." Woodsum guffawed.

"Right, and do y'know why they don't call them mooses? Or meeses?"

"Well—they just don't. They're just moose plain and simple—and simple in the noggin, too. I tell you what. They don't eat nothin' in the winter, 'cept willow bushes and such. They come up here in these high elevations and wreak havoc with them trees." He pointed. "They strip the bark from the small ones. We got a big old ugly moose who likes to hang out down by the pond. I shoo him away ever' chance I get."

"We've got a big bull moose out behind our farm in the bog where we go hiking." Angie added. "He comes up through the marsh on Goochie Pond. You can hear him come crashing through the trees."

"They don't know how to be quiet, do they now?" Erin offered, "I'll agree, Mr. Woodsum, they are kinda dumb."

"My two cents—they can stay right down in the bog with you two hikers. And how!" he huffed.

"Can't abide moose, Mister Woodsum?" Angie kidded.

"Nope. But it's no bother to me as long as they stay put. Ha!" he snarked loudly. Woodsum used hand-hewn ski poles made of wood and hemp rope that had seen decades of use. Gliding along the trail like a pro on his ancient cross country skis at a leisurely pace, he stopped occasionally to talk about points of interest like a most personable tour guide. "We got lots of good stuff in these parts. Down at Plymouth Caverns, that was a rendezvous for counterfeiters—you know, crooks on the lam. You never heard about that? Why, I been in them caverns a time or two. Very spooky. Somethin' you'd appreciate. You probably don't know that gold was discovered here in 1855. They—greedy flatlanders," he spit disapprovingly, "pulled all manner of capers and tricks trying to get their piece of gold." He motioned, "And over that way north is where the Saltash Mountain meets Amherst Lake and the foothills. During the worst winters in the 1800s, that road was cut off by many an avalanche. Everyone was stuck there till the local men got through the road."

As they broke through the woods he stopped to catch his breath, looking up at the messy sky swiss-dotted with snowflakes. Hazy patches played tricks with the daylight. A snowy trail running perpendicular to the inn trail appeared, coming in from the west and wending its way deeper, down the big hill and into the southeastern woods like a long white ribbon. Huge, shadowed trees bent over the trail forming darkly arched, Gothic-like stained-glass prisms of shadowy light. There were track marks, signs of recent snowmobile activity.

At this junction there was a small clearing just off the trail. Two knee-high roundish boulders three feet apart had been topped with a long flat stone slab, strategically placed to create a man-made stone bench where sun and open trails met the dark forest. Carved into the bench's top was one word: **AMITY**, presumably describing this area so filled with quiet harmony. It was a reflective spot, almost reverent, with a stunning distant mountain view of virgin timber.

"'Amity'....peace...goodwill." Angie said thoughtfully, "It fits the setting—I like it."

"Hey, that's so cool." Erin outlined the word with her finger; she gave a low whistle. "Mister Woodsum, didja make this fine seat, now?"

"Yes, I did. Had the slab carved by an I-talian sculptor over Barre way after the war, y'see. Well, after I got out in 1946." He expertly maneuvered his skis and sat down on the bench, then motioned for them to join him. "I call it the thinking bench. Sit a spell and take a gander at that magnificent mountain skyline."

Deeply impressed, both girls sat and sighed, "*Ooooooo!*"

"Amazing view! Where exactly are we now?" Angie queried, on tenterhooks, "Where does this trail go?"

"This here pass is what we call *'The Way In to the Dark Side'*." He pointed, "Y'see, nowadays, it's mostly them dang skidoo-ers that use it in wintertime. And them all-terrain vehicles in the summer. Not that I got that much against 'em; they got to have their sport, don't they? But like you like to say, Erin, in the *olden* days, it was the skiers and snowshoers in the winter. And bicyclers and hikers in the good months. And," he pointed for emphasis, "that's how we got most of our information—well, it was called gossip back then, and meant in a good way—passed back and forth by the grapevine, don't you know. No noise—just the quiet of the deep forest, shadowy and clean, and...all natural." He inhaled, then exhaled, his breath puffs of frosty white. "Truth is, back in the day, we used these trails and the pass pretty regularly to get down to Route 100. Yessuh! Y'see, over that way's bordering Coolidge State Forest—nothin' but gorgeous woodland. And that way a good distance," he raised a gloved hand and pointed to the south, "that takes you to the highway. 'Bout a two-mile walk. Lordy! In the summer and early fall before the snow—it's some beautiful sight to see—what with all them colors, and the sun streaming in! Like them beautiful stained windows in a quiet church—only outdoors."

"Must be kind of like Little Red Riding Hood, walking through the great big woods, all alone. Spooky!" Erin shivered, a sly grin forming. "I like that! Especially if rain comes...aye, I think I could do it! Unless there was a tornado, like in the Wizard of Oz. Or a hurricane!" she said, eyes wide with wonderful terror.

"You just love scaring yourself silly, don't you?" Angie reproached.

"Aye, I do!" Erin oozed gleefully. She wiped the frosty fog from her glasses with her mittens. "Hurricanes! I want to be in one—a real good one! I like being scared out of me wits!"

Woodsum's face darkened a bit, and he sighed. "Be careful what you ask for, missy. Mind you, we've had a few of those in our time, don't y'know. And other such disasters."

"Really, Mister Woodsum?" Erin asked with renewed respect. "Disasters?"

"I've heard Gumpy and Dad talk about hurricanes. They're not too much *fun*, Erin." Angie emphasized.

He nodded in agreement, "That's the truth. Y'see, what happens? All them sweet little streams and creeks along the main roads, they become huge raging rivers when the rain comes in a big way. Let's see...there was Belle in '76 and Floyd in '99. But the Hurricane of September of 1938 was probably the worst! Toppled over trees! Water come right up on the roads. These big craters got formed, didn't they—washing out all them main roads like you read about, making sections of the road impassable! We didn't recover for awhile." His voice became tinged with modest Yankee pride, "It's times like that when you see real Vermont ingenuity. These trails here are invaluable, 'cuz people can travel all the way up and over the mountain to the other side—to civilization, and schools, and the like. Yup. Nice long forest path pretty as a picture. Why, in those tough times I seen a hundred-odd people walk that pass to get to their jobs and go provision shopping on the other side when they got cut off by horrendous calamities with hurricane damage and the like. And then people come together to rebuild roads, bringing in their tractors and horses to help out wherever needed. It's pure joy for mankind when you get a chance to see it."

He sighed, prodding his ski poles around in the snow. "Yup. That's what a disaster does—brings out the best of human nature and yes, the worst of Mother Nature. Been there and it's pretty gruesome, I tell you. Not to be a killjoy, but it's been awhile, and I'd say we're due for another big ol' natural disaster nearer in the future than far. For that matter, a big ol' blizzard, too!" He sniffed the air and gave a wizened look upward. "But don't you worry. Mount Holly Mansion is always ready for whatever comes our way. Through it all. Who knows when? You just can't stop Mother Nature when she comes and takes away. Anything or anybody." He wiped a teary snowflake from his eye. "Listen."

A hush came over the group and no one moved, willing the wonderful silence. They listened to the gentle sounds of the wood. With one's senses tuned just right, it was true—one could hear the *shhhhhhhush* of the snowflakes softly tumbling helter-skelter. They listened to the cracks and pops of the cold teasing the hardwood, heard the rustles and queries of the undergrowth's life force. They heard the whimsical wind, murmuring through the trees, singing a poetic song of its own making....

After awhile, Woodsum whispered with renewed spirit, "'Course, Mother Nature, she's a lively 'ol gal and she can be generous, too. Givin' us back *good* stuff."

"It's heavenly." Angie returned the whisper.

Erin—with equal reverence to the special moment—sighed. "Aye, Mister Woodsum. Surely, and it's…" she searched for the right phrase and found one of his, "just what you say—*the cat's meow*. You reckon you agree?"

He gave a confident nod. "I reckon."

At that very moment the clouds unexpectedly parted directly above. As if on angel's wings, a patch of bright blue sky appeared and the sun burst like an effervescent smile through the light falling snow.

Woodsum said, "Y'see? That's what I'm talkin' 'bout." He grinned. "Now you two go on down and explore that trail together—it's real 'cool'—as you both would say. Me? I'm just goin' to sit here a while and commune with my thoughts—if that's all right with you." He pointed toward the distant thick stand of evergreens whose rich ocean-blue needles were like a cluster of frothy tiny bristle brushes. "I'll be right here when you get back, still pondering, I imagine. Then we'll all be ready for our lunch!"

Chapter X
Solarium Reflections

What a magnificent place—delightfully in the sticks, to be sure, Mrs. Bundle reflected in her quiet reverie, *but oh, so charming!* Outside the windows, the light snow from earlier in the day had commenced again, accumulating like marshmallow fluff on the weighty bows of the mammoth spruce and pine trees. Frosty crystals had begun to cling to the bullseye glass panes; she had a sense much more snow was on the way.

While the girls hiked, Mrs. Bundle had enjoyed more quiet exploration time in the library. Aurelia and Olivia had tended to her foot, first soaking it in hot water mixed with something aromatic, layering a thin coating of salve over the blister, and then wrapping a herbal poultice round the infected toe, covering her foot round and round with a warm muslin bandage and tying it off with two fluffy bunny ears. It was remarkably lightweight for all that coverage. A stylish black cane with ivory-carved handle had appeared from nowhere to complete her ensemble, which helped with getting around. She felt rather ridiculous being cared for in such a way, but the healing effects began immediately as the pain subsided.

As she'd requested, a light lunch on a tray had been brought into the library; she ate alone, enjoying the solitude and the big yet comfortable space; she read and reread **Deegie and the Fairy Princess**, going on the third time. It was colorful and sweet, a treasure she couldn't believe she had discovered. After lunch, she had hobbled into the comforting sanctuary of the warm solarium where she now sat totally relaxed, bundled inside an overly large and very comfy wicker chair. A small pot of hot cocoa (now nearly empty) was close by.

The steaming cup of real chocolate—the old-fashioned kind—had been comforting. It was as good as Tuddy's Diner, where Ger Tudhope used a family recipe that was over 200 years old. "There's truly nothing like a sweet cup of hot chocolate," Mrs. Bundle murmured. Away from all the hustle and bustle of post-holiday Pillson, she emptied the last drop from the pot, swished the creamy liquid round her tongue, and swallowed.

She closed her eyes, feeling completely relaxed. Her nostrils drank in a mixture of scents: pine from the Christmas evergreen wreath on the French door leading to the porch; rich earth smells from the nearby potted geraniums, irises, hibiscuses, and orchids—there was even a variegated tulip reminiscent of the rare Semper Augustus! Intermingling with all the aromas was cinnamon, heavenly and yeasty, emanating from the distant kitchen down at the other end of the large inn. Could that be more cinnamon bread or, she pictured, cinnamon buns baking? Spread with lovely sugar glaze?

Eyes still shut, it comforted her to know the most gloriously untouched, idyllically bucolic, wintry wonderland would be before her when she chose to look. From this elevated observation, distant Lake Nineva's mirror-like sheen was enhanced by the Green Mountains, majestically displayed like confection-dusted, violet-and-viridian-hued gumdrops. Earlier, a burst of late sunshine had poured in and usurped the gray sky for a few precious minutes. It had enveloped her, the southerly exposure optimized; meanwhile, inside was cozy and warm as the red-hot coals in the nearby small stove grate emanated auxiliary heat.

She was actually relaxing!

This particular corner was especially created for privacy, a getaway for anyone desiring a bit of time alone. North Pillson Corners, whose predictable, tedious humdrum could always be counted on, interspersed with the gossipy exaggerations from the likes of fellow

Pillsonvillian, Weezy Bunton (with whom she had an ongoing love vs. total aggravation relationship), seemed far, far away. She certainly was settling in, and settling down. Not quite as skitterish as she had been the last few weeks, she acknowledged. One could almost forget all the tired tittle-tattle of home within the comfort of this very old, very comfortable black rattan wicker chair. Luckily for many, it couldn't pass along all it had "heard" over the years, with its large arms and high back wrapped round her like a protective sheath, a wool blanket wrapped round her knees—why, she was as snug as a bug in a polar bear rug! Happily, all the sensations of the warmest season of the year—summer—surrounded her, even at mid-winter's frosty pinnacle.

Just what the doctor ordered, she thought, pleased they had made the decision to get away—not just to anywhere, but to this magical, off-the-beaten-path place. Truthfully, she must now own up that she needed a bit of rest from everything—but especially the busy fall escapade. She stretched her long frame, outfitted in the most comfortable attire: scoop neck long-sleeved tee under a buttoned sweater vest, over which she wore a Pendleton wool plaid shirt, stretchy black, flexible maxi-skirt—and one fleece-lined slipper complementing the other bandaged foot. Quite an athlete in her day, she was happy she'd been able to resume her daily regimen of walking and lifting hand weights, the combination of which allowed her to maintain her sturdiness. The injuries she had sustained in the fall were not going to keep her down, she had thought determinedly, although maybe she had been pushing things a bit? This minor foot ailment had forced her back into inactivity, but not for long.

Tall, hardy, and well-built, she defied the average description of her generation. Her hearty face was softly outlined; dancing youthful dark brown eyes, still sharp and bright, were almond-shaped above a classic Roman nose and square chin—there was no weakness there. Unnamed others still found her striking, a natural beauty. These days she preferred the natural look of no makeup, except for a pinch of blush and a light touch of lipstick. Long, brilliantly silver-brown braids wrapped neatly around her head in an intricate circle, crowning her features. For years, she'd handled sheep's wool, and the natural lanolin kept her hands soft and smooth. Most always, she possessed a natural, calm manner. She was an interesting mix of class and country, with a tad of eccentricity.

She released a long, contented sigh: *Ahhhh...* Her thoughts flitted about lazily. True, this out-of-the-way location was a devil to get to—but worth every snowshoe step in, she acknowledged, knowing now that upon arrival, one could expect to be treated like a long-lost sister, a daughter, cousin, or aunt.

She decided she was totally beguiled by Mount Holly Mansion Inn. It was truly a magical, welcoming place, like a shot of Geritol to her veins, renewing her positive energy; helping to reevaluate her priorities and decide what was coming next in her little world.

Even the lunch she'd been served was different and exciting— some kind of Scandinavian boiled sausage, "Rød Pølse" (Danish for "red sausage", Aurelia had told her) served with a remoulade, fried onions, and pickled sliced cucumber! The sausage, a finely ground mixture of pork, nutmeg, and allspice, was very surprising to her palette and thoroughly enjoyable. It begged the question, How on earth had they come up with that? Who would have ever thought she would be eating something so exotic here in the middle of nowhere, and enjoying it so much? It was nice to step out of her comfort zone and she hoped the girls were having as nice a time as she was.

That said, she came back to her question of just exactly *how* the Pettyfers, at their advanced age, were able to keep up with this mausoleum; how did they get everything ready for paying visitors; how did they run such a large household? Surely, she concluded, they must have help of some kind. Their hosts, constantly on the move throughout the inn, were methodical, always with a purpose, performing their jobs in an ostensibly effortless way as a tight knit, efficient trio. Their relationship with each other was as symbiotic a one as she'd ever seen.

Like it or not, she had a way of knowing when things just didn't fit. Sometimes it wasn't facts that lead her; it was more a feeling.

And she had a feeling, for sure. Just like other feelings that came and went…feelings not directly related, but persistent nevertheless.

Her mind hit a speed bump. Suddenly, a jumble of thoughts cascaded through her mind, thoughts she had unconsciously suppressed the last few weeks, or at the most had attempted to digest but instead, had been compelled to set on hold. She steepled her fingers, placing the tips at her lips as she contemplated the conundrum she had been confronted with at home.

Since her new friend Duke Driscoll had abruptly left town, life in her usually predictable little world had not been the same. She made her clucking sounds of dismay.

When she and Duke had returned from their adventure in October, the first two weeks of her physical healing had been a top priority. He had been there with her every day; she was grateful for his caring nature. As each day melded into the next, discovery, healing, and yes, she had to admit, a goodly amount of playful banter ensued. She and Duke shared stories and thoroughly enjoyed each other's company with no further expectation; the days hurried along through November. She had to admit she'd begun to count on Flaps, his feisty Blue Tick Coonhound/Springer Spaniel, and his visits. Surprisingly, even Cracker, territorial and aloof as he was, seemed to have come to a degree of acceptance of their daily calls.

When she was well enough, he'd begun taking her out for daily drives in his big no-frills truck. Each day he had been there: encouraging her, helping her heal, never asking for anything. His stays were longer and longer as they sat for hours getting to know each other, talking quietly into the late evening.

During one of those private moments, one particularly poignant conversation evolved.

Haltingly, he had said, "You know, *back there*," (the phrase they used to reference the adventure that had drawn them together), "after the capture when we were, ahem, reunited, you were, to say the least, in complete disarray." His hands motioned his upper body, "Clothes ripped, mud and grime from head to toe…you were a real mess!" They both chuckled. He continued, "Well, your, you know, shoulder was…you know, exposed," he hurried on, "and your shoulder…well, I happened to note that pretty recent scar…still red and…very permanent and…?" His voice tone rose in question; she gazed at him intently, nodding to go on. He continued, "Um. I've seen my share of war wounds. It made me quite disturbed to think someone had hurt you so, had inflicted such an injury and to that extent." He reached for her hand, his eyes intensely darkened with anger behind the compassion. "I think I know you well enough now to see you don't like talking about the violent side of…what you do. Heck, I don't like to talk about my…POW years. War is a terrible thing. But you and what you went through…what I mean to say—"

She paused, drew in a deep breath, "Oh! I wouldn't want to diminish the suffering you've experienced in any way by comparing it with my little, em, escapade." She reached out, "No, that's not accurate. It was pretty harrowing. Oh, dang! What happened to me is something I have a hard time…acknowledging, much less talking about—I mean, the danger aspect of it all."

Unconsciously, she touched her shoulder, lightly rubbing the offending spot. "A few years ago…unfortunately, I acted quickly, probably without a lot of common sense, and I took a bullet in my upper chest. I was lucky to survive. Actually, it was the first case Cracker and I took on. Very disturbing. We fought against a criminal who was pure evil reincarnated—vindictive, menacing, cold—a very nasty fellow, that leader. And certainly out of my league as a newbie private eye." Eyes cast downward, the words spilled out first in a dribble, like a rusty faucet being let open after nonuse, and then in a full wash of narrative, as she told him the story in a way she had never described it to anyone, not even Allie. Filling in the sordid details and the challenges she had faced, she described how her nemesis had sadistically hurt three loved ones, murder his primary intention.

She said hoarsely, "So! Thankfully, we all breathed a sigh of relief when he was sentenced with no chance of parole. The last I heard he is in a Pennsylvania federal prison with only the basic necessities, and he'll be there for the rest of his years—right where he belongs. He'll never bother us again here in our little world."

He squeezed her hand, his usually undemonstrative nature replaced with a sweet display of passion. "You can be assured of that, Letitia. That is, if I have anything to do with it." His index finger fondled her chin, and suddenly to her complete surprise, he had leant in and gently kissed her, a most heartfelt, unrestrained and decidedly more-than-just-casual, kiss.

She thought now about that kiss—not with longing or regret, but with interest, trying to decide what it had meant to her. Her mind went unfocused and foggy, an unpleasant experience. Oh, bother! *Awareness is palpable to those who want to see it*—the thought seared a path across her consciousness.

There was a niggling side effect to it all. Through those weeks together, Duke's daily visits to her farm on the knoll did not go unnoticed by the locals. Sooner than later, the scuttlebutt from North Pillson Corners to Pillson Junction to Pillson Falls to Pillsonville (and even townships beyond, she realized) was that Mrs. Bundle and Duke Driscoll were "keeping company." She had said nothing either for or against to dispel the rumors. Let the general populace be filled with conjecture; she could not control the local verbal fodder.

Consequently, the message she received on her voicemail on the first of December was nothing short of puzzling. Duke's usually warm, deep voice sounded terse, impersonal, and…one had to assume in retrospect, rather final in nature. "Hey there. I've been called out of town. I'm not sure when I'll be back. It's been…fun… these past few weeks. Now that you're better…I'm sure you'll be fine. Anyway, thanks for everything…um…" Hesitation had been evident in his voice and the pregnant pause precipitated an abrupt beeping end to his message.

And that, as they say, was that. It all seemed awfully illogical to one with such a logical mind as she; she was used to dealing with common sense and order. More than anything, she had to admit it rankled her *just* a tad. This smacked of poor behavior, which seemed quite out of character for Duke—or the Duke she knew. But then again, she asked herself—did she really *know* him after only those few weeks? Yes, they had experienced quite a few things together that tended to bond people on a fast track.

Without animosity but more with nostalgia, she allowed herself to wax wistful for just these few moments as she reflected on his attributes and not his recently inconsistent behavior. A superb pilot and the owner of Ace Flight Center, Charles "Duke" Driscoll was exasperatingly reserved—downright reticent until you got to know him, and then he was quite likeable. Solidly built, of medium height and laid-back, Duke was one of those men whose face had matured gracefully, aging into first-rate good looks. He had a wavy head of flecked silver-and-black hair full and tousled, as though he'd just fought a battle with the wind and lost. His deeply tanned, mature face was roughly handsome with chiseled, well-defined features: he had a tough chin with prominent cleft; thin, strong lips and firm eyebrows. His hands were leathered and tough, in opposition to his intelligent, sadly soft eyes. He walked with a slight limp, which according to her husband Arthur was related to his incarceration in the Vietnam prisoner of war camp. Although he never talked about his own personal trials, he had proven himself to be quite dynamic in any given emergency situation. And his loveable dog....she reminisced, who couldn't love Flaps? A Blue Tick Hound mix full of energy and fun. Why, even Cracker had warmed to him over those weeks of daily visits.

After his abrupt phone call, she'd set aside the ambivalent feelings and moved mechanically through December towards the holiday season. Days later, when she'd shared this news with Allie (her best friend since middle school, known formally as Althea Swain Kelley, the sole person she relied on to give it to her straight), she expected one thing but got another.

Allie had offered neither advice nor sympathy with their tea. Granted, her perspective was happily skewed, having been married just over a year now, still in the throes of marital bliss with the debonair Ian Kelley. On the other hand, Allie's own journey finding and securing a solid relationship had not been without its obstacles and bumps. In her first career, Allie had been a combat nurse, had found and lost a love to the war. Inconsolable, she had worked on a remote American Indian reservation for many years, then traveled the world, always with a main goal to bring aid and comfort. She had purposefully chosen this path, taking on the roughest assignments — that is, until she decided to return to her hometown of Pillson Falls, replacing constant hard work with art, and making a new life in the process. When she'd least expected it, she'd found the love of her life, someone who held her own incredibly optimistic approach to living.

"Well, I'd say it's not him you have to worry about." Allie had offered when the situation had been laid before her.

In her mind's eye now, Mrs. Bundle could see Althea's kind oval face, her welcoming smile and messy, layered dirty-blond streaked hair, cut short for ease of care. It was her eyes that captivated everyone: large, opalescent green, as round and perfect as a doll's, framed with long ash-colored lashes curling just at the end. Perpetual laugh lines crinkled at the corners.

"Well, I'm not worried." Mrs. Bundle had replied. "I'm more… confused. He was so attentive. He became such a good friend. Quite a special one."

"Right." Allie said, studying Mrs. Bundle so intently it had caused her to shift in her seat; she'd seen that look before, that exact frankness and clarity in Althea's eyes. She added, "Cool as a cucumber."

"Yes, he is, isn't he? Extremely hard to read."

"Good grief! I meant you. *You're* cool as a cucumber."

"Oh."

"If you're asking my thoughts, L, I'd say it's you who have to decide if it really does matter — and it appears to me it might — and then if so, how much, and why?"

"What do you mean with all the questions for *me* to answer?" Mrs. Bundle had asked, confused. "I've just told you he's left — at the drop of a hat, mind you, without so much as an explanation of why or where he's gone! Don't you find that odd?"

"Not really. From what you've shared, you and your pilot have yet to become…intimate."

"Oh, gaw, Allie!" She blushed, then blubbered, "No! Of course not! And he's not 'my' pilot."

"Well there you go." She shrugged. "You're both free agents. You like to hold your cards close to the vest—Will O'Malley and I know that for sure! That's your privilege. Duke, too, has that right. We all have things that need attending at times. They're commonly called emergencies. And we all need our privacy, too. Call them secrets if you will. I call them challenges. Especially, later in life—sometimes to deal with matters that are unforeseen. Or, things that aren't clearly defined or require clarification. Life can be very complicated!"

Mrs. Bundle's ears were working but nothing was computing between them. From her perspective, she was justified in keeping info from old standby, Sheriff Will O'Malley—their relationship was one mixed with friendship and professional angst, as he often felt the need to be very bossy around her. When working, it had been her experience not to want to bother with specifics or take advantage of either Will, Allie, or anyone dear to her when pursuing a dangerous "situation." Granted, she readily called on them when said situation reached a level of (in her final opinion) an "emergency." Without doubt, both friends were extremely competent: Will, having been Windsor County's sheriff for decades; Allie, whose varied life experiences had been quite different from the satisfyingly boring life in the williwags that Mrs. Bundle had led before becoming North Pillson Corner's ace (and only) detective. She had always been in awe of Allie's life choices and felt lucky to have her nearby now: safe, retired, and right down the road in the little brick cottage, just a stone's throw from the Andersen farm and her farm on the knoll.

Mrs. Bundle knew one thing: Allie's friendship and truth-telling was always a constant, the epitome of altruistic support; she was an open book whose pages were filled with comfort and encouragement.

If she had been paying close attention, she would have also noticed the other constant in her life, Cracker, weighing in from his prime vantage point atop the refrigerator.

Everything about Cracker was sleek and exact: his delicately accentuated ears; a perfectly-shaped triangular nose; prim whiskers and pristine wide mouth—not to mention his luxuriously long pink tongue, which he now obsessively utilized, bringing his daily toilette to an impeccable state. His opinions were to the point, also.

He preened and licked his portly black body to satin sheet perfection and cat-thought with authority, *Having had my own share of liaisons (which you understand, being the gentleman cat that I am I am not inclined to discuss), I can appreciate the let-down you've experienced with the chap leaving so suddenly.* However, this *Lothario* (never one for modesty was Cracker when referring to himself) *more than most knows the old 'cat-and-mouse' game. He's been very crafty managing to capture your interest—very clever of him!* He scratched his nose, sniffed nobly, and arched his back until it was rigid. Pushing down his own mixed feelings, he continued without interruption from those sitting below him, *I'll have to admit his daily visits were starting to grow on us, weren't they? The chivalrous way, the charming attention—it was all very endearing. I know, my dear, it stings a bit. Nevertheless, let's look at the bright side! Isn't it refreshing to get a break from that wild pooch, Flaps? Egad! His nervous twitching, the tongue-lolling, and the constant ear-flapping—it was enough to drive a cat to drink. And that bark—heaven help us!—rattled the windows with earthquake force! So I say—Good riddance and let's get back to our lovely routine.* His glossy, ebony coat glistened in the window's filtered rays of sunshine.

And so, they all three left the conversation hanging in the air of conflicting views.

Mrs. Bundle had deftly changed the subject to their upcoming Pillson Library board meeting and the newest challenge: hooking into the Vermont online library system and the possible funding involved. Of course, this was just minutia compared to the controversy and danger she had experienced a few years before within the same walls of that venerable building. Nowadays, it was a piece of cake tackling the agenda; the board worked together without ill will for the betterment of the community.

However, Mrs. Bundle treasured Allie's friendship and assistance and so, even if reluctantly, had to take to heart her friend's words.

She had decided to put the whole business on hold for now but look at it at a later time. Admittedly, Duke had come into her mind every so often. But, if nothing else, she was stubborn—she could dig in her heels with the best of them! Now that she was here at Mount Holly Mansion Inn, Althea's recommendation seemed to be seeping into her psyche even more. The words echoed in her mind...*I'd say it's you who have to decide if it really does matter—and it appears to me it might—then if so, how much, and why?*

She clasped her hands together with finality and gave a solid *harrumph*. Nope! She wasn't there just yet. She wished the man well, whatever endeavors had caused him to run off like a jackrabbit.

Reshuffling her thoughts, she switched to the present, back to this wonderful, interesting vacation she was having. Yes! This trip to Saltash Mountain was proving to be just the ticket to get her back to her old self!

Adjusting the wool blanket, she *tut-tut*-ed with a modicum of annoyance, tugging to tuck it in. "Oh! C'mon!" She pulled, but it seemed caught on something. Inspecting the rounded left wicker arm of the chair, she issued a fresh onslaught of clucking sounds. "*Geez, Loooo-eeeze.*"

Squinting to find the offending hold-up, she saw that the woven coverlet threads had snagged on the large, curved underlip of the arm. A half dozen unwoven, jagged wicker strands protruded like a bunch of matchsticks, worn away with time or some long-ago mishap. She picked at the blanket threads one by one until all came away except one long strand. She strained to inspect it closer. "Hmm. Almost there. One more strand to go. Much ado about nothing, Lettie." If this was the only issue she would have to deal with today, all was well. She reached underneath and tugged on the coverlet. "C'mon, you son of a gun! Let go!"

She reached further. Her probing fingers landed on a slightly protruding *something* underneath the arm's lip. She couldn't see, but she could feel the object as her slim fingers reached deep down inside the recess of the chair arm underpocket. The tips of her fingernails gingerly stroked at "it": smooth and round, hard...an oval shape—not at all bumpy like wicker or sharp like a nail. This was much more interesting!

Eagerly, she rose from the chair, placing the weight of her bad foot on its heel so as to coddle the sore toe. Clumsy but determined, she stretched the bandaged foot out in front, used her good foot as leverage, and scooched lower and lower toward the floor until she was just inches from falling; her abs were taut with the effort, and when she was close enough to land without hurting herself, she relaxed her body.

With a *thump* she landed inelegantly on her rear end at just the right angle. She pulled the last strand of blanket away from the jagged broken edge of exposed wicker and put the blanket underneath her for a cushion. Most interested in what she was now able to see, she peered up underneath the arm—black, undistinguishable nothing—too dark. She knew something was there. Her slender fingers reached up and in and touched the small but hard roundness again—yes, something *was* stuck inside.

She hastily pulled her hand out and reached up to the nearby tray; she found a useful tool—a tiny teaspoon. Using the other end, she delicately moved it back and forth like a fulcrum inside the minuscule area. Securing it just under the small dark item that matched the black of the chair, she flipped the spoon end upward and *pop*! The little rounded cache tumbled out, spun out of control and skidded along the floor, where it disappeared behind the terracotta plant urn.

Chapter XI
A Tiny Discovery

Gingerly she knelt. "Ouch!" Reaching her hand blindly round to the back of the urn she probed, her fingers searching the floor inch by inch. The tip of her index finger touched it, barely. Success! Now, how to get it out? She grabbed the black cane the sisters had provided, and skillfully probed with the hooked end. "Oh, boy, c'mon...." Agonizing mini-inches later, she was able to first pull it toward her, then tenderly roll it until she could reach in with the other hand and grasp it. "There...got it!"

She brought the item close to her face for inspection. In her dusty palm, it was no larger than a quail egg. Besides the residual dust, it was covered with grime, the kind accumulated over time. She gently blew on it; some of the dusty powder flew off. Lo—it was a small treasure, wasn't it?

It was a tiny, Bohemian-style, black oval box. The top was decorated in faint flowered layers, yellowed with aged decoupage now, each delicate layer sealed with varnishes. The lid top was firmly secured around the lip's point of contact to the lower boxy section with a frayed but sturdy piece of now-dirty white tape. Mrs. Bundle studied it carefully. The tape was so old it was cemented firmly to the box. Predating today's typical black electrical tape or yellow masking tape, she recognized it as original insulating tape, the kind made of cloth impregnated with a sticky compound.

Mrs. Bundle searched for the old-fashioned word deep within the recesses of her mind. What was that called? She exclaimed, "Yes! Gutta-percha!" She knew about it from her grandfather—and her old farmstead. She and Arthur had had constant run-ins with the sticky stuff over the years. The bane of many historical homeowners, this particular type of white electrical tape was used pre-1940s to insulate soldered splices on knob and tube electrical wiring, even as time marched on to more modern options. Sticky and messy, the glue on the tape was called gutta-percha (from the Southeast Asia tropical tree). It was a biologically-inert, resilient latex used from the 1800s and on for insulation until the invention of standard black vinyl electric tape. It was often used in a similar way as duct tape is now—for anything needed sticking. Easily torn off by hand, it could also be written on permanently with ink. She looked closely.

"Oh!" The piece wrapped round the lid had a message! She adjusted her eyeglasses on her nose and read two hand-inked words: **Our Secret.** Underneath was a date: *1/8/1940*. *Our Secret*...oh my, very intriguing; what could that mean? And the date...January 8th, 1940? Was it a birth date, some historic public event...or something more private? Presumably, the date scribed on the box meant the age of the box was at least—she calculated excitedly—sixty-six years old. Wait—how odd! Even more stunning—the date would be *exactly* sixty-six years old tomorrow—Sunday, January 8th.

Holy cow.

What she had discovered was, apparently, something very old and very secretive. Hidden right here in the chair...what a peculiar spot....begging the question—why? Its size couldn't be more than 1½ inches in diameter and likewise the same in height—was there anything inside? She gently shook the little box and heard a muffled tap, tap round the inside surface—yes, there was!

She studied the sealed tape. Accessing the inside of the box properly would necessitate tweezers, maybe even a bit of solvent to gently lift the stuck tape off without damaging the box.

"Oh, dang and double dang!" she declared under her breath, and then the dreaded words, "A mystery." Even as she was dying to peel the old tape off without regard, something essential held her back—her conscience, the same thing that always seemed to predetermine her actions. She clucked and *tsk-tsked* some more as she studied the box and considered her dilemma. "Grrr!" Who did it belong to—most likely, a former guest at the inn? Children playing a game? Or, a couple? Yes, two or more people, in all probability, based on the possessive *Our* written on the label. If it was a secret, one must assume the contents signified something important, or dear, something...prized. She pondered the conundrum.

By Aurelia and Olivia Pettyfers' own account, all the furniture had been here for decades. Apparently, this chair, too—for, if the box was dated 1940, the chair predated the box. Might the box's owner or owners be a young child—or conversely, an important somebody? Both ends of the spectrum could be highly probable, based upon the number of guests who had stayed at the inn and sat in this chair over the decades. Might the Pettyfers know about it—if she asked?

A possible solution. Or not.

Early conclusion: the item had lain hidden deep inside the chair...since 1940. She checked herself. Hidden? Yes, that was the best hypothesis, as yet. Left there...maybe for someone to pick up? Her imagination went wild. It was a very tight, small spot to hide something. Perfect for a tiny item. And, she conjured up, perfect for someone who could have slipped it under the arm because *they* were in a tight spot? Or, maybe they just liked the way it fit so neatly.

The exertion had caused her foot to ache. Dang! She shifted her body and leaned her back against the chair, pondering the riddle from all sides. She came to a conclusion.

Rather than blindly offer it up to the Pettyfers, she decided to wait a bit, to do her own discovery just for...her own amusement. She would make a decision later today or tomorrow about this treasure (for indeed, whatever was inside was a treasure, whether it was of value monetarily or not) and who it should go to. She thought it best to leave these musings for later when she was in the privacy of her room. Removing her lace hankie from her sleeve, she carefully wrapped the item and zipped it in the inside pocket of her Pendleton shirt.

"Hmm." This certainly gave her something to ponder besides her present pity party, leaving her own predicament with Duke to simmer on the back burner.

She shivered. This slate floor was darn cold! And outside, the falling snow was even more furious. Unable to prevent it, she yawned. Whatever time it was, she was tuckered out! She rose at a snail's pace, using the cane. Her knees groaned and she favored her foot. "Oh, the old bones do creak and crack." She hated to admit it, but her toe, wrapped up like a mummy, was hurting, her body overtaxed by the activity. She might need a nap before the girls returned. Yes, that sounded lovely.

She left the room with her tiny prize. Fighting the twinges of dull pain, she made her way slowly up the grand stairway (the black cane lightly tapping as she went), unaware of the nearness of another.

Olivia Pettyfer's fretful gaze followed her every step, the long shadow of the dining room doorway shielding her. "Good gracious me," she whispered raggedly, nearly dropping the meat cleaver from her shaking hand. "Cousin Milly was right. You are a clever one."

Chapter XII

A Quandary...and Growing Pains

Upon their return mid-afternoon, Angie and Erin listened at Mrs. Bundle's closed door but, hearing nothing, concluded she must be napping. After a hushed game of Parcheesi in Angie's room, Erin retired to her room; both settled down for some quiet time reading and napping before teatime.

A bit later, there was a knock at Mrs. Bundle's door. "Mrs. B?"

"Hello, my dear." Wiping the sleep dust from her eyes, Mrs. Bundle greeted Erin. "Ahhh. How was your hike?"

"Oh, t'was wonderful. That Mister Woodsum is *so* nice! We went cross-country skiing all over the mountain; we sat on this really cool stone bench he made in the wilderness. He helped me collect twigs with all different needles—pine, spruce, fir—he knows *so* much! It smells *so* lovely in me room! He brought this big old thermos filled with hot chocolate—it was *so* yummy! Y'see now, Mrs. B, after our picnic we came back here. It sure is snowing out, isn't it? Mister Woodsum measured it with his yardstick. You were sleeping." She gave Mrs. Bundle a detailed report of their hike around the property. As she concluded, she spied the wooly creature at the end of Mrs. Bundle's leg. "Blimey! How's that pesky big toe, Mrs. B?"

"Oh, it's good. The Pettyfers have taken good care of me."

"Does it hurt?"

"Only a tiny bit. What did you do when you got back from your hike?"

"We were totally knackered, too—fact is, Angie's still dead to the world. Like this—*Arrrrrrrh…phfft, phfft!*" She gave an exaggerated loud snore and giggled.

"Oh, my!" Mrs. Bundle drew the drape back to reveal the oncoming early Vermont twilight amidst the flurry of snow, "It's really coming down out there, isn't it?"

"Mister Woodsum says it looks like we're gettin' a good ol'-fashioned blizzard. Yahoo! And, Miss Aurelia said we're to come to the *dining room* for teatime. They have a *surprise* for us." She paused, twirling her hair and fidgeting while her right foot tapped impatiently; meanwhile, her twitching nose caused the twin butterfly eyeglass frame to dance like two ballerinas.

Mrs. Bundle knew those signals. "What's on your mind, Erin dear?"

"Well, em, Mrs. B, I think we need…em…a good chinwag, don't we now." She flounced onto the bed, a bundle of nervous energy.

"What's up, luv?"

"Well now…I was wondering. C'mere, d'ya think things about this place are a might…fishy?"

"Fishy?" Mrs. Bundle chuckled. "Hmmm. What makes you think that?"

"Well now, I've been watching. And observing what goes on—like you always do with your detectin'. Sure and away, there are some very interesting *clues* to pick up. I'm starting to keep track, y'see?" She tapped her temple. "Up here."

Mrs. Bundle knew it didn't take much for Erin, prone to suspicion and intrigue with a strong admiration to be just like her, to keenly ferret out mysteries at the drop of any wayward abnormality. Added with an unquenchable thirst for allure—like Mrs. Bundle—Erin also possessed intuition beyond her years, and she went on, "Clues, Mrs. B, clues! First, there's the cat. Or," she held up fingers in quotes, "no cat." She fixed a very pessimistic look. "Who doesn't have a cat in a big place like this? Right? I know when I hear a cat. I'm very keen on cat sounds. And I definitely heard one. Aye, there was a cat or something that sounded *exactly* like a cat out there!" She pointed an emphatic index finger toward to hallway.

"Hmmm. I hear what you're saying. From my perspective, I didn't see or hear a cat. I did hear a few strange sounds, though I can't put my finger on what it was—could just be the old house creaking. That said, I believe you did, or think you did, hear a cat. It's certainly something to mull over, but I wouldn't hang my 'good ol' mystery' hat on that." She tweaked the freckled, flushed cheek. "What else, Private Eye Corrigan?"

"Well, she seems sad, doesn't she now? I mean, Miss Aurelia. She's got some, em, trouble nagging away at her. I reckon she has a secret, something big. That's one. Fact of the matter is, Miss Olivia acts like kind of a sourpuss. But really, she's hiding something, too. Maybe something that makes her worried so she acts like a sourpuss but really she's nice inside. That's two. Then, there's Mister Woodsum, he's like a little boy. But he's old—really old! He acts so much younger, doesn't he? Sure, and he was a handsome divil in those olden days! I'll give you that." Clearly, Erin was smitten, in point of fact, had fallen hook, line, and sinker for the elderly gentleman. She went on, "Blimey, he's a hoot—he's got all those funny sayings!" She threw her head back and imitated him in expert style, laughed gaily, *"Hardy har har!"* Instantly, she turned sober again. "Aye, I'll just bet he's got some secrets, too." She braided her fingers together expertly. "Here's something—how come he never went off and got himself a wife like other normal gents do? D'ya think he ever had a sweetheart, even maybe on the Q-T?"

"Oh! Well, Erin, I couldn't begin to speculate on that. In my experience everyone has secrets of some kind: some small, some big. The Pettyfers, well, they certainly, by all appearances, seem to have lived quite a sheltered life up here in the williwags."

"Aye, sheltered. And very long lives they are, wouldn't you agree, mum?"

"Uh-huh. So the likelihood is quite favorable for…secrets. Wouldn't you agree?"

"Aye…the longer the life, the more secrets," she stroked her chin in deep thought (a trait she'd adopted since reading *The Complete Sherlock Holmes*). "None of them married, am I right? Miss Aurelia and Miss Olivia—*Misses*, not Mrs. like married, c'mere now."

"As far as we know. But a good detective never assumes anything. We only know that they appear to have been…single…now and before—and going by their original surname of Pettyfer. You see?"

"Aye, that's true. Hmmm. I believe that might need some research. And, why wouldn't the lads be sweet on them when they were young? I'll wager they were quite fetching then. Right, now—but it's not just that." She lowered her voice, "Ach! Here's the last clue. Have y' noticed the way they all run this inn, getting all things done so efficient-like? How d'ya think it could be possible, them bein' so ancient and such? Without any servants, way up here? They're *ancient!*" To Erin, these were walking Methuselahs. "Even if the time stands still up here. And, surely," her eyes widened, "it's such a weird wonderful place." Her hands flipped to palms up. "Weird and wonderful, wonderful but weird. Ach, it's too peculiar; I feel just like bloody Gumbo!"

"Gumbo?" Mrs. Bundle laughed uproariously; Gumbo was Aineen's pet hamster. "Oh, my word, Erin, you are a pip! Why do you feel like Gumbo?"

"Aye, don't laugh too soon, Mrs. B. Think about that hamster in one of those mazes she goes through. And think about like, here at the inn, we're allowed to go here," she motioned wildly, "or here, and down here," her hands were flying. She jumped up from the bed, "But, mind you, we can't get over *there*, 'cuz if I do," she threw up her hands in frustration as she reverted into the first person, "it's off limits. For some *strange* reason I'll not be understandin' for the life of me. Why, I ask you? All swings and roundabouts is what it is! With everything so danged perfect! They're all so nice—even Miss Olivia when she forgets herself, aye? So, why are *some* of the doors locked? And the attic, too?" Her voice rose a pitch, "What the divil do you suppose is up there? All kinds of ghosts from the past? Secrets!" she pronounced; her eyebrows shot upward. "Blimey, there's one thing

I know for sure! I know a dang cat sound when I hear it, even if *they* don't abide cats!" She was fired up now, babbling with soapbox fervor. "Which, surely now, who doesn't like cats? They're sweet, and smart. Ach, it's surely maddening! *And*," she made her final point soundly punching the pillow, "you can *be sure* our Cracker-Cat wouldn't have any of that, not one bit, would he now?" She plopped herself down in confusion and fatigue. "So, those are me thoughts, mum. It's just not like real life here. It's...a wee bit of the phony baloney."

"Now, now." She reached over and hugged the girl. What Erin had articulated in childlike fashion echoed some of Mrs. Bundle's earlier gut feelings. Her hands itched to share the little box in her pocket, but she held off, not wanting to rile up the youngster any more than she already was. "Calm yourself, dear girl. Believe it or not, I *do* understand what you are saying." She leaned back, locking eyes with Erin. "I have also given some thought to most of what you've mentioned. We are on the same page, you and I—there might be some mysteries here with some secrets. However," she drew her wool shirt close to her, "we're here as guests in this idyllic spot deep in the forest on the top of a very remote mountain. We don't know this place as they do, as they have their whole lives. This isn't just an inn to them, it's been their home—forever. It's likely they want to keep their private life—and their secrets, mind you, if they have any—private. We need to respect that, don't we?"

"Well, I suppose."

"Meanwhile, we can still...be observant." She gave a quick wink.

"Mum, wouldn't it be *so* romantic to have a mystery happenin' here at Mount Holly Mansion? I reckon there's something dark and sinister, something very....*crafty*...going on. Maybe something ghostly! From the past." She lowered her voice. "I feel it in me bones. D'you, too?"

"Hmm. Do I believe something *might* be going on? Possibly—but wait—I don't know how dark or sinister it is. Or, for that matter, whether craftiness enters into it. But I'd suggest you keep a log of ideas."

"And didn't I bring me wee journal with me, too! A stroke of luck if ever I saw one!"

"There you go. Keep a log as you did when you solved the Clancy twin's garden mystery. It's very helpful and will keep you," she almost slipped and said *occupied* but recovered with, "organized. And we can confer on this matter later. Shall we? Meanwhile, I would urge you to keep all this pondering under your hat. We certainly wouldn't want to upset the Pettyfers."

"Oh, no!"

"And, no snooping around on your own anymore—got it?" She extended her little finger in agreement.

Erin extended hers and they executed their pinkie promise, a very serious pact in their world. Mollified, she said, "That I'll do, for sure, Mrs. B. But just in case, I'm going to keep me eyes open at all times for anything dodgy. I'm watchin' *everything*. Aye, and I'm listening, too!" She made a motion of knocking three times on the wall. "Just in case....be ready!"

"Right-o!"

She gulped some air and suddenly flopped like a ragdoll back on the bed, almost losing her butterfly eyeglasses to the wind force in the process. She stared at the ceiling languorously. "Ahh…me, oh my."

"So! Is there…anything else on your mind, dear?"

"Well, aye, now that you ask. It's a bit hard…to discuss. I was going to ask me new friend Loralei—you met her at the Christmas concert—she wears a bra and everything and her Mum, Pastor Holly, is good with most any predicament. But…you've done for me before when I'm in a pickle. This is kinda like a pickle but *personal*. And you know a lot about…well, pretty much everything. See…." she paused.

The key words "predicament" and "personal" opened the door for many possibilities. What startling revelation was about to burst forth now? It sounded like Loralei (and possibly Erin) had already utilized Reverend Holly's expertise; she was inclined to investigate that when they got back. For now, Mrs. Bundle just proposed, "Go ahead, luv."

"I've got…" Erin blushed, a phenomenon she experienced only when completely flummoxed, which was seldom, "em…feelings."

Mrs. Bundle nodded encouragingly. "Uh-huh. Feelings."

"Well, y'see…em…sometimes…right here in me tummy." (Fidget), "And then…all over…not sick, but…"(shiver), "kinda *quingy*-like."

Ah, yes, thank goodness — a Walterism, Mrs. Bundle thought. When in doubt, she, too, often borrowed from Walter Andersen's unique vocabulary of made-up words that suited a myriad of situations; those words were often the best way to express ones' feelings. For example, *quingy* (one of his most-used) meant feeling out of sorts, not oneself, downright peckish. *But, oh boy.*

Caught off guard, Mrs. Bundle wondered if now was the time for The Talk — the same one she'd been given by her mother around the same age as Erin was now, when those type of feelings surfaced for her — one and the same, accordingly given to her daughter Karen and, just a few years ago, to Angie, who Mrs. Bundle had often been called upon to mother, growing up as she did surrounded by only men.

Erin watched her reaction as if her life depended upon it. "Would you be knowin' anything about that kind of peculiar ailment, mum?"

The key here was to know just how much to share. "Yes, I think I do know something about that."

Erin leaned in, breathless and all ears. "*Aye, and..?*"

"Well…Erin, as you know, since you were a youngster we've talked about many things. A lot about changes children make as they grow, and learn about themselves and the world around them. And, of course, there have been our ongoing discussions about using restraint, educating ourselves, thinking first before we jump in and speak — these kinds of things. Which ultimately, helps us become more independent. Right?" She smiled and touched the little hand beside her. "In addition to that, my dear, you are on the precipice —" she paused, thinking that word difficult.

Erin said in a rush, "Yes, I know *precipice* — the brink, the edge — go on, Mrs. B! I'm all ears."

"You are on the precipice of some wonderful events that occur only to us—women, that is. Your body is giving you little signals… signs for these… milestones or stages that occur as a girl transitions into womanhood."

"Oh!" Erin offered thoughtfully. "Womanhood. I think you might be talking about these bits and pieces Angie's been tellin' me about. The personal yucky stuff." She shrugged, wiggling her fingers in the air idly.

Mrs. Bundle gave a firm nod. "Yes. One and the same."

"Surely you don't mean that monthly thing that happens whether we lasses like it or not?" She sat up with a jolt. "Ach! And I'll wager about having babies, too." She reached over and patted Mrs. Bundle's hand reassuringly. "It's okay, Mrs. B. I'll be *twelve* in April."

"Uh-huh. The thing is…there are things that we, as mature ladies, should learn about, and even embrace. Growing pains are all part of the process." She smiled thoughtfully, recalling her own reaction to this news as a young girl.

"But, mum!" Erin wailed. "Why do we lasses have to go through all this sufferin' and tribulation? What about the lads? Why, they just get to slide by and have all the bloomin' fun!"

"Well, boys go through…other things." *Wait,* she told herself, *breathe, and this one may go by.*

Erin gave a disbelieving sideways glance, "Ha! Do they now, and who gives a hoot anyway? Angie told me *I'll* be fancyin' *boys*"—she grimaced as if spitting out dirt—"once I get to me womanhood. Sounds like bollocks to me! Me *brathair* Jack is the only mate I need." Her head shook violently. "Surely and *you* know I just can't *abide* boys—especially those knuckleheads—" her head waggled with disdain and her curls shook in accord. (Mrs. Bundle knew exactly which knuckleheads she was referring to) "who I *wish* would keep their big gobs closed. Ach—so aggravatin'!" She sighed and tapped her knees impatiently. "Y'know?"

Mrs. Bundle clucked with understanding and allowed some time to gather her thoughts. What could anyone say in favor of the infamous Clancy twins who were forever getting on Erin's last nerve?

Suddenly, Erin quirked her head in light-bulb-moment mode, "'Course now, *Anthony* Clancy—not to be taking a side, mind you—he's not such a bad bloke, is he? He likes to read a lot—like me—and he's funny, too—in an odd bookish way. I like talking to him at the library. Did'ja notice he wears spectacles like me, too? Now, he's a *proper* mate." Erudite Anthony Clancy, a much older version of his brothers, was indeed one of Mrs. Bundle's favorites, too. "Not to get all googly-eyed and blushy about, mind you, now." She sighed resignedly, "Aye, all me growin' pains surely are a bloomin' pain in the arse." Her hand shot over her mouth. "*Oops*! Sorry, mum. It's just a big pain all around, I reckon."

"Excused this time, dear. However, you'll just have to be patient. It's a waiting game."

"That's it?" She was a freckled mess of bewilderment. "I just have to wait for it all to happen to me?"

"Exactly."

"Will it come like a smack to me noggin when it hits?"

"No. It comes gradually. In fact, it's better if you don't over-think it. It's rather an ongoing process. Like how a flower bud opens and then slowly blooms. Before you know it, you will feel quite… womanly. Trust me." She quirked her eyebrow and smiled.

"Really, now, that's how me womanhood comes? I want to put me head around it, but it's truly mysterious." Her tone was skeptical. "Okay. If you say so, I'll trust you, mum."

"You can come to me anytime—or, Angie, too. Whenever you have questions."

Erin flipped her hair then rubbed her speckled nose vigorously. "*Hmmpph*! For now, I'm going to concentrate on me school work and chores, me ukulele, and some good ol' detectin'."

Mrs. Bundle gave a double thumbs up. "Those are good priorities and goals. Y'know, we're all very proud of you."

"Whoa! Didja hear that now?"

Downstairs, the loud gong echoed resonantly—*Teatime!*

"Ooh, boy! Sure and I'm so hungry I could eat the hind end of a skunk!" (Another one of Gumpy's sayings, proving no one could keep Vermont from infiltrating this Irish lass.)

"Me, too!" She gave Erin a quick wink. "Mum's the word on our detecting. We'll keep an eye on things even while we relax and enjoy the rest of our time here."

"Right-o!" She stretched and gave Mrs. Bundle a quick peck on the cheek. "Thanks ever so, Mrs. B! I better go get—" A nearby door opened and closed, followed by footsteps. "Angie!"

Angie appeared, yawning widely, hair mussed, cheeks flushed. "Ooooh, jeesum! Just what I needed—more sleep! It's like taking a magic potion here." She stretched, beautiful and rested. "I dozed off big-time. So cozy here, even with the cold outside." She looked out. "Wow, it's really coming down now!" It was true; the snow was falling with more intensity; however, all was so very nice inside. "Anybody else besides me totally famished?"

Chapter XIII
High Tea or Not?

When they entered the dining room, it was quiet—and very empty. No tea or dainty concoctions had been laid out; all was as empty as Jacob's kettle. Their energetic hosts were nowhere nearby, causing them a bit of panic. Whilst dusk descended outside, a blustering wind whistled and whined like the dickens.

"Mercy! It's beginning to sound quite gloomy out there." Mrs. Bundle's solo pronouncement fell flat in the catacomb-sized room. She raised her voice, "*Helloooo!*" It echoed off the wall and came bouncing back.

Angie was quiet and watchful. "Where *is* everyone?"

Erin skated over to the large French window and pulled back the drape. "Wow! It's darker 'n a deep pocket,"—another one of Walter's favorite sayings—"and snowing like the dickens! Can't see much of anything out past the side yard here." She turned back. "D'you think now, they've all *left* us here to fend for ourselves during this *monstrous, terrible* blizzard?"

"Just wait..." Mrs. Bundle said; they stood listening on tenterhooks for any signs of life.

"This is kooky..." Angie spoke; Erin added, "And...kind of spooky—"

With sudden abandon, the kitchen door seemed to come apart and Woodsum appeared big as life, clacking two wooden spoons together in merry reverie. He shouted, "Hear ye, hear ye! Calling all guests! Change of plans—no formal tea today. Because of this big storm a-brewin'!"

"No tea?" Erin made a face like she'd just swallowed a dose of bitters.

"Now, wait a minute. It's okay!" he insisted. "We're changing the program and it's good news. Yes, to tea. No, to formal—y'see, we're just gonna hang out in here—casual-like."

"In the kitchen?" Erin stood on tiptoes trying to peer past him."Really?"

"Yep! C'mon in," he gave a flourishing bow, and then straightened, pointing the wooden spoons toward the unchartered territory, "to where *all* the magic happens, missies! C'mon, now! Shake a leg! Well, exceptin' you, Mrs. Bundle. You just take your time."

Aurelia, who appeared just inside the sanctioned area, stepped back, then tiptoed backward further and pronounced, "We'll have a proper *kitchen* tea today. Cozy as all get-out!"

The designated food preparation area was large and very old—a true vintage kitchen in all respects. The lack of abundant lighting (there was only one window, and a lone but welcoming gas lantern hung on the wall) gave it a snug, subdued ambiance. They were met with warmth and sweet smells—phenomenal!

Their eyes, bright with wonder, took it all in. Here was the heart and the true pulse of the home where marvelous culinary delights and all things incredibly edible dwelled. The ancient cast iron kitchen cook stove was handsome. Fine lettering spelled out *Windsor*. This was the circa-1920s steel range whose daily creations issued aromas that reached every corner of every room of the large dwelling. Gracing the stovetop were three steaming kettles: two, with water for tea and one for cooking. Two other big pots spluttered and boiled away.

Possy the Royal Grump lay on a gigantic cushion near the stove, snoring away, ignoring the hustle. His snores were so lively that the lone rocking chair beside his cushion rocked to the rumbling rhythm. On the other side along the wall was a ribbed-topped porcelain counter complete with two deep enamel sinks and pewter fixtures. Both sinks were piled high with pots and pans. Someone had been hard at work!

Olivia, wearing a full apron and brandishing a carving knife of intimidating proportions in one hand and a ball of jute twine in the other, stood at the helm of the very hefty farm table located in the center of the room. Her cheeks were flushed with heat from the nearby stove. She greeted the girls. "Well, now, how're you all doing?" She pulled out a yard-long strand from the twine, pulled it taut, and neatly sliced the string with the knife.

Angie exclaimed, "Oh! We're…just wonderful!"

Erin added, "Fan-tastical!"

"And you, Mrs. Bundle? How's your foot?"

"Oh, much, much better. Thank you for all your kind ministering. That salve and poultice have worked wonders!"

The knife flashed as Olivia's attention focused on the large piece of raw meat before her; the blade deftly peeled away stray lumps of fat, then sliced the pork tenderloin in half lengthwise, skillfully leaving it uncut completely through. She vigorously rubbed it down with salt and pepper. "Your afternoon was, I trust, relaxing and uneventful?"

"You bet. Words cannot adequately describe the benefits of good ol' afternoon napping!" She watched with interest, "I hope you haven't been slaving away all afternoon. When do you get a break?"

"Oh, no, no. I got in a little nap myself. Right there through that door are our quarters," she motioned with her chin while she worked away, rolling a layer of basil and garlic, sun-dried tomatoes, and cheese within, "and you already know that back stairway goes up to all the guest quarters." She patted the meat, folding in the narrow end.

"Yes, Woodsum told us. He also said they were a bit dicey to negotiate." She chuckled and gave a little kick in the air with her bad foot. "I doubt I'll be using them."

"Blimey, that stove is a monster, isn't it now?" Erin was enamored with it all. "Wow!" she cried out gleefully, "It's like being way, way, *way* back in time here."

They watched Olivia skillfully, with loops and knots, tie off and then deposit the beautiful specimen into the roasting pan edged with finely diced potatoes, onions, and carrots. Meanwhile, she explained, "It's a Windsor, best there is. The fire's stoked at dawn's first light. We get it readied for breakfast and all the hours of work, and then our pretty little 'Winnie' continues to put out heat throughout the day." She opened the oven door to show them. "There's the two shelves above the six burners, with a warming closet, a waterfront and reservoir all lined with tin for heating our range water, mind you." The range shined as though new. "Always spic and span; always ready to serve the cook! There! That oughta do it." She slammed the oven door, straightened, and turned to address the task at hand. "Isn't that beautiful?" She stepped back and admired her handiwork, then landed the roast with aplomb atop the cabinet in front of the window, which had been opened just a crack for fresh air. "You know what they always say, missy?"

By now used to Miss Olivia's axioms, Erin paid attention, knowing she was ready to impart another. "No, Miss Olivia, what do they always say?"

"They always say 'the quickest way to do many things is to do one thing at a time'. There! All set for dinner later on." She winked. "Now—what's next?"

"Tea?" Erin asked hopefully.

"You bet!" Woodsum said.

The long wooden work table was quickly cleared of all utensils and paraphernalia and wiped clean. A large tray of cups, saucers, silverware, and cloth napkins magically appeared, along with a pot of sweet dark winter honey.

"You're all going to *choose* what you'd like to have for tea treats today!" Woodsum said. "You can help yourself."

"Really?" Erin asked, looking around for all the delicacies. "From where?"

"Right over here through this magic door." Aurelia stood at the far end of the kitchen, waving with a warning finger. "We just *cannot* abide anyone going hungry!"

Woodsum chortled, "For all sweet tooth emergencies, enter here!" His grin was wickedly fun, reminiscent of the Big Bad Wolf.

"And—you can help yourself anytime you've got a hankering, just like Homer and Milly always did when they were here." Aurelia beamed with pleasure as she opened the pantry door and stepped aside, motioning them to join her where delightful aromas combined with heavenly rays of colored light like a prism. Was it fantasy or real?

"That's right. Make yourself to home." Woodsum added. "C'mon Erin—you too, Angie!"

Suddenly old Possy was at his side, knowing from experience that when that door opened, something very special was up. He barked a short directive: Har-*rummppphh*! Pushing his scrunchy nose against Erin's heels, he nipped impatiently.

"Oh, lordy, lord!" Erin exclaimed.

Now was the time the Pettyfers had chosen to reveal all—at least, in the kitchen—and there was not one dilly-dallier in the bunch. The three guests stepped forward.

Chapter XIV
Culinary Nirvana

In its entirety, it wasn't just an old-fashioned walk-in pantry—more to the point, what was revealed was a precious cache of culinary riches. Lined with shelves reaching to the ceiling, the large room just off the kitchen was a veritable treasure trove replete with abundant numbers of sacks, bags, tins, and canned jars, all chock full of everything from dilly beans, chow-chow, sweet and sour pickles, to soup stock and succotash. There was an assortment of berry preserves and conserve, piccalilli, honey, and chutneys. Nearby were fresh breads wrapped in clean linen towels, and a mouth-watering selection of desserts and treats: orange sponge cake, dimpled apple tarts, caramel pudding, gingerbread, rhubarb brown betty, and behind it, yes—

"Is that a lemon meringue pie?" Mrs. Bundle asked, overjoyed.

Nearby, a plentiful assortment of potted meats, fish, and mincemeat were organized neatly on lower shelves. There were faded-from-age-and-use, patterned tin containers, all with colorful scenes with everything from an English foxhunt to the RMS Queen Mary; a playful Humpty Dumpty in a tam-o'-shanter hat and a scene of Old London; and a lovely one with huge roses against a bright blue background. When opened, each tin was filled with a homemade delicacy: nougat; molasses and taffy; nut brittle; hermits; and candied lemon peel.

"Hermits? I love hermits!" Angie exclaimed. "I haven't had one in ages!" There was nothing like a good ol' hermit to put a smile of satisfaction on one's face.

"That one on the top's got your name on it, I reckon." Olivia offered matter-of-factly.

And the prism of colorful light? Lining the top shelf all around the pantry like sparkling jewels were numerous gleaming decanters—a liquid spectrum from yellow to vermillion to emerald green.

"You've had a chance to taste our medicinal brandies and cordials," Aurelia gave a dimpled smile. "Well, let's see, there's cherry, lemon, peach, and blackberry cordial, and apple brandy, and raspberry and oh, peppermint—that's quite a yummy one. Of course, we learned all the receipts from Mother."

"We enjoyed them from an early age—sometimes without Father's full approval." Woodsum snorted, giving Mrs. Bundle a wink.

"But *only* in the evening or on *special* occasions." Olivia corrected him.

"Oh, yes, they're certainly...robust." Mrs. Bundle offered. "And so flavorful!" *It must run in the family,* she thought, smiling inwardly. She wondered if this was where Granny Milly had gotten inspiration for the elixir she was famous for far and wide.

Tall round cracker containers housed dry goods and staples. Clear glass jars of dried herbs were at eye level. Near the door, dark newspaper-lined twin vegetable bins held squashes, onions, potatoes, and various other sundries suited for long-term storage. An old but immaculate three-door oak icebox with metal interior, complete with ice block tongs and aluminum ice cube trays housed dairy goods, a large bottle of milk, and other perishables. Rounding out this virtual survival empire was a butter churner sitting beside the icebox.

Upon viewing this cavalcade of cuisine, Erin, whose eyes shone with delight, heartily echoed Walter Andersen's sagacious saying, "Aye—just like Gumpy says, you surely *can* judge a hostess by what she's got in her *pantries*."

Everyone struggled for control and then burst out laughing as Erin grinned with sweet naiveté.

Returning to the farm table with their chosen treats, they were met with pots filled with tea; the cups, dishes, and silverware had been set out by Olivia in place settings for six. The rocking chair had been moved closer to the table. They all settled in, choosing catch-as-catch-can the small caned side chairs gathered from around the room, just enough for their little coterie.

The centerpiece was a platter of fresh cinnamon raisin buns with white icing.

"Mmmm!" Erin gushed and all were happily silent for the interim. "Hiking sure brings on an appetite!"

Minutes of pleasure passed without as much talk as munching.

As their delightful teatime wound down, Sir Possy's furry topknot popped up from his cozy spot. He whined, focusing on the farthest wall.

"Possy, dearest, what is it? Do you spy something?" Aurelia queried, rising.

Suddenly, he barked as ferociously as an old ruler can, struggling to jump up. He lumbered achingly over to the baseboard grilled vent, fixed his snout in one corner, assiduously rooting around like a Tasmanian boar.

"Yessuh! He's after another varmint." Woodsum cheered, "Didja get at it, ol' Poss?"

"Varmint? You mean a mouse?" Erin asked impishly, "Or a big huge rat?"

With a snarl and a cuss, the dog gave up and ambled back to his warm spot.

"Yes, something tiresome like that. Best house mouse killers around. It'd be a badger if he was outside." Olivia said, pursing her lips. "Dandy Dinmont Terriers are famous for digging large holes quick as a wink. You should see them go! Don't leave them anywhere near small varmints like mice and hamsters. They'll ferret 'em out like the devil possessed." There went that chin, jutting out with conviction. "And swallow 'em whole."

"Now, sister, don't get all wound up. True fact is, them Terriers got lots of moxie." Woodsum informed them. "Now, Possy here, he barely gets around. They always had issues with them short legs all the way through the dynasty—it's the first thing that goes." He gestured toward the sorry-looking animal, "The days are long gone since he can travel upstairs. But back in the day, he was a pisser, just like all the sires before him! Uh-huh."

Olivia added. "Why, most all our Possies challenged foxes, too, don't you know. And," she puffed up proudly, "They were just aces going after stray cats."

Angie whispered close to Mrs. Bundle's ear, "*Hmmmph.* I'll bet our Cracker could give him a run for his money."

Patting him fondly, Woodsum snickered, "You're just a swell ol' bum, ain't ya, just like the rest afore you!" He reached into a nearby box and treated Postlewaite the Eighth and Great to a special mail-order diabetic dog biscuit. "Here you go, ya big galoot!" He clucked, "Yuh, yuh. There ya go." He passed a biscuit to Angie.

"Pretty ferocious, huh?" Angie asked, taking it. She gestured doubtfully at the dynasty's surviving member. "He sure wanted to tussle with whatever he got wind of over there." She reached out and tapped his paw with the biscuit; he snorted, grabbed the morsel, and begrudgingly snuffled her hand.

"All ours were the same, some more ferocious than others. Our *very first* Possy—he was the biggest one—remember, sisters? Gaw, didn't he just hate that old corner wicker chair in the solarium with a passion! Went after it time and again!"

"The black wicker chair?" Mrs. Bundle asked, sitting forward.

"Yessuh." He chuckled, "One day, he got a bee in his bonnet that some critter was hiding in there. So, he gets up on the seat somehow and gets to gnawin' at that wicker arm like there was no tomorrow! Chewing it near off just to get at some itty bitty mouse hiding underneath the crook!" He slapped his knee and guffawed. "Ha! That little fella—ferocious as all get out! Remember, sisters? Yuh, yuh. That was our first Postlewaite. 1939."

"Foolish dog!" Aurelia sighed, her voice tinged with sadness. "Ah, yes. Good ol' memories, for sure. Possy the First was a corker."

Olivia sniffed.

Hmmm. Mrs. Bundle knew well the chair causing Sir Possy the First's ire so long ago. She held her excitement in check. "I... happened to notice that chair arm today. In fact," she stopped, not sure she wanted to give it all away, "my...lap blanket caught on the sharp corner of the arm."

"That's the one." Woodsum said blandly.

As well as, Mrs. Bundle thought, *finding something quite noteworthy inside.* What a coincidence—and what was she to do? *Not just yet,* her intuition spoke loudly to her.

There was an explosive *Baww-w-wppp!* below their feet, followed by the rhythmic *thug-a-thug-a-thug-shoooosh*-ing they'd now grown accustomed to hearing.

"Mister Woodsum, I'd like to know," Erin inquired, "what that thumping racket is that we hear every now and then? It's like a babby's howlin' just before a soft lullaby." She pointed below as the unmistakable sound pounded away like the dickens.

Woodsum's countenance was joyous. "Oh! So you noticed? Why, missy, that's our Bensie! Sweetheart is what she is. She lives deep down in the dark, dark cellar!" He quirked a teasing eyebrow at her. "Huh. I'll just bet you'd enjoy another exploration." He lowered his voice spookily, "How 'bout a tour of our old subterranean crypt? You and Angie?"

"Why not, you ask? Seems like you've got a funny name for everything, Mister Woodsum. Aye, another adventure for us—*what a day!*" Erin's eyes gleamed—and maybe another clue, too? "Aye, how grand!"

Chapter XV
What...Evil Lurks?

And so they ventured into the unknown once again, this time down, down, into the cavernous basement. Head dipped to avoid the low overhead clearance, Woodsum brought them through a labyrinth of crowded darkened pathways past the root cellar, his cluttered workshop, and the cramped storerooms of the dirt-floored cellar. With only the light of one dim lamp, the girls stayed close to their leader, who fearlessly pressed on deeper and deeper until they reached the furthest end. It was like another world, one that serviced the underbelly of the inn, a world where one could imagine (if minds like Erin's were allowed to wander) fiery dragons and monster bats and wooly beasts of all sizes. The deeper they went, the louder the sound...thumpa, *thumpa, thumpa.*

"Aye, it's a bit like a castle dungeon, isn't it now?" Erin whispered reverently, checking behind her at every turn. The *thumpa thumpa* gained intensity like jungle drums—wheels turning, metal against belt, and then—a distant screech! "Shush, now! Did'ja hear that?" They paused; the only noise: the *thumpa-thump.* Her eyes were huge, magnified through her glasses. "C'mere now! I heard it... something very....peculiar, wouldn't you say? Like a banshee... cryin' out somethin' terrible!" Her shoulders hunched in fear, "From beneath this deep, dark dungeon cell!"

Angie nudged Erin from behind and she jumped like a skittery cat.

"More like lions and tigers and bears—oh my." Angie said dryly, ribbing her. "I think someone's imagination is running rampant."

They came to a stop before the loud, huge contraption dominating the full corner: it was a beast of a machine, churning and chuttering away.

When Woodsum spoke, his voice filled with awe and reverence. "There she be—Sweet Bensie, our prized furnace! Ain't she just the bombdiggitty? *Heeeee*-haw!" Immediately going into detail, he pointed and gesticulated. "That there is a top-of-the-line, warm-air heating plant! It's a beauty. Very, *very* economical. Coal or wood—whatever your little heart desires! It was considered a luxury when it was first installed long, long ago. Winter water," he explained, "was dicey for most homes back in the day, but this solved the inn's problems for a clean, healthy, plentiful supply." He further indicated an old spring-fed well provided water to both the furnace and the monstrous attached hot water heater, which was then pumped upstairs by the original Bensen's hydraulic water ram.

Emanating from the heart of the furnace and networking throughout the basement was yet another unparalleled feature— in Woodsum's opinion—the massive piping system. "Yessir! Y'see now, Father bit the bullet in 1930 and upgraded to this state-of-the-art system." Six lengths of extensive piping exited the furnace top and ran to each end of the house, providing heat through a vented system. He took the time to point out every vent, signifying which room they were each connected to, then explained how the piping was channeled judiciously up through the first floor walls to provide auxiliary heat to some areas on the second floor. "That's what you're hearing and why there's lots of echoes through the inn. Sheer luxury in heat!" he snorted gleefully.

"Yes, I see." Angie did her best to feign interest, not one to offend. "Wow. It's quite the system!"

Erin's voice quavered as she asked, "Is there....anything else down here?" At his elbow, she looked around judiciously, crumpling the bridge of her nose and breathed, "You know...like magical things?"

Woodsum scratched his head. "Well now. Magical—like what, missy?"

"You know, like some mythical creatures like in King Arthur's court…dragons and such…or wily monsters ready to carry maidens off to unknown lands? Or, right!" she snapped her fingers and cackled, "A *wicked queen!* Ach, wouldn't that be the *bee's knees!*"

"There she goes again." Angie sighed.

"*Heeeee*-haw!" He slapped his thigh. "Well now, that's a good one." He pulled himself together. "Missy, I can't say as I've ever seen any of that here. That ain't to say there ain't none, 'specially if you believe in those things. Anywho, I expect by now you've seen most everything down here—and at the inn. Officially! I'm of the mind you've got the picture and then some. Had quite a day, haven't you?" He gestured upwards, "Well, it ain't over yet! I got a wicked coin collection, silver dollars like y'read about. Why, I even got a 1914-D Lincoln penny—and Olivia's been collecting stamps forever. Her albums'll make your head spin—wanna see 'em?" He led the way back to comfort.

With everyone having such a gay time, little notice was given to the outside world.

Covering two thousand miles in girth, the storm from the west that had reached monumental status and earned the apt name "Midwest Monster" was now smack dab in eastern New York and little Vermont, having worked its magic from west to east. Early indications were ominous but it had already proven to be cross-your-fingers time for anyone in its wake. Widespread outages were rampant. For now, if residents had milk, bread, toilet paper, and beer they were lucky. Thousands of flights had been canceled at most airports while crews treated runways glazed over with ice. Roadways were devastated with huge amounts of snow; travel was treacherous and almost nonexistent as drifts and whiteout from blowing snow made moving anywhere virtually impossible.

On the eastern seaboard, there was more treachery on the major highway of I-95 as the bear of a Nor'easter barreled its way northward. Traffic was sluggish at best; New York City was in gridlock. The monster winter storm stretched up the coast to Maine. Its nasty center had already whipped the seas to 21 feet at the Diamond Shoals buoy off Cape Hatteras. The sheet of ice had turned to snow as it moved north, roiling westward to New England like a gigantic smothering blanket. Most stores, if still open, were sold out of ice melt product, flashlights and batteries. The National Weather Service was already calling it "the biggest blizzard of the millennium." Worse yet, what was predicted to come afterward were deep freeze temperatures that would thrust everyone into more turmoil after the snow had stopped.

Even in the Connecticut Valley, the bear of the Nor'easter would have a leg-up on even the hardiest New Englander as it slammed into everything in its wake with a force to be reckoned with. On the local TV weather report (for those who still had power), experts said the worst was yet to come—when, by early morning, it would converge with the Midwest Monster.

Both snowstorms, they said, would collide in a colossal mess of ice and snow with a rumble and jumble of mammoth blizzard proportions the likes of which had not been seen in Vermont since… exactly sixty-six years before.

Chapter XVI

Darkness Brings Forth Dinner, Games...and Times Past

After a proper dinner of succulent roasted pork, the guests moved into the informal den/game room where they were joined by the Pettyfers.

That evening was spent in wild revelry—that is, Mount Holly Mansion-style. Games were the ticket, along with tale-telling. By nine p.m., Angie and Mrs. Bundle had finished a rowdy game of checkers by gaslight. Next, a nail-biting card game ensued, to which Erin exclaimed, "This is more fun than anything, isn't it now!" as she slapped down the final winning card in Crazy Eights.

"Oh this ain't nothin'." Woodsum said, "You want some real fun, pull out Pick Up Sticks or Tiddley Winks—that'll get the room a-hopping. A good ol' game of Parcheesi never hurt anyone, did it?"

"Don't forget about Pin the Tail on the Donkey, brother." Aurelia sang out. "That's a good one."

"Or, 'course, there were the scavenger hunts where we'd go looking for Uncle Ernie's Civil War sword or the missing dinner gong." Woodsum added.

"Or the armadillo! Ha, ha!" Olivia chortled, "Remember the armadillo?"

All three chuckled.

"You had an armadillo?" Erin asked.

"Well, it was stuffed." Olivia said. "It got hid most every time we had a scavenger hunt—till we had to retire it. Someone—" she jerked her head in Woodsum's direction, "dropped it in the pond running back to the winner's circle. Ha!"

"Ah shucks, I'd a thought you'd of forgotten that after all these years, sister. We did the scavenger at every birthday party. We'd search all over creation finding oddball utensils and gadgets. Whatever foolishness we could come up with. It was swell!"

"'Course—speaking of the pond—for fun, there was always swimming." Olivia said. "Cannonballs."

"Or skating. Figure 8's—and crack the whip. Oh, what a lark!" Aurelia added.

A relentless wind howled through the darkness and trees. Conditions outside were blinding, but they were safe within four sturdy walls and it didn't seem to matter. In fact, it seemed to amplify their sense of adventure and fun as they discussed a lot more old-time pastimes, most of which now gone by the wayside.

Woodsum and Erin, however, found they had a common love for a rivalry still in style: spelling! They began testing who could spell the hardest, longest, most unusual words. It started out with the word *pneumatic*—Woodsum's challenge to Erin—of course, easily executed by Erin while the others watched.

She countered with *millennium*, which Woodsum breezed through slick as a whistle.

Each challenging round became harder, all of which were verified by the impartial judge, Angie, partnered with a big old Webster's Dictionary.

Ossified was followed by *lollygagging*.

"If I didn't know better, I'd say you're quite the *snollygoster*." Woodsum needled his opponent.

"I don't know what that is but I'm sure I can spell it." She grinned defiantly.

"Shrewd! Oh, you're a shrewd one if I ever did see. You remind me of sister," he nodded in Olivia's direction, "She was quite the speller in the day. Won the county bee, didn't you?"

Olivia pursed her lips in thought, "Yessuh. Eighth grade. My one claim to fame. Represented Rutland County in the Regionals over in Windsor. Won a banana split for all my efforts."

"We love banana splits—especially Gumpy. Don't we, Angie?" Erin said.

Angie nodded. "You bet. All the Andersens do—it's a tradition Gumpy started eons ago."

Aurelia added, "Oh, those countywide functions were such fun. Spelling bees, bike races, ice cream socials, and the like. It was pretty much our only outside socializing. We always met the nicest boys from over Windsor way. Just plain nice—some pretty good-looking, too. Mind you, that was a fair distance to travel back then. My, my."

Olivia's forehead creased in thought. "Y'know, I recall that spelling bee like it was yesterday. Tough competition, for sure. And, as you say, sister, one such 'nicest' boy lost to me. Frankly, I think he let me win. And don't you know, I shared my prize with him—that *huge* banana split." Her tight mouth relaxed into a rare smile. "We sat on that hardwood floor—never gave it a second thought. He was a very funny fellow." She smiled wistfully. "Oh, to be young and foolish again."

"Smart as a whip, you were." Woodsum praised, "Just like this little firecracker here."

"Aye well, Mister Woodsum," Erin smiled, "you can thank Gumpy for me spelling so good. He makes sure I do my drills every night. He's a stickler for spelling. Funny thing is though, if *he* can't think of a word, he just makes one up to suit himself." She slapped her knee and, like her new friend, snarked, "Hardy, har, *har!*"

"Our Father was such a stickler. Like a tyrant." Even Aurelia's face in frowning mode was endearing.

"Oh, my Gumpy's no tyrant. He's a sweetheart. Like you, Mister Woodsum." Erin batted her eyelashes.

"Don't go tryin' to snowball me with your charm." Woodsum chided, squinting at her. "Let's get back on track. Next round. What have you got, missy?"

"I bet you don't know this one." Erin blew up like a blowfish on helium. "*Cyberphobia!*"

"Wal-l-l...hmm," Woodsum stalled, "I know the phobia part, but what the hang is a *cyber*?"

"You won't find it in that old dictionary. It has to do with using computers."

"Computers? Bah! Heard tell of 'em. Can't abide 'em. Okay, I'll give it a stab," he countered, and did successfully.

It was full-out battle mode. Woodsum compared notes with his sisters and cackled, "Hee-hee! I got you skunked now. Spell *Lake Chaubunagungamaug!*"

"Blimey! *Lake Chau-bun-a-gung*—what the *divil* did you say? There's no such a word, I'll wager."

"Oh yes there is, girlie. It's the Indian name for Webster Lake in Massachusetts!" He enunciated slowly in sequence, "*Lake Chaubunagung-amaug*—and no lolligaggin', now."

"Chau-bun-a-*gung-a-maug*." She took a deep breath and began, "C-H-A-U-B-U-N..." she paused, wrinkling her nose. "A-G-U-N-G," she debated, thinking very hard, "A-M-A-U-G. *Chaubunagungamaug!* There!"

"Correct!" the judge pronounced.

She beamed, "I did it! I did it!" Her nose quivered like a bunny.

"You shred it, wheat!" Woodsum said; she stared at him. "What?"

"You said it," Olivia said. "It means you said it. Speak English, brother."

"Attagirl! Give her the Bronx cheer!" Woodsum croaked, sputtering out a very hearty raspberry.

Mrs. Bundle and the sisters vigorously joined in.

Erin, convinced she could finally stump her opponent, challenged, "Your turn. Spell this one! *Phlegm.*"

"Oh, you're cagey. I got it, don't you fret—now wait...okay. P-H-L-E-G-M. Run for the hills!" He crowed, "Bawk! *Bawwwk-bawwk!*"

"Darn it! You sound just like Chester—my rooster. *He* gives me a pain, too!"

"Erin," Mrs. Bundle interjected. "You know you love Chester, especially when he sings."

"Now, missy," Woodsum rubbed his hands in glee. "I got another one for you. Start weeping." He drew in a deep breath, paused, and clamped his mouth shut. He squeezed his eyes tightly shut, "It's another phobia word. Here goes! *Hippopotomonstroses-quippedaliophobia.*" His eyes opened wide. "There y'go!"

"*Jaysus*, Mary, and Joseph—so you say!" Erin exclaimed. "How can I ever spell that? It's longer 'n a cat's purr! I can't even pronounce it."

Angie looked up from the heavy tome. "Beg pardon, but that *can't* be a real word." She closed the cover. "It's nowhere in *this* dictionary."

"Oh, but it is real, young gal!"

"Okay—then what does it mean?"

Woodsum breathed on his knuckles, shot the imaginary dice, and cooed, "Fear of long words."

Who could top that?

After the spelling bee, the volatile weather finally crept inside, morphing into an expanded discussion about the pros and cons of the Vermont seasons. With the sun, long, long gone, what remained were eerie-murky shadows, swirling-whirling snow, and lonely, howling winds.

Olivia poured herself another apple brandy; the glass stopper clinked as she replaced it. "You know what they always say…'In New England we have nine months of winter and three months of darned poor sledding.'" She asserted with certainty, "In *my* opinion, here in Vermont, one has to learn to appreciate the good that *each* season brings us *every* day."

The cordial had flowed freely amongst the adults—Mrs. Bundle (who herself was enjoying a second thimble of the cherry variety) thought the Pettyfers might be tipplers—*unless* this was considered one of the afore-mentioned '*special occasions*'? It certainly felt very special.

"Even freezing winter?" Erin asked. Sleet made tinny tinkling sounds against the windows.

"Especially winter. That's when everything lies dormant under the surface, welcoming the snow cover and waiting for the new spring rains. When the snow melts, it gives us plenty of daffodils."

Aurelia looked up quietly from her crocheting and pronounced. "With winter can come sadness. And death."

Olivia interjected, "But spring is such a beautiful time of rebirth."

"Summer is the funnest time of all, I'll wager." Erin interjected. "We go swimming in Goochie Pond, lily pads and all."

"I wholeheartedly agree. Summer *is* the funnest." Woodsum said. "Good word, by the way."

"It's one of Gumpy's." she replied.

"Fall stirs everything up," Olivia went on, waving a bit too grandly, "sending seed pods hither and yon, promoting new growth. Everything is magnificent—Indian Summer, all things to be thankful for."

"And Halloween—and pumpkins. Don't forget those. I love autumn in Vermont." Angie added.

"And then we're back at winter, again." Aurelia added petulantly. "Can't get away from it here."

"You're right, sister. We can't. It's in your face like you read about. And storms put the ice-ing—get it?—on the cake. This one is a big'un, biggest in a long time. I can tell. Couple-odd feet of snow already, and more to come." Woodsum nodded. "Just like the old days." He stood up expectantly, "Whilst we was out today, I got one of my feelings. I told sisters when we got back, 'this is gonna be a big one.'"

There was a sudden rapping at the window and they all jumped.

"Who's there?" Erin moved closer to the group.

Woodsum said calmly, "Oh, pshaw! Ladies, that's just the storm gearing up. Worst of it will be tonight and into tomorrow, I reckon. We might even get snowed in."

The wind screeched and there was a deafening crash outside.

Peering out, Angie cried, "Jeesum! A big branch just came down."

Woodsum shrugged nonchalantly, peering out into the darkness. "No worry. Must be the weight of the snow on the trees. Reminds me of another time just like this. Back along, oh, 'bout sixty-six years ago, I reckon. Just before the war. World War II." He sat down, joining them again at the table.

"Aye, I do love all your stories about the olden days, Mister Woodsum." Erin begged. "Tell us, please."

"Matter of fact, I got it all right here. This'll trip your scary trigger." He reached into his vest and removed an envelope. "This here's from the *Miami Beach Sentinel* way back when." He squinted. "Yep. Sunday Edition, mind you. A buddy brought it all the way back with him from Florida. He come back from shipping out to Cuba. Said he picked up the newspaper and couldn't believe he was readin' about us way up here in Vermont. Can you imagine?"

"What is it?" Erin asked, trying to be patient.

Woodsum went on nonchalantly, his hand still. "Course, they's no good local record of what happened here on the 8th of January. See, newspapers and most businesses was out of commission for a good week—during and after. From Boston to the Canadian border, everything was down while everybody scrambled. Even the *State Standard*. It was lights out for everyone."

"What happened?" Erin's voice rose in anticipation.

Mrs. Bundle flinched. *January 8th*.

"Look here, kiddo. It's all written down. I saved it, seein' as we lived through it." He carefully pulled out a worn, yellowed news clipping ensconced in the envelope.

Aurelia had stiffened and drew back silently deeper into her chair.

"Yessuh. Here, you gals take a look-see."

Erin and Angie gathered round him and the lamp.

Looking over his shoulder, Erin read the yellowed newspaper headline aloud: "'*Raging Blizzard Brings Vengeance. January 8, 1940: A Day to Remember. New England Freeze Is On.*'"

"1940?" Mrs. Bundle's antennae were up in a flash.

"Yup." Woodsum nodded. "1940. January 8." His eyes narrowed as he emphasized the date. "It was a weekend. Awful bitter cold—I tell you what. Can you believe that blizzard happened smack dab midst our twentieth birthday party?"

"Wait a minute." Angie straightened up and croaked, "January 8th! That's tomorrow. Just like then—I mean, now. Weird."

"Yup." Woodsum acknowledged diffidently. "So it is."

Angie said with disbelief, "So, you mean *your* birthdays are tomorrow?"

"Bingo." Woodsum nodded, whilst neither of his siblings reacted either pro or con.

"You never said!" Erin clapped her hands gleefully. "Yay!"

Olivia sat pokerfaced and Aurelia looked as though she was on the verge of crying—not celebrating. With difficulty, she whimpered, "Yes, sad to say, it's our birthday tomorrow."

Olivia coughed, subdued. "We'll be…ahem…quite old."

"Our Angie's twentieth is this Thursday." Erin said with glee. "C'mere—she'll be twenty, too! Just like you back then. Blimey! What a coincidence." She paused, "Hey now, shouldn't we be celebratin'?"

"Oh, no, no! We don't make a big thing of it. Truth is—" Olivia began, but was interrupted.

"Let me guess." Angie broke in, "You can't abide birthdays, right?"

"Right." Olivia pronounced with a sharp nod.

Mrs. Bundle took up the article from where it lay on the table.

"How extraordinary." She inhaled deeply, forcing herself to settle down. *A huge storm the weekend of January 8, 1940—the same day and year as the date on the little decoupage box.* This news more than puzzled. It felt too quirky to just be a coincidence. Her curiosity was piqued for sure, enough to hear more of this story first—before she could reveal her own find.

Quite logically thinking, it certainly couldn't be just a coincidence, could it? Were these almost 86-year-old triplets trying to tell her something? If so, they were master poker players. She handed it back to Woodsum.

Facts before her: the "find" earlier today...the storm of monumental proportion bearing down on them...their birthday. Haphazard events, strangely coincidental to something that occurred decades ago? Weather certainly wasn't planned, unless the Farmer's Almanac had grown angel wings and divinely intervened—but here she and the girls were, visiting the inn smack dab midst a killer storm on the eve of the Pettyfers' birthday. Two momentous occasions—what was this all about?

Was this part of another premeditated ploy to deliberately heighten their guest experience at the inn? With the dim lights, the outside cold whistling, were they part of a tableau, a staged event? Another game was what it could very well be, she reassured herself. The Pettyfers knew more than they were willing to offer (at least for now), and so she sat back, most interested in watching the show that was about to unfold as her skeptical side stepped in.

The girls were enthralled, completely drawn in, particularly Erin, whose itching fingers were prepared to tear the article from Woodsum's grasp if he didn't get on with it.

Squinting through eyeglasses inadequate for the lighting, he peered at the article and drawled, "*Waa-alll* now, lemme see." He coughed. "Dang it all! My eyes are more tired 'n a roller coaster on nickel night. Who's going to read it aloud to everyone?"

Erin raised her hand as if she were in class.

"Ah, heck. Here you go, missy." He passed it to her. "Have at it."

"Oooohhh, aye, just so! I'd love to!" As the wind howled and the fireplace crackled, she sat close to the lantern and settled her glasses firmly. "Ahem. If everyone is ready?" She cleared her throat and began. "'Beginning the Friday of the first weekend of January through Sunday, January 8th, a storm of record intensity with high winds, rain, sleet, and snow lashed out over all of New England, breaking all communications with the rest of the country and dumping massive amounts of snow on areas already reeling from three December blizzards previously.

"Poles blocked roads, trees were felled, roofs caved in under the snow and ice pressure, causing mayhem and making for complete isolation. As yet, undetermined number of deaths related to the storm are rumored. Off the New England coast near Martha's Vineyard, a freight steamer went aground in the tempest. Heavily battered Portland Harbor, Maine is littered with damaged craft.

"'In the most devastated state of Vermont, ten-foot drifts blanketed villages, with tallies of new record snowfall in most mountain communities. In the valleys, the snow turned to a heavy wet mixture followed by freezing temperatures leaving a treacherous sheet of ice coating everything and cutting them off from the rest of the world for days.'"

Woodsum interrupted, "Here comes the good part."

Erin looked up. "Right, this part that you've circled. I reckoned it's pretty important."

"Let her read it, brother." Olivia shrilled. "Gaw!"

Aurelia said quietly, "Let's settle down, please."

He replied, "Okay, okay."

Erin raised her hand and waited patiently—like a school teacher in front of errant fourth graders. "If I could continue?" she asked, blinking earnestly. "'Thirty-six inches of snow was recorded in the high region of Plymouth, Vermont and nearby Mount Holly.'" She paused for effect, enunciating. "'Officials say it is *the most* snow in one storm ever recorded.'"

"Don't y'know that was *my* yardstick made that reading. Mine!" He puffed proudly. "Actually, it was a touch over that—close to 37"— but I didn't want to be braggin' on it when I was giving the stats to Skeet Littlefield from the *State Standard*. He had the horses and sled out, pushing them through the high drifts. He passed the info along to the town bigwigs who gave it to the state highway department and they approved it as 'on the record'."

"All the way up the chain of command." Olivia offered. "To make it official."

"Wowser!" Erin, duly impressed, continued reading, "'In the vicinity of St. Johnsbury, *over one thousand* electric power and telephone trunk lines were carried down and disabled. All telephone circuits went out and now, days later, have yet to be restored. Thousands of broken tree limbs litter the roads, making travel virtually impossible.

"'The freighter *Treblinka*, aground near Woods Hole, was refloated yesterday, and returned to Boston Harbor. Four sailors from the *Sarah Jane* fishing boat were lost overboard.

"'Diminishing winds and colder temperatures are hampering all of New England as it tries to dig out from this massive storm.'"

Erin drew in a deep breath eagerly. "Whew! C'mere now, quite the vexing storm, I'd say!" She fixed the oldsters with a gape of ghastly admiration. "And you all lived through it? Wow."

"Hen wet your apron—you betcha we did. Ice damage shut everything down. It was a corker." Woodsum said. "Ever'one started diggin' out just like we do, finding people who couldn't get out. We just went on as usual. Well, sort of, I daresay."

Mrs. Bundle made her clucking sounds. "It sounds quite amazing, ravaging the area like that. Back then there were no TV weather predictors to say there's a huge storm on its way."

Aurelia breathed in raggedly. "I remember everything. It was awful. Just *awful*. Everything was cut off over on the dark side of the mountain. The King family's son Atticus died in the storm. Froze trying to get to the cow milking in the barn."

"Two clapboards below zero is how cold it was." Woodsum said. "That barn was only about as far as from here to our back shed. They found him in the spring about a mile into the woods."

"I'm spooked. It's so odd…being tomorrow is January 8th. Isn't it bizarre?"Angie asked.

Woodsum spoke in a low voice, "They say if you listen real good, you can still hear his ghostly cries from up on the top of the Saltash."

"Up where we were today?" she asked. "C'mon. It's just the wind howling."

"Makes you wonder. Heard tell of many a ghostly tale about others who perished during that storm, and after, too."

"A ghost tale? Oh, Mr. Woodsum!" Erin stopped as the mood seemed to change, becoming as cold and dreary as outside. "*Oooo!*" She shivered, rubbing her arms. "I've got me a chill."

"Yup. Life's right tragic, is all you can say." he said.

Olivia added from the shadows. "We were young. What should have been a wonderful time was…tragic. There were many who suffered."

Woodsum said with longing. "Well, it should have been our time, y'know, to find—to find out who we were and what we *really* wanted." His statement cast a wide net, more a declaration about their lives.

"Did you never find a special someone? Not the one of you?" Erin asked before Mrs. Bundle could squelch her.

Olivia laughed harshly, "Find a special someone? Keeping company—that was what we called it back then. Keeping company." She stared out into the darkness. "They say you can't always tell by the looks of a toad how far he can jump."

Woodsum added, "It was pretty much all work and no play."

From the darkness came a small voice. "There was one." Aurelia's cheeks were as rosy as the cordial, but her mood seemed morose. She cried out, "What's that?" Unexpectedly, she straightened like a steel rod and waved an accusing finger at the group, "There were others lost during the storm!" Her eyes were wild.

Woodsum said, "Well, sister, we know it was a doozy."

Olivia shook her head. "Shush now! That's enough about the storm. It's upsetting sister now."

Aurelia thrust out her lower lip like an injured child and she shouted, "He's gone!"

Angie asked, "*Who*…Who's gone, Miss Aurelia?"

Her hands clasped together as though trying to communicate something most difficult. She breathed in and then, with a harsh, "Mhhm-*mmm*," exhaled a moan like the wild caterwaul of a keening fox. An eerie sob, like precious mist on a lonely moor, left her frosty, bluish lips.

The fire crackled and popped; spirals of sparklers exploded wildly—and then suddenly were extinguished to eerie shadows. A chill of vast scope seemed to envelop the room, strangling the air, causing agitation.

A gasp of pain burst forth; she tried to stand up and she shrieked, "Oh! Won't you come back?"

Sadness, fear—something terribly unresolved and painful—that was what Mrs. Bundle saw on Aurelia's face, heard in her shaky voice.

The lantern and candles, nearly snuffed in the flare-up, suddenly recovered their light.

"What...was that?" Angie looked round, feeling the unknown presence, as if someone or something had joined their cozy group.

"Who's there?" Erin's body was rigid; she followed Angie's searching eyes. "Miss Aurelia, are you ok—?"

The woman, pale as a sheet, dropped back in the chair with a thump. Her head sagged like a spineless doll, resting on her chest, motionless.

"Oh, dear! Miss Aurelia!" Erin cried out. "Help her, Mrs. B!"

They moved quickly to her side. Angie got there first, "Miss Aurelia? Who—what do you mean?"

Olivia took charge. "She's had these spells before. Let's get her down on the rug." She pointed at the divan pillow. "Give me that, and the wool blanket." Mrs. Bundle complied; they moved her efficiently. Olivia propped her head up and rubbed her sister's hands vigorously. "Got to get her blood going. She'll be all right." Woodsum wet her lips with water and she gasped, revived, and grabbed Woodsum's hand.

"You're all right, sister." he said, "Calm yourself."

Slowly, her energy returned. "Heavens...to Betsy." A delicate lace hanky appeared from her sleeve cuff and she dabbed at her eyes. "Excuse me. Please, I want to sit up." They righted her in the chair. Her hands shook and her voice was unsteady; she muttered to herself, "Happy times...never the same. Pleasure...sorrows. The Lord giveth...oh, give me strength."

Olivia put a protective hand on Aurelia's wrist. "Careful now, sister. We're here."

Aurelia noticed them all watching her and assured them faintly, "I'm fine, I'm fine."

"What's wrong, Miss Aurelia?" Erin asked. "Has the divil got his clutches round your throat?"

Olivia repeated, "She has these spells, every now and then."

"She looks peaked. Aye, right peaked, I'd say!" Erin was concerned. "Would you be wantin' some more of that cherry cordial?" She thrust the decanter at them.

"Good thought, Erin." Mrs. Bundle saw the residual signs of distress in the elderly lady's face. She poured her a glass. "Easy now…take your time."

"Better, yes." She drew in a less stressed, stronger breath. "It's Time…that is unforgiving."

"Y'know what?" Woodsum put a protective hand on the chair. "Sister's just tuckered out from a long, busy day. Everyone needs a good night's sleep."

"Yes, I agree." Mrs. Bundle said gently.

"On that note, it's time for bed." Olivia said brusquely. "Come along, sister. With this tempest, who knows what we will wake up to in the morning?"

More prophetic words could not have been spoken.

Chapter XVII
Contents Revealed

Assuring Olivia that she was capable of tending to her foot on her own, Mrs. Bundle, back in her room, removed the bandage and took stock. It was remarkable how quickly the toe was healing—it was not quite so angry looking now—as though the salve and poultice together held some magic power, as fast a track as any modern-day antibiotic. The dishpan with all the necessary items within was in her room and she redid her dressing. "There, almost better!" Frankly, she wished all was as well with the Pettyfers. Something festered deep within them. She couldn't help but be compelled to get to the bottom of it.

She prepared for bed. She removed the Pendleton wool plaid shirt and tried to remember Erin's exact words earlier today as she described in her innocent way the way things were at the inn, the way the Pettyfers acted. She had said, "Even if the time stands still up here." As a side note, the photo of Woodsum and his friend somehow troubled her, too. It was the words on the back—*Happy Times*. A normal friendship by all appearances. The Pettyfer Triplets had grown up with a life surrounded by lots of guests, engaged with people with experiences from around the world. Yet, they had chosen to not move into the future, into the modern world. And then, she recalled Aurelia's chilling voice: "It's Time…" she had said, "that is unforgiving."

It was as though everything had stopped in the year 1940.

By the time she had donned her flannel nightgown, she realized something quite startling. If she looked carefully, she could tell the bureau drawers had been rifled. The other slipper had been moved just a hair. Her coat, hanging on the hook, was askew. Someone had been in her room...searching? My, oh my. Desperate measures.

What had changed for them? Why choose to live in a bubble and refuse to accept the modern conveniences of the world? Was it choice, or was it something more? She thought so.

Sitting on the edge of her bed, she unzipped the inside pocket of her Pendleton wool plaid shirt and removed the little box hidden there since this afternoon.

She inspected the little decoupage box, reading the date on the tape once again. She knew now the box must belong to one of the three Pettyfers. The coincidence to their birth date was too profound to ignore. But which one? And why?

Was this what someone had been looking for in her room? Granted, the list was a short one; there were only six people in the building—that is, that she knew of. However, it was a mausoleum... again, her nagging thought—*who was here at the inn besides Aurelia, Olivia, and Woodsum?*

The box felt hot to the touch, burning an imaginary hole deep into her palm as if it was on fire with secrecy. Should she open it? Should she turn it over to the Pettyfers unopened? Could a guest have hidden it there? There was a secret here at Mount Holly Mansion Inn—a mystery—and, like it or not, she had been dropped like the proverbial bloodhound right into the middle of it. How serendipitous was that?

And then it hit her. Dang!

Could it all have something to do with the 'kerfuffle' Granny Milly had let slip that day at lunch before clamming up?

She looked round, realizing divine providence had provided the tools she needed, tempting her. Beside her on the bed were the items used to clean and wrap her wound: rubbing alcohol, cotton batting, small cuticle scissors, and the basin. In addition, she had brought her trusty detective fanny pack—thank goodness habit precluded her from leaving home without her sleuthing essentials. That said, its contents were more sparse than usual—her intention to take a break from it all here at the inn—hence, inside were just the basics: her reliable high-powered ultra professional magnifying glass, some dental twine, and Arthur's trusty Swiss military penknife with all thirteen tools attached: reamer, wood saw, tiny tweezers, toothpick key ring, large blade, small blade, Phillips screwdriver, can opener with small screwdriver, cap lifter with screwdriver, and wire stripper. The tweezers would help tremendously with the task at hand.

With a firm nod, she decided to begin. First, she took the magnifying glass and re-read the script on the tape around the decoupage box: *Our Secret. 1/8/1940. Confirmed.* Now, how to keep that intact and still access the box. She inspected the gutta-percha, some of which had seeped out from under the tape. She broke off a small piece of the batting and drenched it in the alcohol, then dabbed gingerly at the tape gummed with age. Little pieces of glue began to fleck off, which she then removed gently with the tweezers. The tape appeared to be loosening quite nicely. She used the reamer to gently push it. Careful not to disturb the lettering, she continued the painstaking process hoping she could slip off and unravel the tape from around the box in one piece. Once she had a good half inch, she was able to softly tug on it halfway around—until it stuck. When it wouldn't budge any further, she used the waxed floss, pushing it gently on the underside of the tape. Slowly, it dislodged; the final piece of ¼" was so cemented in, she made a clean cut with the cuticle scissors without destroying any of the writing on the tape. This made a little hinge for the lid, which she pushed up on lightly and it suddenly popped open.

"Ahhh." She peered inside to see what had been hidden for decades. It was a lovely gold ring, crafted especially for a woman's dainty ring finger...a friendship ring...or, better yet, an engagement ring? There was nothing else inside the box. She ran a finger inside the ring; she could feel the slightest depression within the inner band. She arched an eyebrow and examined it closer to the hazy lantern light. She could see delicate, slightly sloping script... yes, whatever was written was in italics.

She needed something better to see. She reached once again for the fanny pack and found her magnifying glass. She moved the lantern closer, focused the magnifying glass, steadied her hand, and continued, holding her breath. The inside rim was clean as a whistle—brand new, it appeared, never worn—was that possible? Yes...

She could see four words. She spelled out the first inscribed word slowly, "M-I-C-H-E-L-apostrophe-S." There was that name again. And the other words? "Let's see...W-A-H-L. *Michel's Wahl*—period." The mystery person's first name. And the Wahl part, was that a surname? Or was it another word?

She whispered to herself, "Michel—*Mee-khahl*. I'm listening."

She read the final two words inside the ring: *Goldener Wunsch*.

The bits and pieces were coming together slowly. Without knowing exactly why, her heart was suddenly overcome by a sense of sadness and despair.

Chapter XVIII
Some Enchanted Evening....
You May See Some Strangers

Meeeeoooowww...
It was the faintest of sounds. Erin's eyes popped open. *Meeooowww.* There it was again!

Erin's sleep had been dominated by a fitful but dramatic vignette: her, a poor orphan, struggling, slogging through the high banks of snow, pulling a sled...soldiering on, all while carrying the most darling little kitty inside her coat. She knew *that* part was a dream... so how, with her eyes open, was she still able to hear the plaintive meow? She was so sure it was real! A strong gust outside caused the window by the bed to rattle. She squinted through the curtain; It was very dark outside against the stark whiteness of snow—much too early to rise yet.

What time was it?

She lay still, listening, waiting. There it was...faint, barely discernible, there it was!

Meeooowwww.

She jumped out of bed and tiptoed in sock-clad feet toward the sound. Where exactly was it coming from?

Meeooowww.

Like a dog on a bone she ferreted out the sound, searching the room's perimeter until she paused just by the mammoth-sized wardrobe built-in beside the open shelving. She placed her ear to the twin doors and held her breath. Yes, there it was, faint, but distinctly cat-like! There was a key in the armoire lock; she turned it slowly and it finally gave way. She opened the big cupboard door, revealing a jam-packed variety of period coats and costumes, all hung neatly in a row. "Blimey!" Below the clothes were pairs of old-fashioned shoes, some of the hook and eye variety, all lined up nicely in two long rows.

Anxiously, she searched the inside area for the cat—nothing. Stepping up on the protruding bottom lip of the cabinet base, she spread the clothes apart, listening again, and there it was—the same little sound! She jumped up and climbed inside, reaching all the way in until she touched the back side. She was enveloped in darkness, the large stifling cavity filled to capacity. She pushed the shoes to the far sides of the cupboard, knelt down and, placing her ear against the back far wall, listened. Yes, there it was distinctly—a mournful but very weak *meeeowwww*! Using her index finger, she felt along the back; there was a slight crack in the plank.

She put her lips to it, whispering, "I'm here, little one. Hang on." Seconds passed on the other side; the meows became fewer until finally…silence. Confused, Erin postulated that the wall was common with Angie's room; it didn't make sense that Angie hadn't heard the cat, too. She tapped lightly; the sound that came back was dead and empty. Angie must be fast asleep. "Ach, what should I do?"

She must find a way to the other side! Frantically struggling with the weight of the coats and dresses around her, she removed them laboriously from the rod above, tossing them to the floor with a thunk, thunk, thunk until the cavernous closet was empty. "There!"

Nimbly stepping out onto the bedroom floor over the bumpy pile, she scurried to the night table. With steady hands she removed the glass globe of the kerosene lantern, lit the wooden match, and replaced the globe. Its soft glow illuminated her steps back inside the wardrobe. "*Hmm,*" her voice echoed in the gaping space. "Let's see." With the lantern, she inspected every inch of the back wall. In an instant, she found what she was hoping for—a wrought iron latch at the top of the wardrobe wall!

On tiptoes, she pulled it down; it clicked. Suddenly, a skinny, long door opened! Before her was a small landing the size of a broom closet off of which were stairs…yes, she could see it dimly…small steps leading upward! Without a thought for anything other than finding the cat in jeopardy, she held the lantern tightly and squeezed into the space. Placing the lantern on the landing so her hands would be free, she contemplated her next move. Her nose ignored the musty odor and she straightened cautiously to her full height of 60 inches. Reaching her hands outward to break a fall, she stepped up one step, then the next, and the next, each movement becoming dimmer as she moved away from the lantern. At the fifth and last step, she paused, squinting to see, ignoring everything that might deter her, intent only on what was there before her. She was right! Behold—the scrawniest kitten she'd ever seen: not a newborn, but only weeks old and surely unable to fend for itself: gray dappled body and head with overly large ears, pink nose, big oval cat eyes—staring out blankly—dull blue with a helpless look. It opened its dry near-lifeless mouth and nothing came out.

"Oh, doar!" Whispering, she clasped her hands to her chest. "Ceann beag bocht! Oh dear little one…" In times of stress, Erin's speech often reverted back to her native Celtic. She reached down and gently scooped it up with little resistance from the tiny bundle. "Me poor, poor little kitty. Where's your *máthair*? You're lost, aren't you now?" She snuggled the cat gently to her chest and could feel only the feeblest of heart beats. "Oy! You've not been cared for, for sure. *Cnámha*! Bones—that's what you are! Wee bones." The cat shivered uncontrollably and closed its eyes. "Aye, you're famished, aren't you now? Milk is what you'll be needing!" She burrowed her face in its scruffy bony head, deciding she would find the cat some sustenance post haste. Holding it close, she found her way back without stumbling, down the narrow steps, through the cupboard portal and into her room. She wrapped the sweet limp body in the discarded soft turtleneck atop her bureau. She retrieved the lantern, placing it carefully on the bedside table beside her eyeglasses, and rushed back to minister the kitten.

Against all odds, an intermittent, soulful purring came from within. She grabbed her quilted bathrobe and put in first one arm and then the other. She would awaken Mrs. Bundle. She raised her arm to tap on the wall—but wait... it was then she remembered Mrs. Bundle's foot injury; there was no way she could make it quickly down the stairs with her in tow. And Angie was always warning her about being nosy and going where she shouldn't—aye, that might be a bit bothersome, too. She decided she would have to make the trip alone. It was just a wee bit away, down the back stairs—how spooky could that be?—and then to the kitchen to get the poor babe some warm milk. She knew exactly where it was, right there, in the old icebox. Hopefully, the scoundrel Possy wouldn't be there to eat the poor kitty alive! And, she pondered, she would have to avoid the Pettyfers at all costs—they had made it clear they abhorred cats of all varieties, even harmless adorable little kittens, she imagined.

She held the small body close to her and rationalized her mission—hadn't Miss Aurelia said just hours before from the pantry entrance where she was now bound, "you can help yourself *anytime* you've got a hankering." *Anytime!* And dear Mister Woodsum had said last night "make yourself to home." And she *distinctly* remembered Miss Olivia saying the kitchen was off limits *except in an emergency*. So there it was—her opportunity. At home, she would take the initiative—didn't Gumpy always say, "One of your best *attriboots*, girlie—and failings, mind you—is that you got some spunk!" (She put little emphasis on the "failings" part at the moment.) Never fear—she and her spunk would be the little one's protector. There was no time to lose!

She paused, reconsidering: should she wake Angie? With a bouncy and confident bob of her head, she decided she *would* wake them and tell them her great tale of danger and intrigue—when she got *back*, that is. She moved quickly and silently out the door with her little bundle, tiptoeing with stealth past Angie's room, traveling further down the long hall to the back hallway, the quickest way to the kitchen. She put aside the Pettyfers' warning about non-abidance of any type of feline—they couldn't possibly mean *this* poor little darling of hers who had somehow found her way into the deserted attic above her room and was *without a doubt* on death's threshold!

Oh, double dang! She silently chided herself, realizing she had left a most essential item back in the room—her eyeglasses! Seeing up close was okay, but distance was a problem, especially in the dark. She gauged the task ahead, feeling the little body against her chest, and deciding it was too late to turn back. She could do this if she moved carefully. The hallway darkened as she passed the final bedroom on the right, the one called *Golden Desire*. Bravely ignoring the eerie darkness, she moved with considerable difficulty through the cavernous great space. Too late, she was upon a large dome—a boulder, suddenly placed in the unlikely path near the back stairs! Holding the kitty aloft, she skidded to avoid the obstacle, but the dense carpet caught her stockinged feet together in a jumble. Awkwardly, she tripped, falling over the large low roundness, listing sideways against a cushioned ottoman, then bouncing back like a drunken sailor, her body spinning out of control toward the floor. She protected her priority—the kitty.

"Oommpphh!" A plump, overly large, orange silk floor pillow of the Indian variety sprung up and met her, colliding with her forehead and breaking her fall sideways. Barely grazing her chin against the rug, her eyes closed tightly in the jarring motion and she fell with a thud flat on her chest—but she was still holding her precious package above her head! She lay frozen. *What in the divil was that?* Her eyes adjusted at murky floor level and searched. The large mass that caused her to trip and fall had disappeared! Even as it happened so quickly, the way now seemed totally clear and free of any debris. For a second, she wondered if she was in some kind of weird dream. She gathered herself together and kissed the kitty's head; it meowed weakly. Yes, this was real and she was still hell-bent on her mission.

As she struggled to sit up, she stifled a scream! *Oh, Lord!*

Inches away near the corner of the ottoman, two shriveled, beady black eyes watched her. "It" stared in frozen stillness, assessing her, ready for action. The eyes were dull, set deeply into a hideous scaly head attached to a crusty stick-like neck, which snaked seemingly forever from around the hassock's corner, the rest hidden behind the ottoman. Unexpectedly, it blinked and the head pulled back sharply into the darkness.

"Ohhhh, jeeeeezum!" she gasped. She was up now, fear driving her; she moved quickly, bent on leaving the dreadful monster behind in the immense dark shadows. "No t-time for f-foosterin' about," she stammered breathlessly, "That's what Jack would say, to be sure." She cushioned the kitty inside the front of her robe and secured the tie at her waist.

She vowed nothing would stop her. She reached the stairway huffing and puffing and gasping for air, proceeding down the first step, straining to see. It was difficult, but she pressed on without a care for her own safety. Picking her passage so no sound would disrupt or waken anyone, even as the little animal's purring evolved into tiny desperate whimpers, she labored on, knowing time was critical.

"Shush, *daor amháin*. Don't have a care, now, we're going to get you some milk. Don't you worry, now." She ventured further down the winding narrow back stairs, stepping quietly on each Oriental rug pad meant to soften the old abode's creaks and groans. Convinced this was an important mission of humongous proportions, she whispered comfort to herself, equally bewildered and in awe at what a strange place this mansion was! By hook or by crook, she would make it to the kitchen. She made a promise: when her charge was safe, she would find out all its secrets, including what or who exactly that monster was lurking upstairs.

She reached the bottom landing, knowing to turn the corner toward the right—and keenly aware that a turn to the left would bring her to the closed door of the innkeeper quarters—and disaster! "Shhhhushh," she comforted the kitten tucked within her robe. The warmth of her own body seemed to be helping the waif; she felt a rhythmic purr. "We're almost there."

In the darkened back hall, she pushed her shoulder against the swinging door and entered the kitchen—much too early for breakfast, she hoped; surely, no one would be up at this hour. The sole kitchen window was illuminated, emanating a hue of unnatural brilliance. Devoid of curtains and securely latched, it was like a photo showcasing buckets of the luminous snow falling outside. Erin still felt like she might be dreaming...was that oddly fluorescent night sky real?

Focusing her eyes, the deep warmth of the cook stove reached her. Surprisingly, a large pot of something that smelled like vegetable soup simmered on top of the stove, and the sturdy cast iron kettle was boiling to beat the band, too. There was a shawl hanging off the back of the rocking chair. The chair...was moving.

Instinctively, she froze, realizing she was not alone.

"Sir Possy?" she whispered, hoping the grumpy old dog would let her be. If he was anywhere nearby, he would definitely cause a ruckus. Not a sound, though—hopefully he was safely ensconced in the Pettyfers' quarters. Resolute to complete the task at hand, she moved across the scuffed linoleum floor toward the pantry, where she knew she would find the icebox and the milk. Abruptly, she felt a cold unforgiving draft of...outside wind! Her eyes adjusted again, searching, seeking out where the rush of cold air—outside air— was coming from. And then...she froze in her tracks and gasped, wrapping her arms round her chest and the kitty protectively.

What, on earth, she thought, *is* that?

Straining her weary bespectacled-less eyes to see all the way through to the darkened summer kitchen shed, she made out the shape of an overly large...figure. It filled the doorway thirty-odd feet away—an unmoving, formidable shape! In the calm of darkness, Erin could faintly make out the large outline all wrapped in white: a plait-like halo; ethereally-broad shoulders; round, trunk-like limbs as bulky as the nearby farm table. Was it a man or a woman? All of a sudden she was reminded of Uncle Carl's old horror films the Andersen household watched regularly on movie night and a similar figure flashed before her eyes. Yes, that was it! Her imagination went berserk and she was mesmerized at the enormity of this...big...*white*...creature before her. Strangely, the being, whose massive hands were placed together in the universal representation of prayer, with a fluffy iridescent halo hovering above its form, didn't intimidate Erin. It was beautiful! As stunned as she was, she could discern a bulky mantle of sorts—blowy white. The creature's gunboat-sized feet were covered in layers of soft cotton—batten-like—like, like…"Oh, my Lord!" she eked out in alarm.

The apparition shrunk back as though being pulled into the heavy snowfall. The snow banks were massive, like a cave forming around the walkways.

Suddenly, the sky flashed with an unnatural glow. There was a hugely loud, CRACK! and a massive BOOM! as the kitchen, housed in the back ell, shook to the timbers. The thunder crashed with a vengeance, followed by a second streak of bright lightning. *Thunder snow!* Such a rarity in winter and created by a turbulent combination of positive and negative electric charges, the phenomenon was terrifying but swift, lasting only seconds. The winter thunderstorm was in full force—not rain, just massive flakes of snow bursting like pinwheels of white circles.

Throughout the flash of thunder, the figure had lingered. Long, ethereal fingers formed wraithlike round its pale, round countenance. "Shhhhhhhh…." a sigh emanated from the frosty mouth. With a soft *whooosh*, the eerie outline moved away, disappearing into the dense snowfall.

 Spellbound, Erin, in these milliseconds, had managed to stifle a scream—more from surprise than terror. She let out a pent-up breath. Oddly, the figure had not provoked fear in her; more present was curiosity and a strange feeling of compassion, like a warm glove had enveloped her body. She reached out her free hand in friendship. "Wait!" she cajoled, "C'mere….don't go. It's only me… and my kitty!"

The door swayed indecisively with the fickle gusts, back and forth, and then shut with a gentle *snap!* All was quiet; the apparition had evaporated into nothingness. The dim, quiet atmosphere returned, providing the first light of murky dawn.

Spooked to the max but desiring more, Erin moved forward. Suddenly, she reeled on her heels as a cold hand grabbed at the nape of her neck, pulling her back. Nothing could smother her spine-tingling scream, one that undoubtedly would reach even the furthest ends of the mansion. Her lungs refilled instinctively and she let loose another good one. "*H-h-help!*" Just as swiftly, a second hand put a strangle hold on her mouth, overpowering her.

Chapter XIX

Abominable Activity

"Stop screaming! What are you *doing* down here?" Angie rasped in her ear, gripping her even tighter. Erin struggled to speak, hampered by the hand over her mouth. "*Shhh!*" She glared. "You'll raise the dead with that caterwauling!"

Erin gasped, pointing. "Let me go, will y'now!" She thrashed about, wrestling from under Angie's grasp. Her eyes were wild. "Over there! Did'ja see it, Angie?"

"*Shhhush!* For pity's sake, I told you—"

"Please, Angie—let me go!" Erin squeaked and pointed, "it was there! In the doorway! Did you not see it, too?"

"See what?"

"The abominable snowman!!! Just like Uncle's old horror film! Did'ja *see* it?" Erin's body squirmed, "Oh, no! What's that now?"

A loud *crash* came from the opposite direction—followed by numerous thumps and excessive thrashing. A shattering din of dueling sounds from different directions approached simultaneously, those coming from the back stairway and the other from the innkeeper quarters.

"We're in trouble, aye—" Erin gulped just as the door burst open and a familiar lanky figure barreled in.

"*Mayday!*" Woodsum Pettyfer hissed, wielding a large baseball bat in skeletal hands. "Mayday, Mayday!" He was a sight from head to toe, beginning with the Pippi Longstocking hat dangerously askew atop his head (wisps of hair sticking out every which way) to the unlaced ancient work boots; in between, a faded red long-john night suit—a one-piece wonder—which hung loosely on his scarecrow body. Discretion prevents further description (in particular, the garment's posterior hatch).

"Jay-sus, Mar-y and Joseph!" Erin declared, blanching.

"*Mayday?*" Woodsum assumed a battle stance, scanning the darkened room and the two figures within it.

Loud, lumbering, galumphing noises followed him and Mrs. Bundle appeared, out of breath and struggling on her one good foot with ungainly hops and leaps as she tumbled through the doorway. She struggled to gain her balance as one strong arm pushed past his tall frame; she gasped with aggravation, "Move, Woodsum! Out of the way! Where—are my girls? Erin? Angie?"

Their eyes grew accustomed to the light—and the girls.

"Hold your horses, Mrs. Bundle!" He peered out, "Holy cow—it's you *gals!*" Lowering the bat, he said firmly, "What in tarnation are you girls up to?"

"I came down to get Erin." Angie attempted calmly, then faltered. "Gaw! What a mess." She was still holding on to Erin and repeated her query, "What in the heck *are* you doing down here? First, I hear a big thump outside my door. Scared the bejeesus out of me. By the time I put on my robe and slippers, I see *you* disappearing down the back stairs." She scolded, "I tell you, all that late night TV causes these illusions you're suffering from."

"Illusions?" Mrs. Bundle asked.

Angie dropped her restraining hands from Erin's shoulders. "And where are your *glasses?*"

Ignoring her, Erin moved to the back shed door and pulled it open. "Oh me, oh my! It was here!" She fully expected to catch another glimpse.

However, no evidence of anything—real or imagined—lingered outside, save the escalating blizzard and huge gathering mounds of snow. Colossal snowflakes, heavy with freezing crystals of water, stung her face and she backed up, studying the distant landscape, searching for anything, ghost or not, abominable snow something or…what? "Come back! Don't be afraid!" Beseechingly, she turned back; that which had exited so quickly was gone.

Angie pulled on her protectively. "Jeesum crowbars! Calm down and get your breath. Don't you realize it's a blizzard out there!" She pulled harder and closed the door.

With wardrobes hurriedly pulled together (by the looks of their dishevelment), the two Pettyfer sisters joined the unfolding scene.

"Mother come rump it!" Olivia's face was filled with pure dismay and fear as she exclaimed, "What on *earth* is going on?"

Mrs. Bundle hadn't heard that saying since the time she'd been caught with her hand in the honeycomb jar by Grandmother—at the tender age of nine. She stifled a kneejerk giggle, surveying the scene for more distress or damage. Yes, she wondered, *what on earth was going on?*

Woodsum gave Olivia a warning glance and cautioned, "Wait now, sister, looks like no harm's done here."

Eyes darting everywhere, Aurelia tugged with one hand at her shawl, underneath which she wore a buttoned-to-the-neck nightgown; dainty ballet slippers peeked out beneath. Her fluffy hair was mussed with slumber; her cheeks were flushed and pink. She held a flannel plaid bathrobe in her hands, which she pressed on Woodsum, shielding her eyes. "Here, brother. Don't catch a chill, now."

"Yes, yes." He said, bashful as an ingénue. He leaned the bat against the doorway and pulled the bathrobe round him.

Erin gathered herself together and with the mastery of a Dale Carnegie trainer soothed the group of adults, "Nay, nay, it's all right, isn't it? Aye, no need to worry, folks! It was just a wee emergency I had. Right, look here, now!" She peeled away the lapel of her bathrobe, magically uncovering her dear commodity. "See here, I found our precious, *darlin'* little kitty, didn't I—and she's real, for sure!" She opened the satiny quilting. "Her name's Tuffy. She's very hungry—starving even!" As if on cue, the victim gave the sorriest little whine and coughed weakly. "Aye, aye, my dearest little one, we're all here for you. Don't you worry, now." She held her out and made her urgent request, "We can save her, can't we?"

They were all reduced to mush.

Chapter XX

Escapades Can Have Their Ups and Downs

"Well, I'll be danged. A cat. Here in our house. How she got past Possy I'll never know. He's shirking his responsibilities now that he's an old guy." Woodsum gazed with unexpected warmth at the little cat, now peacefully in deep sleep and unaware of the raging winter storm outside or the secrets still held within Mount Holly Mansion Inn.

After the hullaballoo of discovery, instant movement had ensued. Aurelia had gathered her shawl and wrapped the kitten. Olivia quickly filled a small pan with milk and warmed it on the stove while Aurelia rocked the kitten in the rocking chair. Mrs. Bundle found the teaspoon in the sugar bowl as instructed by Olivia; Angie fetched the water bottle and refilled it from the kettle.

Olivia poured the warmed milk into a coffee cup and grabbed the little tea spoon. With ultimate care, she lovingly wet and then spoon-fed the cat. They all watched in anxious anticipation. Methodically employing massage, Aurelia stroked the little one's belly, legs, and paws, all the while whispering what a fine and beautiful baby she was.

For all intents and purposes, the Pettyfers' "We don't abide cats" belief seemed to have flown the coop and been replaced inexplicitly with high regard and even...affection! Without doubt, they were, in fact, enamored with the adorable kitty. Tuffy, true to her newly-anointed name, revived with a bang; now, with a full tummy, the little dear slumbered, nestled within the warm shawl.

While the Pettyfers fawned and fussed over the diminutive cat, Mrs. Bundle took Erin aside; they sat down by the pantry.

"Oh, Mrs. B!" she expressed urgently, "There's skullduggery afoot. To be sure." Angie joined them and she continued, "Aye, and I know what I saw in the doorway, Angie."

With Tuffy in such loving hands, all was fine. However, the rest of the secretive goings-on were yet to be explained.

Angie nodded soberly. "I think there's something weird going on, for sure."

In a low whisper, Erin told them everything from the time she discovered Tuffy until the unfortunate stranglehold.

Mrs. Bundle said, "I have an idea." Keeping their voices low and discreet, she directed the plan of action they should undertake.

With Mrs. Bundle's encouraging nod, Erin stood and addressed the group.

"Ahem! Miss Aurelia, Miss Olivia, and Mister Woodsum." They looked up; she spoke evenly, with unexpected maturity. "I expect you'll all be wantin' me explanation."

Woodsum's furry eyebrows shot downward in a white V of concern. "You have our rapt attention, missy."

"So then, here it is. First, see, I heard the kitty inside me bedroom wall. She sounded pitiful. I found her by going through the *magic cupboard*—aye, you know—it's there in me room. Once I figured out the *secret* compartment, I discovered the attic stairs—the ones no one's supposed to know about. *Hmph!*" (She couldn't help the minor editorializing.) "Anyway. When I found Tuffy in the cold attic she was in a sorry state, to be sure. I knew I needed to get her some milk. I didn't want to bother anyone, so very quietly," she emphasized, "I gathered her up. So, here I was, hurrying through the great room. By *accident* I tripped over the big ottoman and fell—aye, fell face-to-face with a *monster serpent*. His eyes were shinier 'n a penny in the darkness. Aye, that spooked *me*, to be sure."

Gathering steam with her tale, she continued. "But still, I knew I *must* be finishing me mission. So I trot downstairs—fast, but not so as to waken anyone. That's when I come upon something so odd...aye, it really was quite *bizarre*." (Pause for effect.) "Without meaning to, *I* spooked the abominable snowman! Right there, standing in the kitchen door, minding its own business. Actually," she pondered, "it might be the snowman's wife. Right, I'm thinkin' it's more likely an abominable snow-*lady*. She's very big, mind you—but not at all scary to me. I couldn't see that good without me glasses." (Look of appropriate dismay toward Mrs. Bundle and Angie.) "Well, don't you know, I left them upstairs by mistake. Anyway, that was when we *both*—the snowlady and I—got spooked by the terrible, *terrible* thunder snowstorm. *Bam!!* Did you hear it, now? Oh, aye, it shook and flashed, and then some! So, the nice big snowlady runs from the house quick as a wink—and *I* got spooked when Angie spooked *me* by grabbing me by me neck from behind. It made me scream! Ach—I wasn't sure who it could be after all that spookiness. Then, I'll wager *you* all were spooked by my screamin'—sorry, I am—and that's why you came running. So, I reckon it would be nice to know...that is, if you've a mind to tell us," she glanced toward Mrs. Bundle for support, who gave her a reassuring nod, "why there's all this spookin' and *secret stuff* going on here? And why you all don't want to celebrate your—you know—" she put her fingers to her lips and whispered, "—*birthday* today?"

"Gaw! Magic cupboards?" Olivia snorted indignantly, "Monster serpents? Snow ladies? Who's next—Tonto?"

"I'm not sure who that is, mum. Is he in hidin' here at the inn, too?"

A nervous giggle escaped Aurelia's lips.

Woodsum's coloring was reddish purple as he grabbed his nose and clamped his mouth shut to stifle a wheeze of laughter.

"I believe Erin asks some very valid questions." Mrs. Bundle said, adding, "I, too, have seen—and discovered some bits and pieces—that are quite peculiar. And, maybe not by happenstance. It sounds like last night's ups and downs may have accelerated the process a bit. I'll be willing to share all of my experiences," she paused, "on one condition. All *three* of you must agree to share, too." Mrs. Bundle took the opportunity Erin had handed her on a silver platter. "Since our arrival, I couldn't help but notice a number of quirky inconsistencies. But let's back up a bit." She pushed a wisp of hair back behind her ears. "The fact of the matter is, I believe it was your wish for me to come to the inn. Maybe to solve a very old mystery, or maybe to help you all, to possibly put some matters to rest?"

Aurelia was the first to respond. "Cousin Milly told us to listen to you. I hoped we could find..." she paused. "Yes, we need your help."

Mrs. Bundle coaxed, "I think you have things you would like to share. Your own special account—a mystery from long ago." The woman turned a shade paler. Mrs. Bundle turned toward Olivia. "I daresay there are some old matters that need a good airing. Olivia, maybe it's time to clear out the cobwebs?" She gestured with hands open, "I believe it's why we're all here now together. Rather than keep it all hidden," she appealed to Woodsum, "shouldn't we put it to bed?"

The Pettyfers, to a one, were visibly uncomfortable as they passed nervous glances between them.

"With all due respect, Woodsum," Mrs. Bundle continued, "this can't be put off any longer. That is to say, if you all want some peace."

His face dropped and suddenly he looked very old. He gave a nod. "Peace. I'll wager the jig is up. You've been detecting since you arrived. Am I right?"

"Not on purpose. It seems as though things have been falling into our lap. Like a game."

"Ah, gee whiz. We figured once we got you settled in, we'd consider all the options and decide, y'know, whether to go forth and share. We didn't figure on the blizzard. That was sheer luck—or a freaky coincidence. I guess it all happens the way it's supposed to happen."

Erin tapped his shoulder and consoled him. "Aye. It's true. The jig is up, mate."

"Well, now. I daresay you've done your job, super sleuths." Reluctantly, he stood, adding, "It's been a long time coming. Sisters? What say you?"

The tension was palpable as silence was all that filled the air.

Olivia stammered. "I'm not in full agreement. To rake it all up... after all these years? Why?"

"It's up to all of you." Mrs. Bundle encouraged, "You brought me here by sheer will, I think. Timing is everything. We're safe. There's no bogeyman, is there? We certainly have nowhere to go." Palms up, she gestured at the shards of morning dawn attempting to strafe through the swirling, blinding storm outside. It was a harbinger of the wintry, wild day ahead.

"That's for sure." Woodsum's ears waggled in agreement but his face was gloomy. 'We ain't going anywhere in this super duper blizzard. So," he said unenthusiastically, "I vote we just hunker down and be done with the whole mess."

Olivia quibbled, "Brother, I doubt it will make a difference. What about sister here? I'm not sure she can take it."

"Oh, my. Oh—my." A tear trickled down Aurelia's cheek. She blinked back the tears and murmured, "We *must* do it. It's time to put it all...to rest."

This is going to be painful, Mrs. Bundle thought. "I will try to make it as easy as possible for you all. Presumably, to forgive and, hopefully, start anew?"

Olivia drew in a deep breath and sniffed. "We'll probably regret it. However, 'a journey of a thousand mile begins...with a single step.'" Her eyes softened, and she sniffed again. "And Cousin Milly said we should trust you, Mrs. Bundle."

Her siblings nodded.

Woodsum said, "That she did." He repeated, as if wanting to believe it, "That she did."

"Well then. I suggest we start slow." Mrs. Bundle established her game plan. "Let's begin with the 'monster serpent' that Erin—and yes, I, too, saw it—upstairs."

Chapter XXI
A Half Hour Earlier (Loose Ends)

When Mrs. Bundle had awakened she knew things weren't right. Instinctively, she reached under her pillow for the small box, even as she tapped on the wall with her other hand. She had decided she would sleep on its contents safe within; the next morning she would try to tackle the Pettyfers and their long-held secret. She shook the sleepiness off, waiting, trying to calm herself. However, instinct feathered into mounting uneasiness.

Erin? No reply came from the other side of the wall and she tapped three times again a bit louder.

There was no answer.

She knew she must check on the girl. She rose quickly, then remembered her lame foot and took more care as she put on her robe and went out into the hallway. Erin's door was slightly ajar. Poking her head in, she perused every corner; the room was empty. By the looks of disarray, it was clear something was going on: the floor, covered with clothes, as if Erin had had a midnight modeling marathon; the wall cupboard doors, wide open. She peered inside—nothing, except…there! In the darkness, she discerned an opening—a wall access. She listened. Not a sound. *Cat's granny, where was the girl?*

Not yet panicking, she moved quickly back into the hallway, reached Angie's room and without knocking, pulled the door open.

Not finding her either, she trusted they were together. She cocked an ear for any sound and whispered, "What are you both up to?" The window was cracked open a hair the way Angie always liked to sleep. She looked out fearfully. The wind whistled and moaned through snow banks astronomical in size, drifting in huge mounds that reached far above the ground—the highest points now within inches of many of the trees' branches.

No, she assured herself, nothing would ever make them go outside in this tempest.

The bathroom? She left the room, clumping down the hallway as quietly as possible. No need to wake anyone else up. Nearing the end, she heard a queer, uncomfortable scraping sound like chalk on a chalkboard. The guest room door called *Golden Desire* nearest the great space—Erin called it the forbidden room—wasn't just unlocked, it was slightly ajar! She peered inside. Just a few feet away, in the dark blush of dawn breaking and the pallor of escalating white snow, a very large, very alive, very long neck hovered close to the floor. Her line of sight was limited but suddenly, the elongated head extended. Beady eyes stared back at her and just as quickly, the head pulled back like a collapsible telescope, waiting, it seemed, with curiosity. Mrs. Bundle searched the dark corners, took a deep breath and pushed in further. The door squealed, opening a hair more.

"Oh my word!" She pulled back as the head pushed out again, longer, then longer still reaching up toward her until it was two feet in length, from deep within a disc-sized center. It was soundless, massive, and entirely awesome! Suddenly two scaly round and stompy feet with big claws clicked on the wood floor, moving toward her. Its teeth snapped around something pointy and sharp—spikes on a slab—*what was that?*

Undeterred, she pushed the door open in full to reveal the monster's huge round hump.

It froze.

She didn't move an inch—waiting—and neither did "It." A standoff occurred, with the only sound the wild, whistling wind.

There was nothing like it in these parts. Strange, utterly mind-bogglingly, fantastical!

Suddenly, there was a blinding flash in the sky! Loud bangs and the sheer brilliance momentarily impaired her vision. The house shook on its foundation and she rocked in place. She reached out, grabbing the door frame to steady herself.

It was then she heard Erin's terrified scream from the distant downstairs. At that point, there was no question that anything could or would stop her. Hobbling along, she took the steps with the lickety-split-edness of an Olympic marathoner. When she heard Woodsum desperately hissing the distinctive military emergency call, "Mayday!" she went into overdrive. That, my friends, was all she needed to discern something must be terribly, terribly wrong. Red hot on his heels, she burst into the kitchen.

Chapter XXII

The Magical Mystery Tour Begins…Upstairs

Aurelia rose, "I will handle this."

She picked up one of the oil lanterns from the table. It seemed surprising that the one everyone seemed most concerned about, and seemed the most helpless—Aurelia—stepped forward to lead the way. "Come along upstairs with me." The others followed, Woodsum at the rear.

At the top landing, she paused and cooed softly, "Yoo-hooo. I'm here now, sweetness. Where are you, my dearest?" She turned to them. "Why don't you all sit down here in the great room?" she urged them as she left, "He'll be out shortly." They settled in and sat quietly, listening to her coo and cluck as she grasped one of the fresh palm fronds from the decorative tin stand, waving it gently; it made a swishing sound. "Hey, there. I'm here. Come along, we're all waiting…" her voice trailed away as she entered *Golden Desire*.

"Will she be all right?" Erin asked the others with concern.

"Don't worry; she knows what she is doing." Mrs. Bundle assured her.

There was a shuffling and scraping.

After a bit, Aurelia exited, walking backward, "C'mon, old thing. Come on out."

Scccrrrattchhh, Scccrrrattchhh, came the ominous dragging sounds.

Suddenly, the lower half of the doorway darkened with a massive hump; a very long neck emerged from the hump; in its mouth was…. not to worry, a juicy slice of…prickly pear cactus! With an inch to spare on either side, the impressive living object slowly blocked the threshold.

"Jaysus! That's what I tripped over?" Erin was gobsmacked. "What kind of creature is it?"

"Let me introduce you to Horatio Testudinidae." Aurelia declared. "Well, his given name is Horatio, but we have grown to love him as our own dear Hoity-Toity. He's a long neck Galapagos land tortoise. Nearly one hundred years old. He was …a gift to me." She sniffled wistfully.

Their combined amazement caused them to stare and not ask the obvious *who* the "he" was that had given her this astonishing gift. The tortoise's impressive carapace (the upper part of his shell) was about 2 ½' wide with raised patterns of greens, golds, and grays within deep tracks not unlike stonewalls surrounding an English country landscape.

"Hoity-Toity?" Erin watched the beast munch the last morsel. "Blimey! He's even bigger than me imaginations."

Angie rose to get a better look. "Gaw! A real Galapagos tortoise? I *never* thought I'd ever see one of these—especially in captivity. They used to be an endangered species, but no longer. They live completely on land, generally are reclusive and shy, but," she scrutinized him, "I've read the domed tortoises are mostly gregarious. At least that's what we'll hope, right?" From a young girl, Angie had always been intrigued with science and particularly lizards, pollywogs and frogs, but especially tortoises, turtles, and terrapins. "The Galapagos tortoises are strict vegetarians, so no need to worry." She nudged Erin. "They're huge beasts but they won't eat you. See?" She moved bit by bit to get a closer look at the large creature. Picking a frond from the resplendent vase nearby, she held it out to the huge tortoise. From his guard station, he looked up, eyes gleaming, and opened his jaws. Leisurely, he snapped off a bunch of the morsel, chewing deliberately.

"Oh, my goodness, mum!" Erin watched. "He doesn't have teeth!"

"No, they really can't bite as a defense." Aurelia explained. "His jaw is lined with sharp ridges—see, it looks like pinking shears. They're very gentle."

"He's actually small for his species." Olivia whispered discreetly. "Most average around 600 pounds and can have a five-foot circumference. But he's just the right size for the inn."

Head askance, Erin asked, "Sure and I'd like to know how you hid this big monster from us."

Aurelia chuckled, "Oh, that. Hoity is really quite easy to hide. He's quite content to stay in one place during the day. As you know from your studies, Angie, tortoises don't need to be in water. In fact, they don't even need to drink water if their food is moist enough. We take care of all that. He likes to make his rounds at night—slowly, mind you."

"He's what I heard the first night." Mrs. Bundle reported. "After we all went to bed."

"Yes. He's our guardian, our keeper of the gate. This is his domain—the upstairs. He's completely docile, even though he weighs in at about 400 pounds."

"The last time he went on the barn scales was years ago." Woodsum added.

Erin stepped forward fearlessly and waggled a finger at the tortoise. "Surely, I was scared out of me wits when I ran into you earlier! But now…" she moved a foot closer. "I'm not at all. Really!" She extended her hand in friendship. "Hi there, mate!"

They watched as he watched them, munching away. At her proffered amity, his head slowly bobbed up and down.

In tortoise thought, he communicated, albeit at a snail's pace: *Salutations. I am Horatio, Lord of the Testudinidae Family, from the wilds of Rancho Primicias, Santa Cruz, an isle in the Great Land of Galapagos. My royal lineage—'The Order of Testudines'—spans centuries. We are the proud Chelonoidis Nigra. Verily, what* excitement there has been since we learned of your visit! I've been waiting to meet you all. Dearest Aurelia didn't think the time was right just yet. Until now, that is. And here we are, together. I greet you all with friendship and goodwill. I've been watching out for you since your arrival yesterday. He nodded slowly, continuing, Don't be alarmed that you tripped over me, child. My ponderous travels sometimes unintentionally put me in people's paths. Other than the occasional run-in, I live an uncomplicated life here, sometimes slumbering sixteen hours in one day. No stress or strain; that...is my mantra. His scaly clumps of feet grabbed the rug and he pushed forward, moving closer. He stretched his neck outward and up toward Erin, further still until it reached halfway up the door jamb.

It was quite impressive and the guests issued a collective— "Oooooh! Look at that!"

Hoity-Toity stretched proudly, as best he could at his ripe age. They got a glimpse of the plastron (the lower part of his body) where his large limbs exited. Unlike a common turtle, tortoises could fully retract their heads into their shells. For now, though, he exercised, pulling his head back to show them the scope of his capabilities.

"He can be a bit of a showman," Aurelia tittered. "Can't you, my dear?"

It's true, m'ladies, like many males of a mature age, he thought-transferred, *I'm used to being admired not only for my size, but my girth—as well, I might add modestly, as my singular prowess and intelligence. There is no one like me—save for you to travel far, far away a great and magical distance to the world from which I came. My undivided loyalty and allegiance was transported to the Land of the Pettyfers—and most importantly, to my dearest Aurelia—many years ago. Our world here...where I have ruled and protected this upstairs domain for decades...is where I belong...and will forever remain.*

"So—that's why you have all the exotic plants." Mrs. Bundle said, putting it all together. "To accommodate his appetite."

Olivia nodded, adding knowledgeably, "Yes. Most tortoises like Hoity-Toity live in the moist highlands of the islands and dine on low-lying shrubs and succulent vegetation like flowers, fruit, grasses, leaves, twigs. So we've learned how to take care of him with just the right diet. And of course cacti is his favorite. That's what all the journals say."

"I think he likes hibiscus best." Aurelia stated firmly. "He smiles so when he gets that."

Woodsum added his own two cents, "It's passion fruit that he really fancies. He goes bananas over 'em."

Aurelia clucked, "Strange to think he was the size of a tennis ball and only a few inches long when he was born. Of course, we first met when he was just a youngster—about a decade old. I fell completely in love with him. "

"You could say...he grew on us!" Woodsum chortled.

"He doesn't cause any harm, moving at night as he does from one side of the house—over there," Aurelia pointed at the room directly opposite the *Golden Desire* room, "to here. Every night he makes his way across the great divide. Sometimes he dawdles, and sometimes, he's just plain curious—like last night, right, Hoity? The fact of the matter is, he brings great comfort to me."

"From *Michel's Choice* to here." Mrs. Bundle murmured under her breath.

Olivia added, "Nowadays, he just hangs around up here. We know just what to do to keep him going. He misses the attention of guests like during the inn's heydey, that's for certain. He always rather liked knowing what was going on...still does. In the old days, we let the guests pat him on his scutes—those plates on his upper carapace. During the summer, we used the dumbwaiter to get him down for a long visit outside. Worked like a charm. He'd spend the summer days napping by the pond. He was partial to the mud holes. Why, he patrolled the area, kept us safe. His armor makes him completely invulnerable to most any predator."

"And if things get dicey, he just tucks in his head, feet and tail." Woodsum continued. "At the end of the season when it got colder, I'd bring him back up."

Aurelia sighed, and her eyes moistened, "At this age, he just likes to be with me...upstairs here, with our memories. What would I have done all these years without my favorite friend...who knows my secrets." She gave a knowing glance at her siblings, "All of our secrets."

"Which, hopefully, you can shed some light on," Mrs. Bundle added expectantly. "If you're ready?"

Hoity-Toity's head raised up with interest; *What? Is it true? Share all the memories—and secrets? Excellent plan...finally. You must tell me everything later, Aurelia.*

She patted his head fondly. "Yes, dear heart." She bent and kissed his scaly head. "Yes, I promise I will come visit later, as usual. You stay here for now."

Methodically, he backed up, then moved (as they watched) toward the corner of the room, where a soft downy blanket had been laid especially for him. He blinked resignedly and closed his heavily-lidded eyes. He settled his mighty shell torso onto the blanket.

Ahhhh...rest. I'll say good-bye for now, then.

Like folding bellows, he sucked in his stubby limbs first, and then his head, until all disappeared and he was gone.

"Whoa." Angie swallowed. "That was impressive." She asked Aurelia lightly, "Can I ask...what's he doing here...in the williwags of Vermont? How did he come into your life?"

Erin added less delicately, "Aye, why couldn't you just tell us about him when we first got here?"

Aurelia coughed gently. "You see, that is why we kept him a secret. We wanted to tell you. But all the questions...that, my dears, is complicated...it's rather a long story that involves others—including sister and brother. It's all a bit topsy-turvy." She pulled her shawl tightly around her and shivered. "My! With all the excitement, might I remind you that we are all still in our nightclothes?"

Erin said, "Right you are, Miss Aurelia."

She smiled wanly and looked out the bedroom window, a bedroom that was decorated in the softest yellows—a lovely retreat. All was silent as their eyes followed hers: outside, it was a whiteout, with nothing in view except the blizzard's wrath raining down...not unlike readying a clean palette for some vibrant paint. There was a tinge of relief in her voice when she finally spoke. "Dawn has broken. I feel better." With renewed strength, she said resolutely, "I'd like to suggest that we first get dressed and then retire to the dining room where we can refresh ourselves with a bountiful breakfast. And then? The story that means so much to us all will be told. The story…" she paused thoughtfully, "about the one who changed our lives."

"With the snow lady, too, I'll wager," Erin insisted. "You'll not forget the abominable tale will you, mum?"

"Ah, dear heart. Of course, we will enlighten you," she said, looking pointedly at her siblings. "That's a promise."

Chapter XXIII
More Truth

Mrs. Bundle had two quick tasks to perform in the short time before assembling for breakfast. Firstly, while all scurried to ready themselves, she discreetly took Woodsum aside; they consulted briefly and he said, "I'll be danged—how did you figure out—?" then stopped at her knowing glance.

She had replied, "It will be fine," and whispered her carefully-chosen instructions into his ear, to which he resignedly nodded.

"Yup. I guess I can do that, if you think so," and he quickly left.

Secondly, after her toilette, she made a clandestine jaunt to the library before joining everyone in the dining room. Her foot, newly bandaged, was feeling remarkably well considering the early morning's intense activity.

Within the quiet mahogany-paneled chamber filled with books, she was as familiar with the Dewey Decimal System classifications here as she was at the Pillson Public Library. She knew what she was looking for, and quickly found class 400—*Language*—high on the top shelves.

Sliding the ladder into position, she awkwardly climbed up, one foot, then the other, until she could easily reach the top shelf. She paused, studying the books, passing over the first few divisions impatiently, "Language—no—Linguistics—nope—English and Olde English...um," she reached to see, "almost there." She pulled the ladder along, winnowing the search down closer to section 433.

"Okay… here we go." She studied the four books, and grinned. "Ah! Got it! There we go."

She had found just what she was looking for—a translation dictionary. She looked up the two phrases that had stymied her since reading them late last evening. "Let me see…yes. There now. *Wahl*. Huh. Just as I surmised." And then the last two—confirming *Goldener* was easy; the fourth word, not so. She looked it up and rolled her eyes. "Of course!" It made sense now.

She put it all together. These facts further corroborated her budding hypothesis. "Which means—" Suddenly, she felt the ladder tremble beneath her, and she grabbed on for dear life, looking down.

Olivia was at the foot, one hand firmly on the middle rung. Mrs. Bundle noted with some concern the pair of large-handled scissors in her other hand. Its sharp blades were pointing directly upward in her direction as though poised and ready.

"Hello…What are you up to up there?" Olivia asked.

Mrs. Bundle closed the book, prepared for her part in the next hours. "Well, I had a bit of research…I needed to do." She eyed the woman, wondering for a second if she really was a threat. "Are you… all right, Olivia?"

"We knew bringing you here might be dangerous. But here we are. You ask if I'm all right? At this point, I really don't know." She had a look of apprehension, even dread. "You'll need help getting down, won't you? Especially with that bum foot."

"Oh, no. I'm quite fine. You could…step back, if you would." She dismounted carefully down the ladder and came face-to-face with her. She looked her square in the eye, ignoring the oversized scissors, still poised. "I suspect these walls have seen…and heard a lot."

Olivia's eyes shifted: first, toward the closet door where Grandfather lived, then back to Mrs. Bundle.

"Don't be afraid, Olivia." She smiled sympathetically but exhibited strength behind her intent look. "No matter what you believe…I hope and pray things will be better. Don't worry. Today…when it's your turn…you must do your part in this and tell your story."

Olivia's body suddenly went slack and she collapsed into a nearby chair. She heaved a huge groan, then burst into tears. Suddenly her body was racked with sobs, as though inconsolable, and she wailed like a widow.

Mrs. Bundle stood by, unflinching, and waited as the minutes went by; waited until the sobs subsided and turned to sniffles. Olivia looked up with inquiring eyes. "You've found it."

She gave a slight nod. Removing the small, gauze-wrapped bundle from her inside pocket, she handed it over to Olivia and said gently, "You know, like you, my mother had a penchant for old adages—especially those she had learned from her mother—my grandmother. One of their favorites was, 'If you lie, you'll steal—and vice versa!' I'm entrusting this to you. *You* must do with it what you think best. It's not my tale to tell. It's yours." There wasn't time to talk further. "Now. Shall we join the others?" Disclosure, confessions— all had to happen with the willing participation of all three.

As though she, too, was aware of this, Olivia pulled herself together and stood up, nodded fearlessly, and left the room.

Alone with her thoughts, Mrs. Bundle knew this was going to be tough; she, as facilitator, would referee if need be, and only present what was so important to their healing. She knew the little decoupage box's story, its ownership and whereabouts known to someone all these years. Such a shame. It would be essential to handle this delicately and in a productive way. She squared her shoulders, believing she was up to the task.

It was a quiet breakfast. Woodsum was noticeably absent. The guests, filled mostly with anticipation, waited as patiently as possible as the table was finally cleared and readied for discussion. Erin, barely able to contain herself, was under strict orders from Angie to restrain her urge to ask questions.

Mrs. Bundle tapped her fingers lightly on the table, but assured them, "The Pettyfers will tell us in their own way on their own schedule."

The wind was blowing like the dickens and the whiteout was so intense that, for that view, they may as well have been on a desolate iceberg as they waited…and waited a bit more. A quarter hour ticked by slowly.

"Where are they?" Erin asked. "What are they doing? Are they coming?"

All of a sudden, from the kitchen, came the dull heavy bumps as more than one pair of boots banged onto the old linoleum floor. Low voices could be heard as though last-minute discussion and prompting was taking place.

Mrs. Bundle nodded. It wouldn't be long now.

Woodsum joined them first, seeming even more edgy than earlier. "I been up and down and all around creation. It's a holy mess out there!" He huffed with exertion. "Finally found what we was looking for, what you asked for, Mrs. Bundle."

"Good. We're ready whenever you are."

He turned sideways and reached a hand through the doorway; he pulled gently and enunciated, "C'mon, now. Don't be afraid. It's all right."

One of the most extraordinary women they had ever seen stumbled willy-nilly into the room. In totality, she was as pale as a new snowfall: her skin, the color of alabaster; her hair, cornsilk-white with a plethora of silky wisps and pulled back into a lengthy braid trailing down her back to her waist. She was dressed in an immaculate white shirtwaist dress and short capelet, apron, and soft neutral lambswool stockings. Her ingénue silhouette was wraithlike: at the crown of her head, melting snow crystals glittered off a pointed white maid's cap, casting an ethereal aura; her eyes were focused downward; her shoulders slumped in timid apprehension and lack of sophistication.

Her size was remarkable! She was all of 6'5" and solid, her physique sinewy and strong—all in direct contrast to her demeanor. As large as she was, she was meek as a titmouse and clearly uncomfortable. Extremely nervous, she peeked up for a split second and they were further surprised by her eyes: her eyelashes were colorless, the irises pink. Her face, as pasty and smooth as unbleached dough, contradicted the fact that it was the countenance of a middle-aged woman.

"Glory be!" Erin gave a low, astonished whistle. "It's me snow lady!"

Woodsum said, "This here is Elga Mae Daewald. We shortened it to May-day because she's our emergency girl. She comes every other day but more when we're in a pinch."

Mrs. Bundle laughed, calling out, "Mayday! Yes, I get it—an emergency for sure."

"She's the last of the Daewald sisters from Denmark; stuck together like glue they did when they was all alive. The five of 'em could never, *ever* abide crowds. Crowds being more than one or two! Loners, they were, the lot of 'em. All of 'em big women, just like Mayday. One by one they passed on." He took the woman gently by the elbow, looked at her full on, and spoke slowly. "They ain't goin' to hurt you, Mayday. They're nice people."

The Pettyfer sisters poked their way through, and with their efforts forced her forward gently. With all three surrounding her, the scene was endearing, yet oddly suggestive of a skewed fairy tale where old tiny minions protect a misplaced giant.

Mayday gave a shrill giggle, made a curtsey and then put her hands over her eyes.

"We were lucky to find her back then. She lives alone down in the hollow over on the dark side. It's been twenty-odd years since she joined us as the only kitchen staff ever. She comes in like a ghost in the night to take care of us, especially if we're in a pickle with guests."

"And she's the one, I'll wager, who made the Rød Pølse—the Danish red sausage I had for lunch." Mrs. Bundle said. Mayday remained in her timid stance, but Mrs. Bundle expressed her comments directly, "It was wonderful!"

"Don't mind her, she can't communicate too good, but she's one heck of a cook!" Olivia said. "She makes the sausage, not to mention she's responsible for the preserves, the majority of the baking, the stews, most everything. And she helps with any heavy lifting, and does the linens, and—oh well, let's just admit it! We're just plain old now and struggle to keep up with it all." She said begrudgingly, "We like to be perfect. Always have."

"That's where our dear Mayday comes in." Aurelia said, "She's a lifesaver!"

Olivia went on, "She solves all our problems."

"All done under the cover of darkness." Woodsum said. "Arrives at 3—3 AM, that is—and cooks, runs a mop, cleans, whatever we need done, quiet as a mouse, and then leaves before dawn as the house begins to wake up. She enters from out back along the main trail, where she leaves her snow machine. Brings all the supplies with her and travels down the path. When she goes home, it's back down the dark side to her little cabin in Plymouth. No one, and we mean *no one*, knows she comes to us. We like to keep our business *our* business. We've always been self-sufficient. But as time went on, something had to give. So, we made this nifty arrangement and it's worked just dandy." He gave a thumbs up. "She knows we like our privacy; that's why she skedaddled when she saw you, Erin. Didn't want to blow our cover, y'see."

"Guess we never thought we'd get caught!" Olivia said. "Shame on us for trying to pull one over, especially on you. 'Course, they always say," she looked at Mrs. Bundle, "The biggest secrets are the ones you can only tell a stranger."

They are proud people, Mrs. Bundle thought, *even more like truant children—arrested development rearing its ugly head once again. Old habits die hard.*

"What about her coat?" Erin asked. "She left without her coat on!" She asked the woman, "Weren't you cold?"

The woman's gaze shifted slightly as though confused; she didn't answer.

"It's an odd thing, but Mayday's never cold!" Woodsum answered for her. "Are you, Mayday? Never cold?" He hugged himself and shivered.

She shook her head, then pushed up her sleeve and flexed, revealing a bicep Popeye would be proud of.

"She's deaf." Angie whispered, stepping forward, and asked the woman directly, "You read lips?"

The woman looked up. Angie smiled and asked, moving her fingers niftily. "Do you read lips—or, use sign language?" The woman grinned broadly, and they were off, communicating in bits and spurts in ASL.

Angie, who had first learned limited sign language in middle school and became more proficient later with a college roommate who was deaf, was clearly enjoying her conversation.

"Yup." Woodsum watched them. "We love her like a daughter. And that's the real story."

"She says it nice to meet us but she really wants to finish up her work in the kitchen." Angie said.

"I'll get her going and be right back. C'mon, dear heart." Aurelia put her arm through Mayday's as they left the room.

"Well that's one less secret." Olivia wiped her brow.

"Aye, and that one was a doozy!" Erin declared. 'All but as good as the Hoity-Toity one, to be sure."

As Aurelia left the room, Woodsum fidgeted, rechecking the dreadful weather outside, which appeared worse than before if that was possible. "Curses to this storm! It's too much like….that winter. Gummin' up the works. What a mess we're in." He muttered between clenched teeth. "I hope sister can take all this stress."

"You mean Miss Aurelia?" Erin asked. "Or does he mean you, too, Miss Olivia?"

"Don't worry about me. I can do this." Olivia replied, shooting Mrs. Bundle a look of resolve. "I pray sister'll be all right, too. She deserves to get some things off her chest."

"Time's passed though." Woodsum worried his hands; his jaw jutted out defiantly. "What you said, Mrs. Bundle, that we're gonna clear out the cobwebs and it will give us some peace? But then, what do we do after that?" He seemed to be losing his spirit; his jolly nature seemed to be dissipating before their eyes. He wiped his damp brow, "Golly! Where the heck is sister?"

Mrs. Bundle marveled at the ebb and flow of the trio's nerve—first one vacillated, then the other. She would certainly be happy to have this over with, one way or another. *With any luck*, she hoped, crossing her fingers, *this process will be the key to unlock their self-imposed time-warp of a prison.*

"I'm here." The tiny-framed woman stood in the doorway. She held her hands together as if in prayer, tapping her fingers together softly. "Brother. It was so long ago but it was like yesterday to me. Is that how it is for you, too?"

"Ditto." he answered. "Can't help but feel we're back there with everything just like it was in 1940."

"We're ready." Erin said, eyes wide with curiosity. "Tell us the story from the beginning, Miss Aurelia, would you now?"

"We certainly don't want to upset you." Angie said, kicking Erin under the table. "It's your choice."

All eyes were on the lovely little lady who suddenly smiled softly. "Yes, my *choice*." The timbre of her voice had changed, strengthened. "It's all right. It's only fitting—and so uncanny—that everything today is exactly the same. We were to commemorate our twentieth birthday in the midst of the madness of that monster storm. I say commemorate because afterward, there really wasn't anything to celebrate. January 8th, 1940 was the worst birthday I ever had."

Mrs. Bundle said with calm authority. "With what appears to be the storm of *this* century upon us now, we're a captive audience. If you're up to it, Aurelia, we're standing with you, to learn about Michel and what happened that night of the storm."

In the glowing aura of the outside, Aurelia leaned forward breathlessly. "You know already, Mrs. Bundle, don't you? About *him*. And me."

"I know some. A lot, actually. But not all."

Olivia reached out and took Aurelia's hand. "C'mon now. We'll all three tell our story—about that time in our lives."

Woodsum, on the opposite side, took her other hand with determination. "*We'll stick together no matter what we run into or how hard things get.* Like we did then."

Aurelia settled her petite back into the big Queen Anne chair at the head of the table and folded her hands together in her lap. She began pensively, "I've spent all these years protecting my memories. You see, like a fleeting dream, he was here for a while… and then…" she raised two dainty fingers and trailed them through in the air, "he was gone."

The air was still, while everyone waited.

Olivia's severe manner had softened a tad, and she said ruefully, "I've *always* believed he was lost in the blizzard. Right, brother?"

Woodsum's face darkened and he struggled to answer, then simply said, "God knows." He turned to Aurelia. "Sister?"

"There hasn't been a *day* that goes by that I don't think of him." Aurelia emphasized each word with conviction and certainty, "You see, Michel Hydrick was the love of my life."

And so, their story began…

PART TWO
Secrets...and Lies

THE FOLLOWING ARE THE INDIVIDUAL NARRATIVES THAT DAY OF THE EVENTS SURROUNDING 1940, BEGINNING FIRST WITH AURELIA'S ACCOUNT, THEN WOODSUM'S, AND FINALLY, OLIVIA'S.

H E WAS WITH US FOR JUST SIX MONTHS—and those were the best months of my life. Every event after that was forever measured by that which occurred that first week of 1940—and the night before we became twenty years old. During that time and after, I experienced pure bliss—and deep agony. It's the bliss I have always chosen to keep within my heart. I want to begin my story with how we first met, to share with you how he changed my life forever.

As young spirited girls in December of 1938, Olivia and I neared our nineteenth birthday a bit foolishly, thinking less about potential suitors than about the daily existence that enveloped us like an ethereal shroud at the inn, protected in a simple life. Because he was a boy, Woodsum had a bit more freedom, but was still limited in what he was allowed to do, or to think, on his own. Our lack of sophistication and maturity was stunted, shaped by our parents, particularly Father, who one could describe as an authoritarian. Certainly, we had little knowledge about how tumultuous and volatile the outside world, particularly Europe, was becoming. We were not encouraged to seek external opinions, nor stay atop current events. We knew little about a country now divided between those that didn't want to get involved, those who did, and those who thought the world was doomed regardless.

Of course, in our little world of Mount Holly, Vermont, we were always defined as three, not one—Woodsum, Olivia, and me—the Pettyfer Triplets. The very condition beginning immediately at birth made it difficult to imagine having an opinion of your own. As youngsters and then later as we reached our teenage years, we were considered special by those outsiders, but we didn't feel as such. We lacked confidence: Father made sure of that; Mother followed his lead.

If you asked a local, they would have surely said the Pettyfer triplets were well-educated, the girls comely—I remember how special I felt with the young fellows lucky enough to be invited for tea. Woodsum, well, he was just a genuinely nice boy, always kind, always gentle. I suppose he could have had a stable of girls who wouldn't have turned down an invitation—but he stayed to himself most of the time. We found enjoyment at the inn—it was all we knew. Our parents were considered by all as local folk who had made good—and kept to business.

As a pensive young man, Norton Pettyfer (our father), had completed two years at the prestigious Massachusetts Institute Technology School of Architecture and Design. While there, he met and soon married our mother Sylvia, and brought her back to Plymouth. He purchased some isolated land at the top of the Saltash with an inheritance from his grandfather, determined to make a go of an area too rocky for decent farming or pasturing for cows, but with the most beautiful views of all of Rutland County and Lake Ninevah. With the latest building designs within his portfolio and his passionate architectural mind set, Norton (joined with Sylvia's strong work ethic) gathered all resources and began their dream: building an elegant Victorian-style inn, an oasis for all to enjoy midst the area's recreational splendor. It took two long years, but as they toiled and created, it came to life. Having poured everything into the project, they reminded us often of their elation when the doors opened for business.

We were born on January 8, 1920. Mother wore her 'Mother of Triplets' badge proudly; we were the light of her simple existence—beside Father, who she adored and could do no wrong in her eyes. We were nine when the Great Depression hit, but little changed in our world. With Father's goal to be ever self-sufficient, we had all we needed at the inn: gardens and fruit trees bloomed in summer; hunting was the norm; living off the land was commonplace, allowing for ample provisions for winter existence. Life seemed pleasant at the inn; we were homeschooled by Mother until age 12, taught only what our parents wanted us to learn, but always encouraged to read, read, read. The library was filled with the Classics, used as tools to encourage and foster the foundation that we were part of a special class, that our bloodline was, as Father put it, 'quite notably white Saxon and Englishmen.' We were taught to embrace our roots tracing back to the Norman Conquest of 1066, where William the Conqueror gave his supporters and soldiers land for service—ours was Worcestershire where the Pettyfer ancestors held a seat. He was always very proud of that legacy, to the exclusion of any other 'distinctive race' as he called it.

While I wouldn't call Father a snob, you must realize that back in the day, a lot of people felt that way. It was more the rule than the exception. In our remote home on the mountain, Father exercised rigid rules and ran a very tight ship at the inn; he was defensive and conservative, allowing us little interaction with the locals. Our world consisted of travelers from afar who came to stay at the inn for a week or more of retreat. He had a penchant for world studies and diplomatic disciplines, and kept a research and drafting room in the back of the barn. We knew it as his getaway, a very secret place that was off limits to us. Locked at all times, it was his sanctuary. As time went on, he became less pensive and more brooding. We saw a side the paying guests didn't see—more often than not, he took his frustrations out on Olivia or Woodsum. For some reason, I was exempt from these tirades. They bore the brunt much more than me.

As we progressed into our teens, we were allowed to socialize a bit more—with tremendous control and direction, mind you— traveling daily down the mountain to junior and senior high school, and then once a week 'downtown' to Ludlow or Rutland for church socials, special school events, and the like. During the inn's annual closing—limited to the week after Christmas through the first week of January—we journeyed with Father on what he called his 'one guilty pleasure' to New York City. He loved the city's sophistication. It gave him an opportunity to connect with a certain group of men that held the same belief system. Consequently, this was our opportunity for a very coveted sojourn to 'the big city' for fun as we celebrated the New Year and our birthday. Immediately after, we knew it was back to our daily remote existence at the inn.

During the early 30s, the US economy was rough. By 1936, the financial system had tumbled into a deep mire. However, our life was comfortable; we always were well taken care of in that regard—'well off' is how it might be characterized. There was always money there for us. Father steered the ship through rough times, keeping his world completely intact. He greatly admired isolationists like Charles Lindbergh who didn't want to get involved in any wars. Of course, others were of a different mind. Father also made no bones about his high regard for Germany's economy which had flourished under Hitler's power since 1933.

Throughout that decade, Father had become quieter, even more serious. Even so, our annual trips always happened without fail. Olivia and I were absorbed with our own interests—we had limited time to enjoy the city, to enjoy the busy days and the exciting night life. There were new hats and dresses to buy, and culture to experience; we went off daily with mother and had a gay time. Woodsum accompanied Father during the day, always returning without explanation as to where they'd been or what they did. We were to assume it was business, and that Woodsum was learning how to be a man with Father as his guide and mentor. Fact of the matter is, he was always tightlipped and sullen as the vacation progressed. We never thought to question where he went. We were having fun. It was a time to be grand, to enjoy our freedom.

And so, it was during what was to become our last trip the last week of December, 1938 on the cusp of our nineteenth birthday, that we learned a bit more of the ulterior purpose of those annual trips.

One night, we were asked to join a large table of Father's friends, all who enjoyed many laughs, fine wine, and heated conversation about politics and the involvement of government in private life and business. Most notably, many of the guests were young men, handsome, charming, and educated.

Mind you, in those days, women rarely shared their own views on politics. We listened, and nodded, and politely supported whatever position was being touted. Of course, we were aware that Nazi Germany and Japan were united against the Soviet Union, that Japan had invaded China initiating WWII in the Pacific, and that Great Britain was being boxed into a corner. We were isolationists. We had learned that term early from Father.

The men discussed politics—sometimes in hushed tones—and we listened in amidst all the pleasantries and Mother's encouragement that we be courteous and charming. We heard one man say quite offhandedly that FDR was a tool of the Jews who wanted us to fight Hitler for the sole reason of saving Jews. This pronouncement shocked me.

Another fellow with downy red hair and flushed cheeks smugly told Olivia and me of an escapade he had been involved in, as one of many who had taken part in a demonstration the previous April on East 86th Street at the Yorkville Casino on the upper East Side. It had quickly turned into a riot that involved five thousand people! Proudly, he expounded the virtues of America First, and another group called the German-American Bund. The others on the opposing side, he scoffed, were proud but very misguided war veterans.

I came to realize these men were sympathizers to the German cause. It was easy to interact on a social level: they were handsome young men of a superior class and style, all with a plethora of opinions centered on their fervor for the German way of life.

In particular that evening, there was a mature-looking man of tall stature seated directly across from me—not handsome, but enigmatically striking—with blonde finely-curved eyebrows and faultless fair skin belying his age, which couldn't be more than late twenties, and serious gray eyes that paused and softened as they rested on my questioning countenance. He had a slight German accent—barely recognizable—which instantly caught my attention. His name was Michel Hydrick. *Such an interesting face!* His erect posture and serious demeanor gave one to believe he had a military background.

He was polite and intelligent, choosing his words eruditely. His wit was keen but dry; he rarely cracked a smile as we exchanged pleasantries across the crowded, zealous banter around us. I couldn't take my eyes off him: he was mature, articulate, and charismatic. He told us he was a professor of ornithology and herpetology on extended leave from Heidelberg University. Herpetology, he explained, was a branch of zoology concerned with the study of amphibians—including frogs, toads, salamanders, newts, and the like—and reptiles (including snakes, turtles, terrapins, tortoises, and crocodilians). 'How fascinating!' I said, 'Please, go on!' In fact, he said he had just returned from extensive field study related to evolutionary biology in the Galapagos. To a young girl such as myself with little life experience outside of Saltash Mountain, I found his story enthralling and told him so.

By way of further introduction, he related his background to me—born in London to German parents, educated in the best schools with study abroad first in Natural Sciences and then at Cambridge where he received two doctoral degrees.

He was well-traveled, indicating his visa allowed him to move freely while he converted his journal to a book to be entitled *The Evolution and Development of South American Chelonians*. 'Oh, my—Chelonians!' I said. He patiently explained with a variety of accompanying hand gestures that chelonians were reptiles with a shell or bony plates, the top of which is called a carapace, the underside a plastron, the two connected by a bridge, whose jaws are covered by a horny beak. They are nocturnal plant animals, generally reclusive; the type he was most interested in were land-dwelling. I continued to listen until he smiled in the sweetest way (I suppose at my enthralled face) and declared, 'Commonly known as…tortoises.' 'Oh!' I stuttered, "Of course!" We laughed together.

It seemed he paid only polite attention to me through the rest of the evening, conversing with Olivia on my right and Woodsum on my left—that is, until I rose from the table to excuse myself, at which point he moved with lightning quickness from his chair and came round the table. In his clipped fashion, he said, 'Miss Aurelia, the pleasure is mine. May I accompany you?' His use of my name fell like shimmering diamonds to my senses—to say I fell instantly in love would be accurate. I blushed, wondering if the group could see my discomfort. Why was he paying me attention, I wondered, as I excused myself. With Father's approval, he walked me to my room. On the way, though, he talked with a passion. The world was changing, he said. He asked me to wait outside his room, saying he had something to show me. When he returned, he had his littlest acquisition, a 'baby' tortoise he had brought back from the Galapagos. It was the size of a round hatbox.

That was my first meeting with Horatio. He was just a youngster at the time!

Michel's eyes glowed as he watched me enjoy the little beauty up close. After a while, he said, 'Well. Shall we continue to your room?' Carrying Horatio like a best buddy, he walked me to the room and said a formal good-night. That was the extent of our interaction, yet it was to stay with me.

I wonder now why Father included us in that dinner with his political friends? Were we being groomed in some way? Was it my purpose to be introduced and meet a young man with the same views as Father?

I learned he was much older; he was a mature man of twenty-six! I spent many an hour day-dreaming about this mature gentleman and our imaginary courting. I carried that musing back to Vermont with me. We returned home to our little world atop the Saltash. I never thought I would ever see this fine man again.

Imagine my amazement one hot day in June when Father announced he had invited Professor Michel Hydrick to come stay with us for what he described as an extended visit. He would arrive within the week! We learned he would do his research undisturbed in father's lair down in the barn. In exchange, he would provide instruction to Woodsum with the intention that he would be accepted at some point for college at nearby Middlebury.

I was intrigued, *nee* elated. My handsome outsider with so much to talk about—coming to live at the inn! Father also implied that we (Olivia and I) would be offered an opportunity to soak up whatever learning we could in his presence. Dare we also hope Father might allow our further education, too? As unbending as he was his political philosophy, Father believed in our enrichment, and encouraged us girls to learn as much as we could from this very important man so that 'you will be ready for the new order.'

A day or so before Michel's arrival, a large wooden box was delivered. I happened to be down at the barn when it arrived. Father was tightlipped as he and Woodsum got it upstairs. As I've already told you, I was always inquisitive. It made me curious, such an odd large box. It was stored in the back out of the way. The next day, when Father went to pick up Michel at the train station, I took Father's key from the ring in his work pants—he would never think I would be so bold—and tiptoeing up the stairs, entered his research area.

The big box was just inside; hay cluttered the floor, indicating it had been opened and emptied. Beside it, a large item was covered by a blanket. I gingerly lifted the blanket and was taken aback to see a strange machine the likes of which I'd never seen: modern-like, with a typewriter of sorts, but the keys were different—odd buttons—and attached below, a set of two odd foot pedals. The contraption reminded me of a pumping organ. I looked closer but could not decipher the funny symbols on each key—they weren't letters in the English language, to be sure. Two large batteries sat on the floor underneath. I wondered if it was in fact a musical device of some kind, a new invention—something to do with Michel's herpetology studies, or something that Father and Michel were collaborating on. To this day, I have no idea what it was. I asked Woodsum later if he knew what was in the box. He said (with a bit of a glower) he had not been allowed to be present when the box was opened. I put it out of my mind. I bring it up now because it stands out in my remembrance as an unusual occurrence of sorts, something to be noted.

He arrived at Mount Holly Mansion Inn with little fanfare late that night with Horatio in tow and settled into his warm, inviting room—of course, he was welcomed into our world with open arms.

From the day of his arrival, time went by in such a pleasant manner—six wonderful months. Because Father thought he was special, and that we should be honored to have him with us, he was given one of the paying guest rooms to live in free of charge. Father's frugality had been superseded by his respect for Michel, who occupied the room in the men's wing nearest the back stairs, the one called *Michel's Choice*. Father said it would be the best, because of his need to rise early and leave by the back entrance to access the barn for his experiments. There were also times when he would leave the premises with Father's approval for a day or two and then return. When he wasn't spending time with us, he was locked in the research room, where Father would often join him. We were told never to disturb them.

Meanwhile, we would meet for our extraordinary lessons daily: invigorating, exciting, field trips; wonderful group activities and scavenger hunts; philosophical coaching and instruction in German. He focused on each of us individually: our interests, our personalities. He was the best teacher we ever had. Over time, we three became four, all of us the best of friends. You see, we let him into our triumvirate—the inner sanctum where no one had ever been allowed. I was to learn later that we all personally thought we were his best friend. I know he made Olivia feel special, and Woodsum, too. However, at the time, I believed that what developed between the two of us was very special, different than with them.

It wasn't long before I fell hopelessly under the spell of this wonderful man. His advances were subtle, yet deliberate. He was very…convincing. Over time, my trust in him overrode every good and common sense trait I possessed. We would meet alone—something not encouraged or condoned in those days. At first I was conflicted; I knew it was a risk; I also knew it was inappropriate. That said, I threw caution to the wind. During the day, it could be a fleeting moment in the library, where we would find a quiet corner. As time went on, it intensified.

We had a special way of communicating. Mother's desk in the library had all those nooks and crannies. Little as they were, we could be creative in what we shared—special things for each other—every day or so. It started during the scavenger hunts with little notes for each other. I owned a special little decoupage box purchased in New York the previous year, in which we would leave each other tiny treasures. A found four-leaf clover; a beautiful smooth stone shaped in a heart from the brook, a sweet peppermint candy. His penmanship was very concise, and he had the uncanny ability to write in a very minuscule script. So, I would find his miniature written messages—often in German, filled with his innermost thoughts—and eventually, his love for me. He told me everyone had choices, and I was his to choose.

As time went on, we would steal down to the barn late at night where we could talk unencumbered. Our sounds were muffled in the grain room. He told me he would not leave me. I was to become his in every sense of the word. He promised me we would be together.

As enamored as I was, I couldn't help but notice the distance growing between sister, brother, and me. Olivia seemed quick to snipe over any odd task; Woodsum, who had initially blossomed under his tutelage, grew quieter, and often seemed conflicted. With those two who had been my world, it was what was left unsaid that seemed most hurtful. We all three seemed to have become secretive, more protective of our private time. We avoided each other, the opposite of what had been the norm our whole lives. I was completely preoccupied. I made a most conscious *choice*—to be committed to Michel and our clandestine liaisons.

That fateful long weekend of the big storm—what Mother called our birthday weekend—had been in the planning for weeks. Father decided abruptly there would be no New York City trip. His only explanation was that it was important for us to be at the inn. Mother, as usual, went along but insisted we have a birthday bash in the same way we would normally commemorate: the night before with a celebration when the clock struck midnight.

The week before was spent preparing—the inn was chock full of supplies in anticipation of a weekend of festivity. By Friday check-in, the place was bustling with guests—we were all busy; there was tension in the air. The influx of guests made it much more difficult for Michel and me to meet. In addition, he seemed preoccupied, more intent on business with Father than with me. However, my first chance to steal away, I met him that Saturday night down at the barn. It was close to midnight, and the fateful storm was bearing down upon us—which made it all the more romantic. There was a sense of urgency, of longing... as always, I was completely under his spell. I remember he said, 'Tomorrow night at this time, go to the library. Look in our place. It will be there for you.' We would turn twenty at the stroke of midnight. Sunday night's festivities were almost cancelled due to the burgeoning storm, but Mother uncharacteristically insisted the party continue—it was our twentieth birthday, a most momentous day, she said.

And so the stage was set and the party began. Midst all the games and the like, I was so consumed with curiosity I scooted into the library and, with no one there, looked inside the cubby. But it wasn't there—yet. I returned to the festivities, gave Michel a mischievous look, and he smiled covertly. We were never alone. As the midnight hour approached, each bong of Grandfather Clock told us our birthday hour neared. Oh yes, back in those days, Grandfather had a place of honor in the front foyer, at the hub of everything so everyone knew the time. Everyone, guests and friends, were preoccupied with the raging storm outside. It had taken on a vengeance—a good ol' Nor'easter, people chuckled nervously. We knew we were safe inside and no one was going anywhere. The wine flowed freely as the minutes ticked closer. Everyone was brought together into the front parlor.

With midnight finally minutes away and a great deal of hullabaloo, the cake was wheeled in midst cheers and singing. I admit I was caught up with it all for those few minutes. However, as things settled down, I noticed Michel had gone missing.

First, I went to the library—no, the little box wasn't there; the space was completely empty. I went to the kitchen—no one was there, but I did notice, his boots were gone! Why had he gone outside in this weather? Brother came upon me and I couldn't hide how upset I was. Where was Michel? I pouted, off-handedly mentioning that he was probably down at the blasted barn working on that strange typewriter instrument—the one he, I assumed, spent time working on until I joined him late at night. Woodsum became madder than I'd ever seen him! He confronted me about being alone with him. 'He's taken advantage of you! You know better! You shouldn't be goin' down there!' he hissed under his breath. I told him, 'This isn't the time to get angry, Woodsum. I need to know he's all right. I love him.' His face was stony but he promised he would try to find him. At the very least, he would go down to the barn in the blizzard and check if he was there.

The party quickly died down. Everyone went to bed. I was worried enough to gather my nerves together and ask Father if he knew where Michel was. He watched my face, oddly, and then said with disdain. 'Haven't I given you everything? The Professor has a purpose much greater than you and our existence here. Go to bed, daughter.' I honestly to this day don't know what he meant, especially about Michel's purpose. His answer only gave me more worry. I stayed up, racked with anxiety as the storm howled and raged.

I roamed the long empty hallway of the inn like a crazed woman, worrying like the dickens. Each time I passed the clock its whirs and tick-tocks seemed to grow more desperate, louder, even more injurious to my waning good sense. I couldn't stand it! I returned to the kitchen to wait at the back door for what seemed like hours. At some point, sister joined me and insisted on knowing what was going on. I told her that brother had gone to look for Michel, that he was gone. Her eyes were frantic, yet she didn't say a word, just sat in the rocking chair, rocking back and forth. Finally, around 4:00 a.m., brother came in with the arctic blast, totally spent from his icy search. He looked frightful! He was chilled to the bone, unable to catch his breath. His fingers were raw and near frostbitten. We settled him by the cookstove and wrapped a blanket round him. I realized how lucky we were that he hadn't perished in the storm. He was reticent, almost grim, confessing he'd been unsuccessful in his search.

'Not at the barn or anywhere?' I asked, near hysteria.

He shook his head and his speech faltered from the chill. He reluctantly admitted to have given up. 'Sister,' he said, 'he's not the person we thought he was.' I covered my ears, but sister agreed, 'He's come between us three intentionally. He has broken us down, one by one.' She shared her feelings, and other things were disclosed about his character, things, quite honestly, I resisted believing. We all cried together—not just at the anxiety of not knowing where Michel was, but at the realization of our loss of closeness with each other those last few months. Even though he wouldn't say, we both knew Woodsum was angry about Michel leaving. Knowing now what we did about each one's feelings of duplicity was overwhelming—and so sad. We got him warmed up, but he still was adamant that we were lucky to be rid of him. Woodsum suggested we say nothing and wait. If Father wasn't concerned about Michel, he likely knew something we did not. In the early hours of dawn, we made a unilateral decision to sit tight and let the chips fall—when and if he returned, his truth or deception could be proven one way or the other. It was just as Woodsum said earlier. We three clasped each others' hands and promised, 'We'll stick together no matter what we run into or how hard things get.'

Michel was gone into the night. The next morning, we searched his room. His valise was gone, along with some of his personal belongings, so his intent was clear. There was no note for me—nothing to indicate he wanted me to know he was leaving. He had disappeared. But Hoity was there, under his bed! He must be coming back, I rationalized. He would never have left Horatio, who he was so fond of, or his plants, his research—but above all, me? He must have my little decoupage box with him, I reasoned. From that day on, I never received any word from him. As we dug out from the horrific storm throughout the next two weeks, I waited and watched for a sign from him. As time went on, my hope diminished. I wondered... had he lost his way in the storm? Would we find his body in the spring? Why, oh why, had he left without telling me? I confess I was in private agony during that time, although I tried to put on a good face. I know in my heart he would not have abandoned our love in such a way, so I've always held out hope that he would return...if he was alive.

No matter what Woodsum tells you, I cannot believe he was doing anything bad. I know someone—probably Father—got rid of that contraption the barn. I don't know what it was used for. I never saw it again. Every remnant of his research was removed, too. Father remained mum, never to discuss where Michel might have gone, or why he might have left, up until his death two months later when the barn burned down. Mother passed just after him—heartbreak is a terrible thing.

After our parents died, we were left to be in charge of the inn. We weren't used to being on our own, sheltered as we had been. I pined for Michel, thought I would die if he never returned to me. Every day I focused on what I thought he might want me to do, about the life we would have had—or have when he returned. We eased into a routine. With my new authority at the inn (by default, mind you), I decided to rename his bedroom *Michel's Choice*— for two reasons (one good, the other terrible to imagine)—firstly, for what I believed would be his inevitable return; lastly, in his memory if we learned someday that he was dead.

At that time, I remember Olivia seemed too apathetic to care. Woodsum was much too busy dealing with the imminence of war and its repercussions. Recruiting had intensified and he had duties to perform here at the inn and elsewhere.

I couldn't bear each day, each month that went by; time became the enemy. The sound of the clock reminded me so much of that night, wandering the halls. Because of that, Grandfather Clock was banished to the closet.

It seemed I was in charge a good amount of the time—something I wasn't used to. Selfishly, I chose to keep a room for myself when it wasn't occupied—the bedroom directly across the hall from Michel's—and renamed it *Golden Desire*. As ridiculous at it sounds, I found comfort meeting there late at night with Horatio. You see, he was my link with Michel. We both loved him, even as he had left Horatio for me to care for. We spent such a lovely time together in that room, reminiscing about Michel—over time, it became *my* guilty pleasure. I prefer to remember him in a good way.

Time has flown by...so many years. So, so long, but my passion is still there!

And that is my story, my reason, my secret.

Did you know the name Aurelia means *The Golden One* in Latin? That's what my Michel always said, 'You are my Golden Desire.' That is what I choose to keep in my heart. Always. That I was his one, true golden desire, his choice, as he was mine. Despite anything different brother and sister have ever believed or told me, or that they will tell you.

Yup. June of 1939 through January 8th, 1940. Quite the time. The best of times and, frankly, the worst for me, as well.

You've heard Aurelia's point of view. Mine in some ways is the same; in others, completely different.

I'll start by telling about that last trip to New York City in 1938. Our family was always governed by one person—Father—and he ruled with an iron hand. Whatever he said, went, at the inn or anywhere else. Mother went along with everything; she was a willing partner, believe you me.

My own beliefs belied the dutiful son actions I showed to the world. Not so much as anyone took notice, but more inside my head. Oftentimes his overbearing nature squelched my creativity but back then, it was the way fathers and sons related. In my early years, I truly did try to please him, to be more like him constantly.

However, over time I realized our differences were too great. I suffered his wrath and displeasure often. 'You must live up to the family name, Son.' Work at the inn was paramount—along with loyalty to him. He allowed me one pleasure—photography. I think he thought it might one day help him in some way. The annual trip was one of the few things that everyone looked forward to—except me. It began in my early years and continued every year thereafter. Y'see, I knew what I would be in store for. It wasn't fun at all for me—in fact, it caused conflict and upset in my life. Certainly, I wasn't the fellow with the sunny disposition you now see here.

You see, Father and I went to *meetings* all day. 'What kind of meetings?' you might ask. He called them rallies—me, sitting on the sidelines watching with little interest, not really understanding; Father, smoking his pipe and joining into the discussions—often with great zeal. There were men of merit at these meetings—pillars in their communities from across the United States who, I learned, followed another political philosophy called the NSDAP—*Nationalsozialistische Deutsche Arbeiterpartei,* better known as the Nazi Party of Germany. The Nazi Party of Germany was organized in eight different layers of strict command called the Ortsgruppe, the first layer governed by the leader of Germany—the Fuehrer, Adolf Hitler. Nazi Party officials had given authority to form an American Nazi organization which, as time went on, became known as 'The German American Bund,' a group of American citizens who were ardent Nazi followers here in the United States who mimicked the structure and beliefs of the Nazi Party.

This was my introduction; early on in my younger years it seemed more like game-playing. I had happily complied, thinking it was a way to please Father. But as time went on, I realized it was evil. Father was intense, demanding secrecy, fervent to the point of fanatical. The Bund held rallies with Nazi insignia and procedures. At these meetings I observed Father exhibit a zealousness he never demonstrated back in our world at the inn. It gave way to confusion for me, as a naive teen. What did I think of this world I had been dropped into? I was introduced to words like 'Nazi' and 'Storm Troopers', used with pride by these fellow Americans. The meetings were opened by giving the Nazi salute—by raising one's arm rigidly, fingers pointed in the air with an accompanying 'Sieg Heil!' At the close of the meetings enthusiastic songs were sung honoring Nazi 'heroes' followed by a triple 'Sieg Heil!' salute. Most importantly, I learned how passionate Father was; his political interests were entrenched in this philosophy. I listened while he and others vilified our President, President Roosevelt, and attacked Jewish groups. I felt trapped, but I played along to make Father happy. Shame on me, but it was the way I coped with it as a young man who felt he had no control over his life.

About that night in 1938 that Aurelia described: I already knew before my sisters that we were going to meet some of these men again that evening—it would be a first for them. I overheard Father making the arrangement with a few of the other Bundmen. It was to be a celebration of the brightest young men and their efforts at Father's expense—and a chance to introduce some eligible young bachelors to his daughters. I wanted to warn them, but didn't. And so, we were joined at our posh hotel for this special dinner, all described to my sisters by Mother as 'men whose views Father so admired.'

I can cut to the chase right here. The most impressive man there who everyone seemed to listen to and admire was this guy named Michel Hydrick. He was described as a world traveler. I cottoned to him because I had never seen him at the Bund meetings so that was good; I didn't know why he was at our dinner but he stood out. He was articulate and had an air of refined authority. He was attentive to us three, as though he was making a special effort. I sure appreciated that and it stayed with me after we returned home.

Y'see, I was a young country bumpkin with no refinement. I felt like I had five thumbs and would trip over my feet. All I knew was what was on top of the Saltash Mountain. When he showed up in our world, I was pretty happy. I thought Father might have some ulterior motive, more than saying he was finishing up his research and getting me ready for college, but I didn't care. Here was a fellow I could learn from. Most of my 'instruction' was hands on—and a lot was confidence-building. We spent a lot of time outdoors—he loved learning about all the surrounding trails so we hiked all over. He constantly was telling me to test myself, to be at the height of my strength. We worked out together. Sports-minded as he was, he was a master rock climber. He taught me the ropes, as they say, and we scaled a number of the more demanding sites in the area—he kept copious notes of those mountain challenges. He loved soccer, and lacrosse, like I mentioned before. And as winter came, you guessed it—ice hockey. He proved to be proficient at that, too. He was good at everything, and good with everybody. He had so much else to offer—not just book-learning, but socially. He was sophisticated. He taught me how to conduct myself. When I was with him, I felt I was the most important person in the world to him. It seemed like he was the first fellow that accepted me for who I was but encouraged me to be more.

He was talkative, amusing, charming. He could hold you spellbound with his stories of travel and adventure. His stories were so vivid, so detailed you couldn't help but believe every word—I often wondered how could someone make that stuff up? He was so engaging you couldn't help but love being in his circle. Well, I can tell you he bowled me over with his ideas. What a swell fellow, I thought. He knew how to make you feel good about yourself, even if you were a rube like me. Sad to say, that's just how I thought of myself. A simple fellow with not much to offer—Father had fostered that doubt in me. But with all that encouragement, I began to believe I was special. One thing I can't deny—even though his views on war were the reverse of mine, I wanted to believe all of his learning and experience had given him the answers I was looking for. I even began to close my eyes to some parts of who I was just so as to be closer to him.

This picture here of me and him together? Olivia told me she showed you this already. We look happy, don't we? I set up the tripod and the timer. It was like that with him and me. He encouraged me to take more photos, to expand my horizons. To be something more. This photo—that's how I like to remember him—engaging. Here he stands tall; he had a strong stance, you know? Like a real man, is how I saw him. How I wanted to be at the time. He was charismatic and so darn smart—but daring, too. See it in his face—no fear there. You see what's wrote on the back? 'Happy Times.' He wrote that, not me.

Now I've painted a pretty picture, let me tell you about his other side I learned about slowly, over time. My sisters and I each held him in esteem in our own personal way. Y'see, he had a way of being who you wanted or needed him to be. But he was so crafty it was quite amazing how he could pull you in and control you. I began to notice the small but very convincing web he was weaving at the inn. For awhile, I admit I wore blinders. Even as we all knew in our gut he was misleading us, he was so darn convincing we overlooked it.

Here's the bad news. He could be arrogant and full of himself. He wasn't truthful—said one thing and did another. I guess that would mean he was a liar. I began to notice things about him weren't...real. Like he had a master plan, or a way to get whatever he needed regardless of who got hurt. For one, he seemed bent on dividing the solid bond my sisters and I had with each other. Looking back over time, I realized he would pit us one against the other in the subtlest of ways. Even worse, I believed he was caddishly playing with Aurelia's heart. One evening in late December, I was shocked to discover them alone down at the barn. Their embrace of passion was obvious. It just wasn't right—in so many ways. She was a sweet, naïve gal. I never said a word. Darned if Olivia didn't seem infatuated with him, too—but in a different way. He gave her lots of attention she wasn't used to. She'd always been kind of taken for granted. He expanded her mind with science books and grandiose ideas; he made her feel special when, sad to say, no one else did.

As he grew close with each of us, we grew farther apart. It was a subtle change. He seemed to know what to say, working on our minds and, eerily, capturing our hearts, all for his own gain.

Besides all this, I noted he would disappear without explanation—sometimes for a couple days at a time. He held his cards close to his chest, that one. He and Father had their secrets—it didn't include me or my sisters. Even though I was supposed to be the one Father should turn to, he didn't, I was sure, for his own particular reasons. Father never really ever thought I lived up to any of his expectations. I suspect Michel was more like a son to him than I ever was. My only logical conclusion was that their affiliation might be due to the Nazi Party—that was when he first came into our lives—so I steered clear of that mess as best I could. I really wanted no part of it. He and Father seemed to be a better fit in that regard, so I made a trade and let it go because Father could be unyielding in his demands—not to mention cruel. And, I overlooked Michel's manipulation as long as I could.

The night of our birthday party confirmed a lot about his character. After Aurelia told me all, I was furious. She begged me to find him and bring him back. I left knowing Olivia had gone to bed in a funk; she was mad at him for some reason—I think because he hadn't paid her enough attention. I kind of started putting things together in my mind and it really started to bug me. I was mad at Father for bringing him here, but I was madder at myself for believing him—and believing in him.

With the rest of the house asleep, I went out to find him.

In the midst of the blizzard, I could still hear the planes echoing in the sky high above. You see, during those past few months, a strange phenomenon had begun to occur nightly. The first few summer nights when it all began, it woke us up, but then we got used to it. Everyone in the Saltash area seemed to politely ignore it, as though it would cross a deportment line to discuss. In the dead of night, beginning around 1:00 a.m., a low steady rumble could be heard in the sky. Plane after plane would pass overhead, low enough to cast a larger shadow as the sky grew lighter, high enough to clear the vast towering mountain trees. We knew they were large armed forces planes, not your typical small engine variety we were used to seeing. The echoing growl, like a band of uneasy tigers, usually went on and on until dawn, at which point the sounds ceased and all things pastoral would return to quiet once again. Yup, we knew something was afoot. I heard whispers here and there at Lowry's General Store and the Grange Hall the few times I was there. However, not one newspaper article ever printed anything about it. No one but no one discussed where the planes were coming from, or where they were going.

The world might be a bustling place but our world here in Mount Holly was small, very small indeed. England entered the war with Germany that September while our country sat on the sidelines watching.

So, here's what everyone knew: the planes overhead must have something to do with an act of solidarity on our part—meaning the United States. It became routine; y'see, back then, no one questioned the big picture. To a man, we just assumed that somehow planes were being used to travel to unknown parts for the benefit of our country—and didn't talk about it.

As I say, I remember the planes that night I went out looking for him in the blizzard and came back without him. The storm was so intense, so blinding—to this day, the wind's echo and the planes' rumble reverberate in my ears, especially when I get overwhelmed.

Sister has told you my condition upon my return. Even though they had no idea the extent of my hurt feelings, like them both, I was devastated he was gone. I told sisters Michel was a scoundrel and to please not give him another thought. I even told them my greatest fear—that he (and by association, Father) might possibly be a spy—an idea they scoffed at. Regardless, he was gone in the night, valise and all, never to return. He took advantage of me and my good nature; he used me. I'm doubly angry at how he used my sisters. And that is all I will say about Michel Hydrick.

It's the aftermath that was most devastating to me.

We lost Father in the big barn fire that March. Mother passed just one month later, never recovering from shock of Father's death. In some ways it is a blessing: they never knew the suffering we would endure those years before the war began—and, not to mention, during the war.

Things got much worse for us all. As the war approached, I was forced to define who I really was and what I believed in.

I realized my only choice. You see, I was a conscientious objector. I was willing to sacrifice myself for my country, I just didn't want to kill anyone! I was what they called a secular pacifist—to me, it was just an unethical and unhumanitarian act to kill. My deep within religious thoughts—if that's what you call them—told me it was just plain wrong. Bottom line—I just could never get my head around killing any living thing—unless it was for food to exist—you know, hunting and the like. Even that was hard for me, but Father believed and said it often, 'Hunting and killing is part of what it takes to be a man.'

Taking a stand like this during that war meant you would certainly be ostracized, even an outcast. It began slowly with the first peacetime draft—almost a year before Pearl Harbor (December 7th, 1941), which then set the stage for every man of recruitment age showing his patriotism by joining up. While others became enthused about enlisting, I was distraught. I lost my appetite and suffered silently through a devastating nervous breakdown—so much had happened...with Michel... losing Father, and then Mother, and the responsibilities of the inn. We—sisters and I—suffered together; we took care of each other. I was in a fragile state, so very conflicted as the war effort reached a fever pitch. How I would live up to what others expected of me? I floated for about two years, working feverishly, helping the local effort. Finally, I was drafted in 1942. When the time came, I knew the only alternative was to ask for alternative service.

After that, I had many a 'friend' turn their back on me. Living in a small town—this is who could become enemies once you crossed the line from soldier to 'conchie.' The next year was a nightmare as I had to make my intention clear to all. I was willing to perform any tasks they could come up with—even medical guinea pig or smoke jumper—anything where I didn't have to kill. Other conchies went to federal prison if the officials thought they were lying. Matter of fact, after the war I learned there were more than 30,000 conchies all over the US who performed alternative service. Hence, I brought my conscience to the forefront and declared who I had to be.

I guess I must have convinced them when I went before the board. I was assigned to a CPS camp—Civilian Public Service—it offered legal alternative service under civilian command. They had one over the line in northern New Hampshire—deep in the White Mountain National Forest near Gorham—and run by the American Friends Service Committee with the U.S. Forest Service. You can't believe every type of human being that was there—doctors, artists, atheists, students, fellas from all walks of life and religions. That was October, 1942. We had one thing in common—our belief that war was just wrong. It was pretty crude there, to say the least. They trained us in timber management, fire control, and maintenance of trails, highways, and telephone lines. Turns out most of the locals would have rather seen their village burned down than use a conchie to fight it. Mostly, they wanted to keep us out of sight so we wouldn't have a negative impact on morale. We were a problem—they said people like me were even more dangerous than common criminals. And they didn't let up, I can tell you that. Some couldn't take it and left the camp in protest to join their comrades in prison—that was the only alternative, unless you were willing to get into the thick of battle as a medic or such.

I heard horrific stories of what they did to those in prison. At the CPS camp, I worked nine-hour days, six days a week at hard labor. We paid the government $35 a month for room and board. My sisters sent the money, even as they ran the inn on a shoestring. I knew it was hard for them—but they never wavered, never complained. When that camp closed in April of 1943, I was transferred out West to Provo, Utah under the Mennonite Central Committee. That was a mental health facility. I was assigned to the insulin and electric shock unit. Yup, I learned a lot about melancholia. Fact is, it made me a better person. We had Sunday school lessons there, everyone sang in the choir, and I met some nice people. I wasn't released from my alternative service until 1946 when that part of the facility closed in

April—a year after the war ended. Actually, they punished a lot of the conchies by keeping them in camps and prisons far longer than the war lasted.

When I returned back to Rutland County I was still Woodsum Pettyfer, but some others thought differently. I was kicked out the door by shop owners I'd known my whole life. People who knew where I'd been turned their backs on me. It wasn't pretty. I held my head high and just got on with things. The way I figured it, I was guilty of two things—my past sins, and my convictions about war. Never looked back, as they say. But then again, it was hard to look forward.

So, that's how the inn became my cocoon; my place of solace; my world in total. I kinda felt like I never grew up, that I was a failure for being so soft. When I came back and put my mind and body to work to make the inn a success, we three became one again. Sisters and I decided we would never talk about my conchie experience ever again. Where there had been conflict, we kept to our promise and came to always be there for each other. We decided to make the best of it, to offer our guests the ultimate comfort—but to do it in a happy way. Not only to offer shelter but to offer sanctuary to everyone without judgment. I figured if I couldn't make a better world out there, I was committed to make a better world here in our little world. So what if I had suffered for my choices? In the end, I think it was a good thing. To tell you the truth, sometimes I even liked it. It felt good to sweat and work hard with others less fortunate—to cleanse my soul. Some would still say today that I deserved it.

My granite bench on the trail? Its message—Amity—means the world to me.

I always had that edge to my personality. I'm sure you've noticed I can't abide an idle mind or body—and I've not much patience when it comes to talking about...my feelings. Woodsum and Aurelia tolerated it, as siblings do. Father, in his infinitely insensitive wisdom, used to say there was a reason mosquitoes never bothered me—too cold-blooded, he said. Imagine hearing that kind of thing from a young age on up through womanhood? In retrospect, I think I just inherited Mother's pragmatic side; I was a no-nonsense little girl, a hard worker, rarely ever time for a smile or enjoying life. I felt most comfortable with inanimate objects—tools, books, and the like—and immersed myself in learning. I grew to be quite cynical and very happy with my alone time. Forget about communing with nature, or loving animals, or reaching out to anyone. That was much too hard of a chore, I concluded, clinical as I was. I had lived my life as one of three—brother was attractive and so kind; sister, so pretty and sweet; leaving me, the quiet one with not much in the looks department—often (but I know now, not intentionally) passed over. I justified my standoffish demeanor logically: I had sister and brother—what more did I need to fill that niche? I could play my part, but no more. Everybody knew I excelled in school, but not in socialization. Consequently, very rarely did I make any friends—such as they were anyway, up on the mountain. As a matter of fact, I could count on one hand who those few were.

That is, until Michel came into our world.

Possy the First was brought as a gift from Michel—he handed him to me the first week and told me it was my *job* to care about something living, and so here was Possy. It was a new experience, taking care of something that responded back. He could be as cantankerous as I was to others—a real upfront study in my own failings. It was my fault that Possie randomly chewed the chair. Truth is, he was mad that I left him alone too long one day when I got sidetracked in the library. I didn't think it mattered enough to care for him. He took it out on the littlest creature he could find, and when I came upon the mess, I saw myself in that little mutt's face. I vowed not to do that again; after that, he followed me everywhere and grew on me. If Michel wanted me to take care of him, I knew it was right for me. Of course, we all fell in love with the little rascal and that was my first good lesson from Michel. It was also how he gained my trust.

The six months we had him to ourselves, he taught me so many things—mostly though, about the world of science, which I loved. I always thought I might have been a doctor, given the opportunity. However, that was never an option. Through Michel, I found I had a penchant for horticulture, plants, botany, and the like—and he fostered this, encouraged my research, made sure I was challenged. There were long discussions on a highly intellectual level—he stimulated my mind. He was the Professor; he loved books like me. In our intimate moments, we shared academic ideas and the way the world could be in the future if scientific progress could evolve without limitations. His field of concentration became of interest to me, also. He put me in charge of making sure Hoity-Toity was well-fed by cultivating plants most suitable for him.

As we became closer, I could envision us one day traveling together far away from the Saltash. I would, I imagined, accompany him on his many explorations to South America and beyond, and one day, we would go to Germany when things settled down in the world. He was a learned educator and I could very well be his assistant—or more. I will admit, I admired him from the first meeting, appreciated his mind…and fell in love with him.

But what did I come to realize? He was a scoundrel, a bounder in professor guise. Subtly, I began to notice his attentions were different toward sister. I observed the way he manipulated her: to my way of thinking, he had Aurelia completely convinced. Even then, I sensed he might be trouble for us three—but he was one of those people you just can't help but want to draw closer to. For Aurelia, he was the handsome prince who she thought was going to marry her. For Woodsum, he was the pal and strong mentor he had never had. For me? I was such a needy moth and he was the indestructible flame feeding my desire for attention and intellectual stimulation. Of course, I look back now and know these are all things I could have readily found on my own...if only I had had the confidence to do so.

Oh, tall tales—he could tell them with the best of them! As winter set in, I caught him in the little white lies—where he said he was when he left the mountain—meeting with professorial colleagues in Boston—what kind of research he was doing in that back room in the barn—herpetology, not likely. Although craftily fashioned, things didn't add up. I was smart enough to know when I was being placated, and still...I allowed him to direct me right up until the time he left. How do you protect yourself and others when they are completely enamored with such a charismatic individual, when they can't see the truth through their own rose-colored glasses?

I was there at every turn, wanting to be with him, refusing to believe he didn't care for me. My mind played tricks on me. On the one hand, I believed he respected me—God knows he told me that daily, how my intellect stimulated his own, how he saw a future in science with me working by his side. He convinced me it was best to keep this quiet, knowing Father might balk at this suggestion.

I left the comfort of my sister and brother's company to steal moments with him. I would follow him, watch him from afar. I began to find creative ways to spend alone time with my professor. After a time, I came to realize it wasn't me or my mind he was smitten with. Oh yes, no doubt he cared for me on some level, more for Aurelia. I wanted to beat her at this game—and, I wanted to protect her. She couldn't help how she felt. And, there was brother. 'Best mates' is what Woodsum would say about he and Michel, but I knew Woodsum *adored* him. He was such a kind fellow, and Michel knew how to manipulate that, too. Over time, my jealously of those two separate relationships got the better of me. I wished *no* goodwill on my siblings. Even as I could see how destructive he was to our relationship, I wanted *him* more than I wanted to mend things with Aurelia or Woodsum.

I was devastated that Saturday night when I followed Aurelia and watched them in the barn. I heard him tell her, in that slight German accent, that she would find something very special—not just a birthday gift, but something that would *change their lives*—in their hiding place in the library cubby. She would have to wait until midnight. With that silver tongue, he soothed her, assured her that they would be together. As I watched, my mind broke in two. I realized how far along their relationship had progressed. I left them hurt to the core, feeling the full impact of that meeting like a sucker punch to my gut.

The next afternoon, the inn was abuzz with activity. The last train had brought in weekend guests. Mother had planned this big bash and was adamant it would go off, despite the gathering storm. The inn was full to capacity and the merriment began. I watched Michel, waiting for my opportunity. He left the festivities; I followed him upstairs to his room. When he came out, he locked the door and tapped his breast pocket distractedly. I scooted down the back stairway and quietly stole into the library.

As we did when we were young, I hid in the closet where Grandfather Clock is now. I could see everything from my vantage point. When he came in I was ready. He placed something into the cubby. So, *that was their hiding place!* I wanted to show them what it was like to be hurting. I wanted to confront him and give him a piece of my mind then and there, but I froze. The closet was stifling; I was filled with a rush of anxiety. He loved Aurelia, or so he said; he had no use for me. He left the library and I was all alone in my misery.

Much later, when I joined Aurelia in the early morning hours in the kitchen, I was desperate. All I wanted was to forget he was ever in our lives. I was so conflicted, so confused. I felt guilty, knowing how glad I was he was gone—wherever he was now was better than causing us all pain here at the inn. What a fool I had been to think he cared for me. He had thrown me so off kilter.

I realize now I wasn't myself that night or for a long time after. I came to believe I could never trust a man ever again. He left us all, but I can't help but feel it was me who suffered the loss the most. When your innermost thoughts enjoy being victimized, there is nothing but self-loathing to comfort you. Right or wrong, I've blamed myself for many years. I wish I had confronted him and told him off good and proper! Not just scurried back into a corner and pined for something that wasn't. Oh, I've given him an earful in my mind many a time! It's terrible being a victim—a role I hate, one that has held me emotionally hostage for so many years—and has turned me into a pretty unpleasant old woman, much as I try.

Of course, we all want to know why he left without explaining. Woodsum had some cockamamie idea that he was a spy, and that Father was complicit. As much as I hate him, I hope it's not the case. We must acknowledge that if Father brought him here and he was doing something wrong, then he, too, was complicit in anything untoward Michel was up to. That's a hard pill to swallow. That's a secret we would hope would never see the light of day here at the inn.

Everyone knows during that time the rumors were running rampant throughout Rutland County about spies hidden away in the mountains, passing information. Hogwash! How in heaven's name could it happen right under our noses?

A part of me likes to think Michel went back to England and died in the war rather than what I do believe—that he died in the midst of the blizzard of the century. Being pragmatic and pessimistic as I am, I know both options would explain why he left, and why he never returned. But they wouldn't explain to me why it meant so much to him to destroy our three lives as he *so* deliberately tried to do. Wielded power can be very cruel.

Our pact that night saved my life in so many ways. To know that we three were as one again was the foundation I would build the rest of my life on.

The years of the war and after are like a fog. I remember working, working, working. Pushing through the pain of lost opportunities—and, I must admit, unrequited affection. I set my feelings aside, hid them in a little imaginary box and pushed through. Cooking, cleaning, tinkering, organizing, greeting and meeting new people—it was my way of moving on. The inn is always here, a comfort in life's storm, a place to put yourself when you don't know where else you should be. And, it will be my place to die when it is time.

It's just as well Father passed before the war got underway. I think he would have been more and more troubled, more agitated and mentally unstable. As it was, he caused enough difficulty in our lives. I don't forgive him for the way he treated us—me in particular. And I certainly don't forgive him for bringing Michel into our lives and causing all the pain.

As they always say, 'the work never fails you.' The inn and the work has never failed me.

And neither have my sister and my brother—ever. They are my constant. Who could I always depend on through every challenge life threw us? We have depended on each other to survive. We did a fine job together making this inn the cheerful, homey place it became; admired by those special few who were invited to join us. We are lucky. Word of mouth gave us a comfortable existence and here we are today. I thank God for my sister and brother. They are everything to me. Our love for each other superseded any of the damage that man caused, even though I know we have suffered at his deception. If I've had a hand in carrying any of that poison these years, I want to make things right—today.

PART THREE

*Trust, Truth,
... and the Future*

Chapter I

Collateral Damage

It had been a long day, without relief, as all three had recounted their tale. The megastorm had hit its stride and now seemed to be marginally subsiding just as mid-afternoon set in.

Erin, who had held remarkable reserve throughout the telling, gave a resounding clap. Her face was flushed with emotion. "Ach! I've never heard such a tale in all me days. It's romantic...but so sad."

"Pathetic." Olivia's voice held regret, "I've always agreed with Woodsum on one point. He was a cad. Someone you would never want in your life."

Aurelia struggled at being confronted with her siblings' stories. "You are right about one thing, Olivia. We all three worked to make the inn a success. Through our twenties, then through our thirties..." her voice trailed off, saddened.

Olivia added, "And...as they always say, time just flew by. How jealous was I. I've known for years it was wrong. I just didn't know how to bring it all to the surface and put it to rest—until you arrived." Her eyes turned wide and sorrowful to Mrs. Bundle. "I know now how important it was for you to help us. I wish it could have happened much sooner."

It's just as I thought, everything about the trip has been serendipitous—finding the secret box, the open invitation to the mansion, and my role in bringing the secrets out. What Mrs. Bundle needed now, she prayed, was helping them sort it all out. "I'm happy to be here with you all. After hearing all three accounts, I must say it appears he did not have any of your best interests at heart—except, possibly you, Aurelia."

"He *never* said he was going away. But there was nothing there. Nothing there left for me—except Horatio. He must have wanted me to take care of him until he came back." Aurelia's look was sad, with intense longing. "He wasn't lost! We would have found him. He didn't run off and leave me. How could he do that? He would *never*, ever have done that. He loved me."

Mrs. Bundle knew it was time; she began, "Olivia—"

Olivia's words burst forth, "It's my fault! He *did* love you!"

Aurelia was startled, "Sister? What do you mean?"

"I've done a very bad thing. I didn't want you to have it. I overheard you and Michel. I followed him and saw where he hid it. I knew it was special, but not...like this. I really didn't..."

Aurelia was struggling to understand her sister. "What? What did you *do*?"

"I did the worst thing possible. I hid it...in the black wicker chair. Inside, where Possy chewed the arm of the wicker away. It—it was the same color. It fit. Afterward, I couldn't bring myself—I just couldn't bear the thought of retrieving it. It's been there all this time." She inhaled with exertion. "Oh, god!"

"Olivia?" Aurelia's shoulders were stiff, taking it all in, disbelieving what exactly her sister was saying.

"I was jealous of you and wanted him for myself." She covered her face with the crook of her arm. "I'm so, so sorry. I let you believe he left with no message for you." She reached out and pleaded with her sister, "I intended to... my heart was broken, too! I harbored a sense of bitterness...all my life. Aurelia—?" Her voice was strangled with emotion as she opened her hand and revealed the tiny decoupage box.

With shaking hands, Aurelia gasped, reaching out, "You? You hid it?" Olivia released it to her sister, who immediately noticed the loosened gutta percha tape and moaned, crestfallen. "And...opened it, too?"

Mrs. Bundle interceded, "Not Olivia. Me. I'm sorry. It should have been you first."

"Geez, Lou-eeezze!" Angie exclaimed. "It's the box?"

"Oh, Miss Aurelia," Erin whispered, overcome with emotion. "Your special gift...?"

Aurelia read the top written in the gutta-percha. "January 8, 1940. *Our Secret*. Oh, Michel." With excruciating care, she removed the top and looked inside. Gasping, she drew out the untarnished ring delicately.

Angie couldn't hold in the "Wow," under her breath.

Blinking back the tears, Aurelia adjusted her glasses, drew in a deep breath, and studied it. "At last," she said. She read the inside aloud. "*Michel's Wahl.*" And then, "*Goldener Wunsch.*"A deep shudder overtook her body—a mixture of elation and sorrow—and she sobbed, "I *was* his choice! Michel's *wahl*—that means 'choice'! I was his and his alone. *Goldener Wunsch*—Golden Desire! That is exactly what he always told me—that is what I was to him. Oh, mercy me. All these many, many years." She put the ring to her lips and kissed it tenderly, then placed it on her finger where, with no doubt or exception, it likely would stay for the rest of her life.

Olivia sighed, completely drained, "I planned on giving it back to him—if he ever returned. He never did. Time went by. I'm sorry. I'm so terribly sorry. Can you ever forgive me?"

"All these secrets and subterfuge between us are over. We are left with the love we have for each other. Of course I forgive you, dear sister." Aurelia wiped a tear. "I now have the ending to my tale. He wanted to marry me." She looked at the group with sanguine eyes, "He had to leave, you see...because he had important things to do...more important than even us. But he did love me. He did." She closed her eyes. When she opened them, her face was serene as she looked at Mrs. Bundle. "Cousin Milly told us you were special. You've helped us. Thank you."

Mrs. Bundle knew her work was almost done.

Olivia took her sister's hand, "It's been a long day. We can all breathe easier now. It's over."

"We've told our truths." Aurelia said. "We've acknowledge Michel changed us *and* even came between us for a while. But we came back together as three again."

"You're the best, sister."

Woodsum added with finality, "Now, let's move on. It's behind us."

"A-*men!*" Erin pronounced. "And maybe, once we're all rested, we can have a party for you all tonight! I'll help!" She snapped her fingers as a lightbulb thought entered her brain, "Couldn't we celebrate *every* birthday you've missed over all these years? Aye, it would be a humdinger, for sure!" She whispered something to Mrs. Bundle.

"I—agree." Olivia smiled a genuine, relaxed grin. "They say every year on your birthday you get a chance to start anew. So, let's do have a party! Woodsum, you can get out your camera and take some photographs! And Aurelia, how 'bout dancing—wouldn't that be fun? We'll get out the old Victrola and all of our favorite 78s!"

"Hey, what say we all get dolled up for dinner? I'll get out my zoot suit! Wait'll you see my duds!" Woodsum added. "And—we'll share our birthday celebration with our girlie Angie here, too. Right, sisters?" They heartily endorsed his idea with clapping as he tapped Angie's shoulder.

"Besides in your cupboard, Erin, there's loads of dresses up in the attic!" Olivia offered. "What do you think?"

"Sounds like a blast," Angie said. "I'm in!"

"Chicken on a biscuit!" Woodsum hooted, "We're really gonna put on the Ritz tonight!"

"We can make 2006 the best birthday ever! Having a party's the best idea I've heard in—*decades!*" Aurelia put her hand to her mouth and snorted, "See? I made a joke!"

The fever pitch was reaching monumental proportions—and the Pettyfer Triplets were…Happy!

Erin, with Mrs. Bundle's permission, was off to the front hallway where she found the striker and, with great flourish, sounded the huge gong. She yelled so loud above the din her Irish lilt reached every corner, "Storm's almost over, folks! And, aye, that's a good thing! C'mon lads and lasses—we're having a *party*! Happy, happy, birthday, everyone! Yaaaa-*hooooey*!"

Chapter II

Still Prisoners Within a Fortress?

The next morning, the good news was that the snow had finally stopped, leaving a winter wonderland of dramatic proportions outside. The bad news: snow banks buffered the mansion like ice-covered marshmallows; some of the peaks reached all the way up into the first floor window frames—virtually 7' high. Egress from the house was impeded from all sides, like a moat around a fortress.

With the previous day so grueling and the evening so hugely festive, all had slept in, rising for breakfast at mid-morning.

After a solid breakfast, Angie joined Woodsum for an investigative tour around the property to assess the damage and impact of the storm. Wrapped in hats, mufflers, and heavy coats and with shovels in hand, they braved the freezing single-digit temperatures; the wind chill on the mountain was -20.

Erin, who first insisted on accompanying them, was sidetracked by Olivia into baking whoopee pies. As a final treat, Erin, after helping Aurelia do the dishes, was off with Mrs. Bundle and Olivia for another expedition—this time officially permitted—up to the attic.

Eyeballing the outside sunshine, Mrs. Bundle agreed to let Angie go as long as they were back by 1:00 p.m., at which point, based on Angie and Woodsum's discovery tour, they would decide how to proceed—and whether or not they would be able to leave as planned. When they returned, Erin and Mrs. Bundle met Angie and Woodsum at the door, both of whose faces were windburned; Woodsum was breathless with exertion.

"What's the verdict? Can we get Junebug out of the barn and down to the main road?" Mrs. Bundle asked.

"Nope." Angie's face was glummer than glum.

"Sorry to say, I doubt anybody's going in or out, Mrs. B." Woodsum said, his face beet red. "We're snowed in here for the duration—sometimes, in the past, it's been for a few days. I didn't want to have to give Angie the bad news. We're just used to it, but I understand why she's upset. She's a young'un with things to do and places she's got to go. It'll take me a fair amount of time just to shovel out to get down to the barn to get it open. Hate to say, you all aren't going anywhere anytime soon."

"And we're happy to have you here as long as it takes." Olivia pronounced.

Angie said miserably, "Gaw! As much as I love it here...but really—I *really* need to get back...Maybe I should try to hike out and down the dark side? How long—?" She paused, frustrated, "Mrs. Bundle?" Angie wiped away what was either perspiration or a tear. "What do you think?"

"We'll need to rethink things. Don't worry. There's always a solution." Mrs. Bundle assured her.

"Now, now. Don't fret, girl. I'll do everything I can to get you back in time for school." Woodsum said.

"Um. Three more days?" Lines of worry crisscrossed her forehead. "Oh, jeesum crowbars."

"And what about the surpri—" Erin froze mid-speech—Foot and Mouth Disease thwarted!—and began again, "What about Gumpy? And Uncle Carl and Uncle Clay? They'll be worrying about us for sure, won't they now? Aye, and Chester won't like it without his Cheerio treat—"(her illustrious and very cantankerous singing rooster, Chester, only responded positively to certain food stimuli) "—and Cracker, too? What will Cracker do without Mrs. Bundle and me?"

"Short of a white knight sledding up and rescuing us, I doubt much can happen at this point." Olivia offered much too logically. "You know what they say...It won't be warm till the snow gets off the mountain, and the snow won't get off the mountain till it gets warm." She saw Angie's eyes fill up. "Now, now, don't worry, my girl." She brightened; the corners of her lips quirked upward, "Say, how 'bout an old ice cream social? I've got a tub of Neapolitan down in the root cellar icebox! Keep a special stash. Would that put a smile on your face?"

Aurelia added, "And we've got hot fudge, and nuts, all the fixings, dear heart."

Woodsum tried to be upbeat, but he really felt he was letting the girl down. "How 'bout it, kiddo? We'll think of somethin'—don't you worry."

Erin wrapped her arm around Angie's waist. "Aye, it'll be okay."

At Angie's valiant nod, Olivia was relieved, at least for the moment. "There now. Okay!" She turned into the model of efficiency. "Brother, if we've got guests for a few more days, there's lanterns that need to be filled, and—"

"I know, I know. No problem—we love having company! Don't we, Possy?" He gathered up the dog and kissed him.

Diversion in action, Olivia disappeared down the cellar stairs into the dark cavern. Meanwhile, Woodsum, with Sir Possy in tow, went up the back stairway to do her bidding. Aurelia entered the pantry in full search mode, ticking off her list in her head.

Before anyone had a chance to discuss things further, there came a tremendous pounding on the back shed door, giving them a start. More pounding persisted, this time more urgent, along with men's voices.

"Who could that be?" Angie asked, opening the door.

At the top of the massive mound of snow were three large men, so over-clad in winterwear as to be disguised—that is, unless you knew them well like they did. The one in front waved a gloved hand.

Angie shrieked with glee. "Are you kidding me? Holy cow!"

With a look as beguiling as Rapunzel, Snow White, and Cinderella combined, she called out, "Is that *you*, my Prince?"

A very snowy Jack Corrigan stepped forward. "Aye, lass, I'm here to collect you."

"You can't even imagine," she drew in a quick breath, "how *happy* I am to see you! I missed you so much!"

He piled into the kitchen and, grabbing her up into his arms, planted a wet one soundly on her lips.

"Gumpy!" Erin shouted with glee at the second man whose face was covered with a scarf. "Is that *you*?"

The man completely clad in rugged red wool plaid outerwear bobbed his head in recognition. From somewhere within, they heard a barely audible, "*Wooo---eee*! It's colder 'n your grandmother's preserves out here. Let us in!"

"Royal? My god, you are a sight!" Mrs. Bundle exclaimed. "How on earth—?"

Walter Andersen and Royal Hudson tumbled past the occupied kissing couple into the warmth of the room. Walter unraveled the overlong scarf wound round and round his scrawny neck, "This ain't much of a storm, is it, Royal?"

Royal followed his lead and nodded amiably. "Nothing we can't handle. Hey, Lettie, how's it hangin'?"

Mrs. Bundle burst out laughing and couldn't stop. She held her sides. "Ouch! Oh, my lord, you two!"

Aurelia, speechless, joined them from the pantry, holding a glass jar of what looked like very luscious hot fudge and a tin of walnuts.

"Miss Aurelia," Erin said, "This is our rescue party!"

Royal grinned, removed his favorite flap-ears hat, and shuffled awkwardly from one foot to the other. "Hey there. Nice to meet ya, ma'am."

"How the heck are ya, little one?" Walter thumped his grandchild on the head, unable to disguise his delight. "Hey, everybody, thought we'd drop in for a cup of coffee." He said dryly, "Well, now, so this is where you been all this time. What a grand trip we've had finding you. We hitched up the tractor on the flatbed and came over with

Royal. That is, we came part way, then up the pass on snowshoes. He plowed his way through the main road and then up the tote road by hisself. Met him just as we both come over the rise. You know—*co-inkee-density*-like. We had a notion where we might find you up here on the tippy-top of God's country in the middle of the Saltash."

"How on earth did you know where to come?" Mrs. Bundle asked.

Jack chuckled, "You left the letter on the printer. I found the map. So it was a 'go' to come find you, wasn't it now? Like one big treasure hunt!" He winked at Angie, who beamed back.

"Guess we were right to come up that old towpath!" Walter said. "Thanks to Royal—knows every back road between Windsor and Rutland County like the back of his hand. Knew we'd find you in due course—just a matter of time."

"Yep!" Royal nodded profusely. "So you said, Walter. So you said. Hoo-eee! You'd never get out of here for days without us. I dragged the snow backward and cleared a path from the barn, then snow-shoed up the path. So, here we are." Royal couldn't have grinned any wider than he was. "It was a hoot!"

Aurelia watched the exchange bug-eyed, still disbelieving they had made their way to the inn.

"Rescuing you damsels in distress, right Erin?" Jack chuckled, his dark eyes focused on Angie whilst hugging his sister close. "You didn't think we'd forget you, did'ja now? We'd never leave you on pins and needles, Mrs. B!" Unable to help himself, he leaned over and kissed Angie again. "Hi, darlin'!"

Royal's eyes searched the kitchen hungrily. "I don't suppose you got anything to eat, do ya?"

"*Do* they—aye, I'll say!" Erin exclaimed.

As if on cue, Olivia popped through the cellar door. Head down, her mission had been accomplished. In one arm, she hefted a gallon tub of homemade ice cream and a scoop; in the other hand, a bunch of bananas. Without looking up, she said, "Whew! Well now, we can at least enjoy ourselves! Who wants a banana split?" She stopped in her tracks when she saw the men. Suspicious, she demanded abruptly, "Who're you and from where'd you come?"

She moved closer and came nose to nose with Walter. Fearing a confrontation of some sort, Mrs. Bundle moved quickly to separate the two, but just as quickly stepped back because the two gasped in unison—not in anger or fear, but in...pleasure!

Olivia squealed with uncharacteristic abandon. "*Good* Lord!"

"Well, I'll be *jibbered!*" Walter responded, removed his cap, and stared at her. It was such an intense moment that everyone froze watching until he spoke. "Now, wait, lemme think. I kept a memory so's I wouldn't forget—it was a name jest like those beautiful sister actresses....em, Joan Fontaine and...the *dee* Haviland one." He paused, forehead scrunched, then spouted like a whale, "Got it! Yes-sir-ee! O-*liv-i-a!* It's you, ain't it? Olivia?"

What used to be Olivia's stern, pinched expression had softened like Silly Putty as she took in the reddened, wind-bashed, awfully-old-but-amiable face of Walter Andersen. "From...the tri-county spelling bee! Really? Walter? Why, you old bean, you," she giggled—yes, giggled! "You used that funny word! I remember. Well, there was no such word really, mind you, but it was so odd! Ha—I never forgot it! *Scrumpled!* That was it!" She blathered and blushed: this new Olivia was young, shy, and sweet! She gave a hoot of pleasure and repeated, "*Scrumpled!* Said your pants got 'all scrumpled up' from sitting on the floor. So," she paused, blushing an even deeper shade. "So, of *course* I had to share my dish—Oh, yes! I never forgot it. My, my." She was so bowled over, she finally shut her mouth and just gazed up at him—gazed, they all observed...adoringly?

He issued his own Yankee euphemism with typical dryness, "Jump-in' Jee-hos-a-phat. Sweet."

Gathering himself up and sucking in his gut, he smiled. And then, totally out of his typical farmer-and-old-sage character, he bowed... youthfully...dare we say, formally? "At your service, m'dear. Yessuh." He took her hand—Erin, in her front row view, was so gobsmacked you could have knocked her over with a feather.

His Adam's apple quivered like a bobber on a line, and he said boldly, "O-livia, I been waitin' seventy-odd years to share another banana split with you. If I'd a know'd where you was, I'd rescued you *all* a lot sooner!"

Gruff and grouchy growls and yowls like the staccato of a broken down machine gun suddenly erupted from the back stairway, interrupting their poignant moment.

"Aurrrrrooooo! Aurrrrrooooo!" The crotchety whines and baying grew closer, mournful as ever.

Woodsum could be heard shouting above the croaky din, "Hold on, hold on! We'll see what's got you all riled up!"

"Aurrrrrooooo!"

"What the heck—?" Walter asked, craning his neck. "Someone oughta put that moose outta his misery."

Erin chipped in, "Ach, there's no meese here, Gumpy. That'd be Possy. He's an ol' bugger who can't abide mice or men—especially if the men wear hats." She affectionately patted the hand that held his hat, passing a sly glance toward Olivia, "He's really not so bad. Oh, aye, you'll get used to all that miserable yowling. We did, didn't we, Miss Olivia?"

Chapter III

Saying Good-bye

Saying good-bye was hard for everyone. Jack and Royal had gushed their appreciation for the fabulous stick-to-their-ribs lunch before they left. Walter gave Olivia an especially fond farewell, with a solid promise for a future ice cream assignation, and joined the other men down at the barn with Woodsum, as they figured out how to get Mrs. Bundle's car out and onto Royal's tow truck bed — much easier than driving the treacherous ride home.

When the girls were ready to join them, they lined up at the door to give them their kindest regards and bid each of the Pettyfers adieu.

Erin gently held Tuffy within her coat; she was ecstatic to have been given Gumpy's seal of approval to take Tuffy home with her. "I'm sure Ainee will love her, too. Aye, we'll take good care of her and make sure she eats a lot and gets her health back."

"Good plan. Got your whoopee pies to give you sister?" Olivia asked. "And your stamps?"

"Sure do! Mrs. B is keeping them in her bag." Olivia had given Erin a 1938 Calvin Coolidge postage stamp to begin her own collection. She placed a silver dollar inside the girl's mitten and whispered. "From brother. Don't spend it, now."

"Oh, aye, I won't! Thank you!"

"And the hermits?" Aurelia asked, "Where's the tin of hermits to take back to school?"

"My favorite? Have no fear," Angie said, tapping her backpack. "They're right here—safe and sound."

Aurelia took Angie's hand. "Such a handsome young man you have. And so polite!"

Angie's eyes glistened. "Yes, and he's special on the inside, too. He's everything any girl could ever want."

"Don't let that one be the fish that got away!" Olivia interjected. "He's a keeper!"

"Well, I'll admit we've got some things to work on," Angie laughed, passing a knowing glance in Mrs. Bundle's direction, "But after hearing your stories, I think Jack and I can weather any storm that comes our way. You're right, Miss Olivia. He *is* a keeper!"

Olivia eyeballed Erin seriously, "We had a good time, didn't we missy? Now, remember this. 'The world is your cow. But you have to do the milking.'"

Erin scrunched her forehead in thought, her eyes rolled with the intensity of a slot's jackpot. "Aye, Miss Olivia. I'll remember that one for certain." She stored it upstairs in that fertile mind.

Aurelia turned to Mrs. Bundle, "When Cousin Milly told us about you, we waited to hear from you. We hoped that you would come someday." Olivia joined in, "And you did come finally, and you put it all to rest." They both hugged her, and then the girls, and were still standing in the doorway waving and hugging each other as the detective and her charges headed down the path to the barn.

Once there, it appeared all was ready.

"Jeepers! I'm gonna miss you dames." Woodsum said between bear hugs. "Don't be strangers, y'hear?"

"Let's get a-goin'!" Walter shouted, jumping into the already crowded extended-cab.

Mrs. Bundle was the last to get in. She turned to Woodsum to say good-bye. As though executing a task, he passed a vintage leather portfolio case to her. "Now listen. We want you to have it. It's your fairy tale—the Deegie book."

"How wonderful of you all! Thank you so much." The air was so cold. She opened the flap and peeked inside. Yes, there it was, the precious book. In addition, a few very thin sheets of stationery were sticking out of the top.

She had expected something like this; warm vapor billowed out of her mouth.

The tip of his index finger grazed his lips. "Yup. You go on, now." He lightly tapped the side of his nose with a forefinger.

She nodded, fully understanding, watching his face.

They hugged.

His eyes, even more electric blue than usual, searched hers. Through the turquoise glimmer, Mrs. Bundle saw tears welling up as he turned away.

Chapter IV
The TRUTH

Mrs. Bundle sat on her own comfy bed in her familiar personal space, thankful to be home with all her creature comforts. The nearby bureau top was neatly laden with all her collectibles: carved wooden and pressed tin boxes holding mementos, cut glass dishes filled with costume jewelry, odd-shaped perfume bottles, her basket of lace hankies, and other little tidbits all sharing her space in happy harmony. Though their monetary worth was small, the intrinsic value was priceless. Now sharing the space, the jar of Olivia's wonder salve. Cracker's glossy black body was curled possessively at her feet. He had missed her and was most happy when he met her at the door that evening. The ride home had been harrowing, a doozy even by Walter's standards, but they had made it. All was well, but she was still unsettled by her experience at the inn. It was the loose ends, always the loose ends that troubled her mind. And there were a few on this case as well, which she hoped to clear up post haste and put to rest.

Once again, she would find those answers within the pages of the hard copy of a book, and one that was long out of print. The first thing she had done when she got home (after showering Cracker with many affectionate kisses and a good share of his favorite Liver Lover cookies to boot) was to scour the library shelves in the den. This had been Arthur's sanctuary and it remained untouched, hers now. When she needed comfort or a remembrance time-out with her husband, this is where she often would come. Her eyes would span the shelves—not one book's location had been altered nor removed since his passing—skimming through the titles of his many prized history books. Huge war buff that he was, she knew his extensive collection included many books about World War II.

A vague recollection from years before was nagging her. In point of fact, Arthur had mentioned something that she now pulled from her memory. It was one of those husband-wife conversations where an exchange takes place but is never fully finished as the runaway train of daily life runs each other far afield. However, she needed to pull that conversation up and conclude it now.

She recalled the day, popping her head into the den to let him know she was just off to pick strawberries at Maxim's Farm. He had a large green book with a thick black binding in his hand. He seemed quite excited—well, excited for Arthur, that was. There was nothing like a dusty history tome to get him out of his staid, matter-of-fact self.

"Say there!" he'd said in that deep voice, "Found something darned interesting. It's all right *here*. I remembered Uncle Stuart up in Plymouth Notch telling me about this years ago. Hit me one day that it would be fun to figure it out. Anyway, what do you think? Here I come back from the Plymouth Library Book Sale with *this*." He raised the book, his index finger wedged between its pages, and she nodded, one foot out the door as he continued, "Uncle Stuart— 'course, we used to call him Uncle Drunkle—spent a lot of time with the bottle after the war, poor guy. I thought he was just…well, joshing, you know, how he always did. But, danged if he wasn't right! Vermonters knew what was coming long before the rest of the country. Everyone kept it on the Q-T. For months before World War II was formally declared, that is."

"Really? How fascinating!" She'd given him a quick kiss goodbye. "Tell me more when I get home." At the time, she was more interested in procuring some of the area's first crop of luscious fresh strawberries, and the details of his find were never brought to the surface.

She scanned the shelves. *Where was that book?* Perusing the section specific to World War II, her eyes lit up when she came across *Investigations into WWII German Espionage and the Effects on the Allied Effort* by Wilson Dodd, 1953. Green with black binding—this must be it! It was heavy and she sat down on the loveseat. Skimming through the preface and first chapter, she went through a cursory overview, learning that Germany's activity and interaction in the U.S. prior to 1940 had been taken lightly—Germans were not considered the enemy by most Americans. The Germans were friendly; National Socialism had grown but seemed to have negligible impact on the average American's life and Hitler's Berlin seemed very far away. The supposed discrimination of the Jews was even further, by all accounts, and often disbelieved by Americans of all classes. As Germany laid a solid foundation for aggression and grew beyond simple diplomacy, Americans felt the rumbling but still were not fully engaged. The author posited that there were many enemy-inspired acts of sabotage that happened within the United States before and during the war; those known acts would be documented in this book. Ultimately, it was noted, German espionage against the United States failed to produce anything of importance.

Most important to Mrs. Bundle's search were the suggestions of what occurred before the War, as she tried to find anything that had to do with Vermont and what Arthur had been trying to tell her years before. And, it was more meaningful than ever now to find anything coincidental to the period when Michel was in Mount Holly, Vermont—June of 1939 through January of 1940.

She dug in.

Before England's entry into World War II, Germany, under direction of the Reich Foreign Ministry, engaged in a number of clandestine efforts. As expected, they were compelled to obtain economic, political, and military data within the United States. Although Germany did obtain some espionage information over a period of months related to future war production, shipping patterns, and technical advances, it was too late, too inaccurate or too general in nature to be of direct military value.

This sentence caught her eye: *Many attempts were made, especially during the frantic months when England was forced into War and long before the United States entered the war.*

Initially, in the late 1930s, German spies had arrived under the cover of benign occupations and recruited those already active in the American Bund or other groups with German sympathy leanings—*(like Mr. Pettyfer,* Mrs. Bundle considered)—to help their secret agents. Clandestine newspapers and seemingly innocuous radio stations were carefully put in place in efforts to establish extensive espionage networks within the U.S. borders. This occurred while most of America was sleeping and comfortable, little knowing that Germany was actively performing sabotage with Der Fuhrer's ultimate goal of world domination. The United States declared war on Japan the day after Pearl Harbor on December 8, 1941, entering World War II; days later, Germany and its Axis partners declared war on the United States, and Germany employed even more desperate efforts to obtain tactical and strategic information on Allied plans.

The most famous spy ring in the U.S. was known as the Duquesne Spy Ring. It was the largest espionage case in United States history and ended in convictions. Thirty-three members of a German espionage network headed by "Fritz" Joubert Duquesne were convicted after a lengthy FBI espionage investigation: 19 pleaded guilty to espionage; 14 others entered pleas of not guilty and were brought to jury trial in Brooklyn, New York, on September 3, 1941. All were found guilty on December 13, 1941 (a very telling date considering the bombing of Pearl Harbor had occurred days earlier). On January 2, 1942, the group was sentenced to serve a total of over 300 years in prison.

She flipped back through the pages until she came to a black and white photograph of a man sitting at an odd, boxy machine. He was holding a small device wired into a typing machine with batteries. The caption below the photo read: *The Pedal Radio a/k/a Pedal Wireless was a radio transmitter/receiver powered by pedals to a generator and was a way of communicating from remote areas. Solely powered by batteries and invented by Alfred Traeger in 1929, it was believed to have been used extensively in Germany's espionage effort* in isolated, often mountainous and inaccessible areas to transmit key enemy data and coordinates. Traeger's ingenious solution was remarkable in that it transcribed in English for the Morse code illiterate. Not unlike a standard typewriter, the keys activated steel arms with a working face cut to required long and short spacings. An oil-filled dash pot produced smooth movement of the keyed arms.

This device fell into the radiotelegraphy category—radiotelephony had not as yet proved reliable or satisfactory for tactical military communications long distance. It looked exactly as the "thingamabob" described by Aurelia Pettyfer. It was battery operated—again, as Aurelia had described. She read on further that all nations on the eve of World War II were employing similar methods of communication for military signaling. Of course, what would have been more effective than this to convey info from rugged terrain long distance? Certainly not visuals like flags, lights, or pyrotechnics. Maybe a homing pigeon, but that would be precarious and problematic in the cold months, and anything that couldn't reach an off-shore destination would have been disregarded. This, she realized, must be the device used to communicate long-range messages to a German off-shore command from one of the highest points in Vermont—the Saltash Mountain!

Mrs. Bundle read on through the next chapter, and the next, scanning the pages quickly. She came upon the subsequent chapter entitled: *The New England Sabotage Effort: Fall, 1939-Winter, 1940.*

Ah! The pages beneath her fingers seemed to heat up with her own eagerness. She scanned quickly, turning the pages through each New England state, and then gasped. There, a modest three-page subsection, entitled *Vermont's Vital Role.* Yes! Here was what Arthur must have discovered and tried to show her—and what she hoped would help her now.

The author contended that hundreds of United States planes, flying low patterns over mid and northern Vermont's massive state forests, had nightly secret missions. Via anecdotal records and post-war documentation by residents from Plymouth Notch, Barre, and the Northeast Kingdom further north, a comprehensive effort had been sanctioned by Roosevelt and implemented, the author documented, with the goal in mind to help with England's efforts in late 1939 and into 1940 as they were forced into war. Dodd posited that the United States knew it was a matter of time before their own entry, so simultaneous to an agreement being crafted officially authorizing same, they were *already* supplying planes and war materials to England.

Noting that the good farmers and townspeople alike in rural Vermont clearly and distinctly heard the nightly drone of planes, the author documented that even as they acknowledged something was up, they never questioned what was going on. Not one mention of this highly covert effort was ever made public in any local newspaper. It seems, as unbelievable as it was, that all rural populace were complicit as part of the bigger conspiracy to help keep things quiet for the good of the nation. It was a provincial world then; these resilient Americans had a sense it was all for the good of the nation; many knew by other means of deduction that America was preparing for war.

She paused after reading the next passage: *The Germans were desperate to know the patterns, the times, the dates, and to have all information garnered and conveyed via clandestine radio signals to the Germans U-boats just off American shores.*

The author's evidence supported Germany's contention that they had obtained information that assisted Germany. An explanation of Dodd's documented timeline was as follows: Historically, the need for secrecy for the clandestine delivery of war supplies to England was significant, because it wasn't until 1941 that the U.S. was legally in place to provide weaponry to England. An act was eventually signed by Roosevelt to aid England's entry into full-out war with Germany. The Lend-Lease Law was enacted March 11, 1941 (a year and a half after the outbreak of World War II in Europe in September of 1939 but nine months before the U.S. entered the war in December of 1941). Under this program, the United States supplied the United Kingdom and other Allied nations with war materials between 1941 through 1945. Formally titled *An Act to Further Promote the Defense of the United States,* it effectively ended the United States' pretense of neutrality. However, it was long before this that much aid was being provided to Great Britain. The administration did not want it made public that which they had already been doing under cover of night in the remote airspace of New York, Vermont, and Canada. Roosevelt's cagey manipulation of the law was to aid England by providing much-needed plane parts and planes, with the terms of the eventual agreement stipulating everything given to the Allies be used until time for return or destruction. (Ultimately after the war, the supplies were sold to Britain at a large discount by the United States.)

Here was where the story got interesting.

Simultaneous to the covert plan's incubation and implementation during late 1938 and the end of 1939, a spy group dubbed *The German Eight* was launched by Germany. Their area of concentration: New England. Arriving by various legal and illegal means on the Northeast coast, these highly skilled and intelligent individuals' mission was to find out as much as possible about American air support to England. They knew America was moving toward war with its own quiet preparation. They knew clandestine aid to England in the form of war parts, supplies, and airplanes, were being flown under cover at the midnight hour from remote northern New York military airbases, through Vermont and Canada and on to the airfields of England.

This large-scale mission was entrusted to eight saboteurs from June of 1938 through January of 1940. They were placed in various remote areas of New York and Vermont. What is known was that their mission ultimately fizzled out and failed. The reason: the dissemination of the group caused by the abrupt disappearance of their leader and organizer of the maneuver—an enigmatic German intelligence operative known only as The Professor. There was a suspected link between this spy and a high-ranking German Nazi official—possibly a relative, and one of the major architects of the Holocaust. Historians regarded the official, Reinhardt Heydrich, as the darkest figure within the Nazi elite. Adolf Hitler himself described Heydrich with admiration as "the man with the iron heart." A folded, handwritten sheet of paper, undated and penned in German signed, "Affectionately your comrade, The Professor" was found on Heydrich's person as he was taken prisoner after the war. In the short, seemingly innocuous note, the writer referred to his recent research in South America and his plan to continue on to a symposium in New York City.

"Bingo." Mrs. Bundle breathed with anticipation. "They knew each other. Heydrich knew Michel Hydrick. Not likely a coincidence. Had he just chosen the English version of his family name, Heydrich? Possibly... And 'Affectionately'...maybe he was this Heydrich's nephew, or brother?" Perhaps; in point of fact, quite likely.

She finished reading the section. The ensuing rounding up, arrest, and conviction of seven of the eight saboteurs was anticlimactic. Their leader, described by authorities as 'tall, light-haired, convincingly pleasant, an impostor whose numerous identities and seamless credentials ranged from pharmacist to an expert in herpetology,' was never captured in the United States, never discovered in Germany, never acknowledged after the war. His true identity was never discovered or disclosed. It was as though he had vanished into thin air.

"Vanished into thin air." She had read aloud, as though speaking it would give her the answer. "Vanished—or not?" An odd sensation came over her; one of treachery at every level and...irrevocable finality.

She absorbed it all, softly rubbing her temples, releasing the pressure in her brain that always accompanied each mystery challenge. For all intents and purposes, she no longer wondered what had happened to Michel; she believed she knew why he had never resurfaced.

And, now?

What she needed to resolve now was what, if anything, she wanted to do about it.

At this moment, here she sat in her bedroom, pondering the next move, one she mightn't find any redeeming quality or solace in, one she might regret.

Cracker had slithered off the bed on reconnaissance in her closet—she determined this by the muffled sounds behind the shoe rack. She had told him Erin had brought back a little furry friend, giving him a compassionate heads up, knowing he might view this competition with some disdain. Best to give him fair warning now before their first meeting.

Beside her on the bed lay her knapsack, the top open, the contents removed. Alongside it, the leather file case, also opened. ***Deegie and the Fairy Princess*** had been placed with care on her bedroom bookcase, a hopeful reminder of her visit.

In her hands was the, as yet, unread note Woodsum had furtively placed within the book. She anticipated with regret what was inside the note and a deep sadness for the brother of Aurelia and Olivia filled her heart. Her fingers closed around the rimless reading glasses at her bedside table. Well, it was best to finish this as best she could.

There were five thin pages, the same lightweight stationery reminiscent of that used in World War II to communicate across the ocean. She read the finely scrawled words aloud to Cracker and the four walls.

January, 2006

Dear Mrs. Bundle…

That clever look you gave told me, for sure, I couldn't pull one over on you. Had a feeling you'd cobble it all together given time. I'm sure you're working on figuring out the why, too, crafty as you are. You've probably already guessed a good amount of how it happened.

I can't ask for forgiveness. What should I have done? Would that I'd allowed him to return to Germany, to do more damage, ultimately to kill many others, including our own soldiers? I say no. I couldn't sit by and do squat. I've fluctuated between being racked with guilt and doing the right thing—more so, as these years have gone by. Nonetheless, it is what it is.

That night when Aurelia asked me to go out in the storm and look for him, I made my way down to the barn. Everyone was in bed asleep. It was crazy with drifting snow banks—high as my shoulders at some points—the path was covered; it was like being in another world—wild, not the safe, trite one I knew so well. There was a wicked intensity in the atmosphere, urging me on, pushing me toward the barn with a vengeance.

The side entrance door was ajar just a hair. It was dark; the storm was at my back just a-howlin', and my footsteps were muffled as I entered. There was a pair of snowshoes nearby and at the ready; I noticed they were wet with melted snow. I could hear the distant drone of the airplanes above. I knew where I would find him. I went stealthily up the open stairway, following the candlelight's glow to the back room—where Father and Michel spent their time on research—where no one, including myself, was ever allowed.

I knew he was leaving for good as soon as I entered. He had hidden his valise, full to capacity, at the door. He was dressed for winter travel, boots and all. There he was at that blasted typewriter Aurelia had mentioned, just a-pushing and a-pedaling those pedals up and down. There was a whir in the background; the batteries were doing their part.

He had a bean shooter at his fingertips all ready to fire! Even though I had never seen the pedal instrument before, I knew. If I had seen it before, I'd probably been able put it all together much sooner. I came up behind him, close like, enough to see there was Morse code on those keys! The air was stifling with unease. He was referring to a notebook that looked just like the one he used on our hikes and mountain climbs. He muttered under his breath, vocalizing the Geman words he was sending. I held my breath and listened, watched as he sent one last secret message to his Nazi cronies before leaving our Saltash Mountain behind for good. By God, that's what he was doing.

I suddenly remembered our rock climbing adventures and saw red. That son of a gun had been using me to get what he wanted. He had been given free rein by Father to roam our mountain, to gather information, to get what he needed without a second thought.

He's leaving, he's leaving, throbbed through my head, and he's leaving a tremendous wake of damage behind with little care for any of our regard. Worse yet—it was plain as the nose on my face. My best pally, the guy I had looked up to, Michel Hydrick, was a spy. Sending off the vital air traffic patterns of the planes above, secrets that would ultimately help Germany. Who knows what other info he'd already brought to them in this same way and, I put together, on his visits down the mountain. All info that could kill our men—and eventually, impact others here in our little world. I yelled bloody murder and jumped on him, trying to pull him off the blasted thing. I punched him; my anger was intense—nothing like I'd ever experienced. We struggled, and he got me good in the ribs, pushing me back, out of the room and onto the barn balcony. I pulled him with me as I fell. He was talking the whole time, trying to convince me, saying things like, 'You can help us, too, Woodsum. That's what we wanted. Think about your father, and your sisters. Don't ruin this.'

I just wanted him to stop. Stop treating me like a nitwit. Stop jerking my chain. I had wanted to think he was a good man—a man of integrity; not a spy. I had wanted to believe in his soul, that his purpose here with us was pure and not tainted with his own failings. I guess what it boiled down to was he believed in one thing; I believed in another.

He paused, panting, trying to explain who he really was— but I knew him for what he really was: the master manipulator.

I gave him what for and saw the look in his eye when he knew I was beyond convincing. At that moment, I knew if I didn't let him go on his way, it would be me or him. Jumbled thoughts filled my brain; this, I feared, was it. He was not going to let me ruin all the work he had done for the Third Reich while posing as my friend and teacher.

'You're not going anywhere.' I said with an air of finality.

I held up my hands in defense and he lunged at me. I stepped aside almost by instinct and, like that, he was gone, sailing over the loft railing, falling twenty feet below. I watched his surprised look as he disappeared. When I peered down, all was silent.

I took it all in and knew I had to face the truth. In that moment, I think I was glad he had suffered for all that he had done. I was complicit in hurting him. I went against what I believed in—not to ever take a part in hurting, or taking life—my own conscience was clouded, soiled forever.

He lay there, vulnerable now, blood seeping into the layers of golden hay. The pitch fork had driven a hole into his back. I've seen enough poor animals die to know he was near death. His lower limbs, strangely crooked as they were, told me his back was likely broken. His eyes, staring blankly upward, tried to focus. I joined him below.

I'll give it to him—at that point of no return, his views on life were less political. Well, Mrs. Bundle, I reckon fanatical doctrine goes right down the tubes when it's the last breath you'll ever take. As I stood above him with his weapon in my hand, he got right sentimental, the son of a gun did, whispering in panicked bits and starts, 'Captured...between espionage...and love.' 'Love?', I says, pretty disgusted. It was then he said our names, one by one, 'Aurelia.... Olivia... Woodsum'. His lips quirked upward, odd-like, his eyes glazing. I felt compassion for him; not the first time or the last that ever happened, right? He begged, asking me to bring Aurelia to him. 'Really,' I says, 'you don't need to worry about sister—either one, in fact. I'll make sure of that.' In his last breath he uttered, 'Don't worry, brother. Were I in your shoes...I...would do the same.'

Why, you ask, did he call me brother? As God is my witness, I confess—he was like the brother I never had. To be completely candid, he was even more than that to me in a way I can't express...to anyone. Since then, I've pondered his affection a thousand times. Brotherhood to his country versus our own...closeness. How easily evil ways can kill something that seemed so pure and good. Yep, I've pondered that to no end. Who was Michel Hydrick really? Beats me—even after all these years—sad to say...beats me.

I suppose my ambivalence included Father, too—he who brought a traitor on every level into our world and almost destroyed us all in the process. Father, who didn't care enough to protect us, who cared most about Germany. Father, who knew all about Michel's spying; there is no doubt of that. One thing I know for sure, he was a traitor to Aurelia, Olivia and me.

Here's another thing to ponder and maybe weigh on that justice scale when you're looking at the big picture—which I know you will do—you look at it in a much more scholarly way than sisters and I can. I came to suspect Father's connections began much further back. In retrospect, I consider the 1932 Olympics in Lake Placid, N.Y. and that special meeting with the ice hockey players from Germany. Yes, Mrs. Bundle, not the U. S. team, but the German team! I'm sure it was Father's connections with those sympathetic to the growing Nazi influence that got us in to see them—Hitler would be in power in less than a year.

Was my father a traitor to his country? I like to think Father was just a poor misguided, miserable fool—so puffed up with his own importance he couldn't see the forest for the trees. Michel and Deutschland used him for their country's gain. I expect a jury would say so. Without doubt, if the locals had found out enough to judge, they'd have hanged him for sure. We wouldn't have wanted that. And ain't it odd, Father getting to exercise his right of free speech and political beliefs at all those American Bund meetings so much like he could? Good ol' America!

Another odd thing. When Michel disappeared from our world, Father never said one word. He got up the next morning and never asked one question—and didn't answer any, either. I guess he figured Michel got away as planned. For two weeks after the big blizzard, we were so focused on getting our world back on track and helping others, it all fell by the wayside. I busted up the pedal machine, used the batteries for more useful purposes, and destroyed the keys. That must have been part of the master plan; Father never said boo. I drug the body out and hid it.

Three months to the day Michel left our world, Father died in the barn fire, taking with him what was left of that wretched 'research' and any other secrets. I always wondered if he set it ablaze on purpose, knowing the end was up for him?

Late one night in late spring when the snow was pret-near melted and the ground had softened, I fetched that pitiful spy's stored body—wrapped and covered, hidden way in the back of the icehouse. I wheel-barrowed him in the dead of night way, way out into our evergreen woods—out the trail—where I prepared a deep grave under the big rocks. There's only one way in to the Dark Side and one way out. To my way of thinking, he belonged there. Didn't Michel always love that view? Yessuh, I can attest to that.

Nothing good ever came from all them war machines in the world: bombs, tanks, and the like. After I got back from my alternate service, we rebuilt the barn good and proper and rebuilt a happy life at the inn—without any remnants of Michel Hydrick—except the memories. I visit his grave often there at the thinking bench.

AMITY—that's what the world needs to survive: friendship, peace, goodwill. Sisters and me, we were the survivors— the walking wounded—left here in our little world. Those memories kept us prisoner—until now. Aurelia thought she held his heart. Olivia loved his mind and intelligence. Me? I possessed the remnants of his soul.

All these years gone by—better for Aurelia and Olivia to think he left them for whatever reason they can excuse, rather than know the truth. I hope you think so, too.

Even as Aurelia kept hopes he'd come back to her, to become her husband...someday. Even as Olivia resented his actions and grew even more bitter with time. If he had returned, they both would have forgiven him. Not me, though—even though, darn it, he was the best pal ever. Nonetheless, to my way of thinking, he was the Enemy to us all.

I pray for mercy from the only One who will judge me.

A Friend in Peace,

Woodsum

Epilogue

Mrs. Bundle always marveled at the view from her bedroom window, each season spectacularly framed like a Winslow Homer masterpiece within the unadorned white wooden casing. The previous days' winter fury was now nothing short of superlative in its calmness...and whiteness. It helped clear her mind as she absorbed Woodsum's confession. To the untrained eye, the scene might look like a blank palette; some might view its simplicity as bleakness; others might see the splendor, how complicated that white world truly was. As if studying an exquisite gallery painting, she followed the shadowed ivory curves of the road and the champagne-shaded valleys. Bits of bone-colored logs peeked out beneath the stark snow, still untouched by man and his machines. Vanilla white tips showcased the mountain peaks. Random ecru mounds beckoned, leaving one to imagine what might be beneath come springtime. The sky, in contrast, was a brilliant blue—also silent in its inactivity—with not a cloud in the sky, nothing moving, nothing to indicate any history of the earlier chaos.

She reviewed her options. What or who, if anything or anyone, could Woodsum's statement benefit now, in this present world? Arthur always said recorded history proved one thing: it couldn't be counted on as a complete picture of what actually happened at the time. His rationale—that if it was documented at the time, the data was likely skewed in favor of the victors. Conversely, if it was documented independently anytime afterward through the gathering of bits and pieces of records and memorabilia, there was usually an agenda, critical thinking, or hypothesis behind it to prove or disprove what really occurred. Reading this recorded minutia—history—so intrigued modern man—not just as a record, but as a future guide. History was meant to teach, to take heed, to not forget; history was never-ending. Strangely enough, every day created itself anew, ultimately, to become times gone by.

All three Pettyfers, in their own way, had existed in their own private hell for so many years—even as, by all appearances, they had created and sustained a beautiful world untouched by time and modernization. In point of fact, theirs had been a vulnerable existence filled with secrecy, self-imposed privacy, fear, and unresolved longing. At their loss of Michel, the Pettyfer siblings had come back together and inevitably made a lifelong, virtuous commitment to provide sanctuary for their guests—and each other. The Pettyfers had been damaged, even as they tried valiantly to shape an ideal world. Their fears of the outside world had imploded and come out the sides, as manifested in their idiosyncratic lifestyle. Juxtaposed against terrible family secrets, dark tragedy and sordid espionage in their own back yard, was their collective positive contribution to mankind. It seemed more than fitting; it was the great equalizer.

Were the scales of justice even? She believed yes.

"Oh, what loved ones do to protect family, home—and country." Mrs. Bundle removed her glasses and heaved a deep sigh. This was living proof that holding secrets could shape the way one spent the rest of their life: on pins and needles, or torment, or perpetual limbo.

She thought of all that had transpired so quickly these past few days and the ultimate resolution: Olivia's new, freshly soft smile; Woodsum's vulnerability and truthfulness; Aurelia's assurance that she was now at peace. She hoped for peace for them with all her heart, for acceptance of deeds long done with secrets no longer held.

An epiphany slowly unfolded before her, not unlike the thin, fragile layers of skin surrounding an onion's fiery core—it peeled back dormant feelings, exposing the underlayment of her mind's knowledge in opposition to the struggling emotions...of her *own* heart. Instantly, the simple yet powerful message of *Luke 6:37* came through distinctly. She whispered aloud, "'*Judge not, and you will not be judged; condemn not, and you will not be condemned; forgive, and you shall be....*'"

She paused thoughtfully. "My goodness!" A shiver went up her spine as a tangential thought occurred. "Really?"

She couldn't help wondering about another who had recently touched her life, wondering anew about *his* secrets. There was no doubt in her mind that he was holding back. Yes—holding back, for sure. Moreover, there was that nagging sadness around him—holding *him* hostage...smothering him.

Why, until now, hadn't she looked at it from his side? He hadn't offered an explanation; more importantly, she hadn't asked. It was her mistake for intentionally not going there emotionally. Yes. She asked herself, in this moment of reflection, about secrets—and her real feelings for Duke Driscoll. She wondered...*had he gone away, not to run away, but to* face *his demons, to put them to bed? In anticipation of*—dare she think—*moving on with his life?*

She relaxed her body, allowing the stratum of her own life events to leisurely newsreel in progressive sequence through her mind. Long-ago events shaping her outlook, the details of day-to-day happenings (subtle or profound) sliding by, each decade poignant and meaningful...finally wrapping up and arriving at *today*. Today! Right now, she admitted, what superseded *everything* was the thrill of what *could*—what *might*—lay ahead.

The Wondeful Unknown.

The hint of a hopeful smile played upon her lips. *Yes! What was... to come?* She simply couldn't close her eyes any longer to what might be possible. This could be her best year ever.

The Pettyfers were a lesson to be learned and she was thankful and blessed they had entered her life.

She folded the thin fragile papers, tore them in half, folded and tore again, repeating the action, tearing until it was all just ragged bits cupped within her hands. She leaned forward floating her limp wrists above the nearby wicker basket. Slowly, she spread her fingers and the confetti gently drifted downward, landing atop outdated copies of the *State Standard* and *Rutland Daily News* newspapers, all slated for tinder in the woodstove.

With only one last request before putting this case to bed, she lay back on the billowy down comforter, enveloped in its satin warmth. With a new point of view, she spied a tiny black spider within a beautifully spun web in the closest corner of the otherwise stark-white ceiling and requested from the universe what was more a hope than a wish.

She hoped that the essence of perfection, peace, and harmony that those at Mount Holly Mansion Inn had embraced, strived for, and shared with so many over the decades would live on perpetually in others' hearts.

She hoped for amity.

That, she concluded, would be a lovely way to remember this winter adventure.

"Ah-h-h!" she sighed and stretched her arms, "I missed my little world here." She looked around. "Oh! There you are, my dear, sweet luv. Come over here and snuggle with me."

Cracker appeared from nowhere and, with two deft hops, landed lightly in her soft lap.

Ooomph! He licked her fingers delicately, then rested his symmetrically-round head in her empty palms. *Life is tough*, he cat-thought philosophically, adding in his knowing, cat-capable way, *sounds like this was an especially challenging case. I should have been there to support you. Yet, we both know life can be disconcerting at times. You must realize I may not always be around to help. I appreciate your telling me about the new 'kiddy-cat'. I suspect that name, 'Tuffy,'—egad!—is a literal reference to the chutzpah and proclivity for danger the waif may possess—I shall try to reserve judgment until our first meeting. That said, you and I are here now and all is well.* He purred lovingly and lay back, giving her his full attention in anticipation of a lovely belly rub.

"I missed you, too, C-Cat. On the other hand, you were *so* lucky to miss a very ornery dog named Possy. He would *not* have endeared himself to you at all and could easily have become your worst nemesis—even more so than Chester."

Cracker harrumphed indignantly at the thought, gave a persnickety sneeze, and the thrumming within him resumed as she patted his belly and chuckled dreamily.

The two had their reflective moment, their time together—as usual, totally in sync. She rubbed his furry neck and ears, stroked the full length of his ebony coat and his long tail, passing her hands gently over him from stem to stern; he purred loudly, noting the range of her emotions and the giving personality he knew and loved so.

Here it comes, he cat-thought without surprise as his mistress sat up with resolve. *Go ahead, grab the strap on that carousel wheel, and hang on for dear life.*

"Now then," she declared with a passion within she'd not felt for years. "There's something I really must explore. Are you with me, C-Cat?"

The End

RECIPES

BLT w/ CE for One a la Tuddy's Diner
(Bacon, Lettuce, Tomato with Cheese and Fried Egg)

4 slices of cooked regular or turkey bacon
2 slices of Monterey Jack or Cheddar Cheese
2 thick slices of rustic bread, toasted and hot
1 TBSP mayonnaise
3 tomato slices
2 leaves of lettuce
2 teaspoons unsalted butter
1 large egg

Set the Monterey Jack slices on 1 piece of toast. Spread the mayonnaise on the other slice of toast, then top with the bacon, tomato and lettuce.

In a small, nonstick skillet, melt the butter. Add the egg and fry over moderate heat, turning once, until crisp around the edge, about 4 minutes; the yolk should still be runny. Slide the egg onto the lettuce; close the sandwich and eat right away. Multiply the recipe for those most precious in your life—they will thank you and, between mouthfuls, proclaim, "Fantastical!!"

Olivia's Hot Fudge Sauce

1/2 Cup Butter
2 Squares Unsweetened Chocolate
2 Cups Confectioner's Sugar, Sifted
3/4 Cup Evaporated Milk

In a saucepan over low heat, melt butter and chocolate. Remove from the heat; add about 1/3 of the sugar and 1/3 of the evap. milk. Stir in and add half the remaining sugar and evaporated milk; stir again and add the rest of the sugar and evaporated milk. Stir until smooth. Return to the stove and simmer for 8-10 minutes. Makes about 2 cups.

Gentle warning: When making your hot fudge sundaes or banana splits it is strongly advised to place a liner plate below, as the hot fudge oozes over the ice cream dish, forming gobs of the delicious sauce that leisurely drips and pools onto the plate below—to be savored last—Mrs. Bundle's perfect ending!

Stuffed Pork Tenderloin Caprese-Style

1 pork tenderloin, medium size, about 2 lbs
4 oz part skim mozzarella cheese, thinly sliced
1/2 cup spinach, fresh
1/4 cup sun dried tomatoes, dry (add to hot water; then drain)
2 garlic cloves, crushed
10 basil leaves, fresh
Salt and pepper to taste

Preheat oven to 425° F.

Cut pork tenderloin almost in half lengthwise so it opens like a book. Cut each half in half lengthwise one more time. Be careful not to cut through. Pound both sides through plastic wrap to flatten slightly. Rub salt, ground black pepper and 1 clove of crushed garlic on both sides.

Lay cheese, spinach, basil, sundried tomatoes and the rest of the crushed garlic down the centre of the tenderloin, leaving 1" border around the edges. Press gently. Roll the long edge over stuffing overlapping as necessary, and fold in the narrow end. Secure with kitchen string or skewers.

Place meat on a baking pan with a rack and place in preheated oven. Roast for 20–25 minutes or until juices run clear or when the thermometer reaches 155° F. Broil the top on high for another 3–5 minutes.

Remove from the oven. Cover with foil and let the meat rest for 5–10 minutes before slicing. Don't forget to remove the string and/or skewers.

HERMITS

This unique cookie evolved in 1860s New England. Some say the cookies were named because they look like a hermit's brown sack-cloth robe.

Your choice: Baked in a 9 x 13-inch pan, these hermits are like molasses brownies. Baked in a half-sheet (13 x 18-inch) pan, they make 1/4-inch bars. Baked in a jelly-roll pan (approx. 10 x 15-inch), they're somewhat fatter.

1 cup (7 ounces) granulated sugar
1/2 cup (3 1/4 ounces) shortening
1/2 cup (8 tablespoons) butter
1/2 teaspoon ground cinnamon
1/2 teaspoon ground nutmeg
1/2 teaspoon ground ginger
1/2 teaspoon ground cloves
1/2 teaspoon salt
1 teaspoon baking soda
3 cups (12 3/4 ounces) unbleached all-purpose flour, or 100% white whole wheat flour (12 ounces), or a combination
1/2 cup (6 ounces) molasses
1 cup (5 1/4 ounces) raisins, either dark or golden

Preheat oven to 350° F.

In a large bowl, beat together the sugar, shortening and margarine till smooth. Beat in the spices, salt and baking soda. Slowly stir in the flour, then add the molasses and beat well again. Stir in the raisins last.

Pat hermits into a lightly greased 9" x 13" pan; the mixture will be quite dry. Bake for 25 to 30 minutes in a light-colored aluminum pan; 20 to 25 minutes in a darker pan. In either case, <u>don't over-bake</u>; bars should barely be pulling away from the edge of the pan. Remove from oven and cool completely before cutting.

Note: Mrs. Bundle has cut the recipe in half with great success using the following modifications: halve all ingredients, bake in a 7.5"x11" glass pan for 20-22 minutes.

Cracker's Favorite Recipes and Treats

(Please NOTE: these are cookies for CATS and not meant for consumption by men, women, or children)

Liver Lover Cookies

½ cup dry milk
½ cup wheat germ
1 tsp. honey

Preheat oven to 350° F.

Combine dry milk and wheat germ. Pour honey on top.

Add a small jar of strained liver baby food or homemade blended liver and stir together just until everything is mixed well. By hand, form into small bite size balls, place on oiled cooking sheet and then flatten them with a fork. Bake 8-10 minutes.

These are soft and almost fudge-like. Cool and store in an airtight container in the fridge. They will keep for a few days, or freeze them and remove as needed.

Loved by CATS far and wide!

Cracker's Fabulous Kitty Cookies

1 12-oz can salmon with liquid
1 egg
1/2 cup flour
1/2 cup dry instant oatmeal

Combine the salmon and egg in blender. Mix for a few seconds, then add the oatmeal and blend well. Spray cooking spray on a 9"-by-13" inch pan and spread the mixture in the pan. Bake at 350° F for 30-35 minutes. Cool, then cut into cat bite-sized squares. Can easily store in freezer. Makes about 24 treats.

Note: Fine china optional—cats enjoy dining formally, too!

ALLISON CESARIO PATON is the author of six adult "Cozy" Mrs. Bundle mysteries. In addition, she is an accomplished watercolorist, with her own line of Fine Art originals available on the Bundle Marketplace. In 2009, she took a huge leap of faith to write and paint full-time and it's been full speed ahead ever since!

The author grew up in Vermont, lived in Maine for many years, and has a deep love for all things New England. She and her husband owned a circa-1830s brick cottage in a little Vermont village, where they had many wonderful experiences, and which was the inspiration for the **Mrs. Bundle Mystery Series.** She is marketing partners with Bundle Publishing (the exclusive entity that features all the Mrs. Bundle Vermont mysteries and original watercolors).

To order all the Mrs. Bundle books and paintings, visit the Bundle Marketplace at https://squareup.com/market/bundle-publishing.

Allison loves hearing from fans on the Facebook Fan Page (Mrs. Bundle Mystery Series) or at bundlepublishing@yahoo.com — you can help spread the word to all North Pillson Corners kindred spirits!